BRAVE ENOUGH to Love

By Valden Bush

2024

Butterworth Books is a different breed of publishing house. It's a home for Indies, for independent authors who take great pride in their work and produce top quality books for readers who deserve the best. Professional editing, professional cover design, professional proof reading, professional book production—you get the idea. As Individual as the Indie authors we're proud to work with, we're Butterworths and we're *different*.

Authors currently publishing with us:

E.V. Bancroft
Valden Bush
Addison M Conley
Jo Fletcher
Helena Harte
Lee Haven
Karen Klyne
AJ Mason
Ally McGuire
James Merrick
Robyn Nyx
Simon Smalley
JJ Thomas
Brey Willows

For more information visit www.butterworthbooks.co.uk

CATALOGING INFORMATION
ISBN: 978-1-915009-55-5
CREDITS
Editors: Victoria Villaseñor & Nicci Robinson
Cover Design: Nicci Robinson
Production Design: Global Wordsmiths

Acknowledgements

My writing journey continues, but this book proved a difficult stage on the way. Two lots of COVID ensured I needed my wonderful editors, Nicci Robinson and Victoria Villaseñor. They rescued my muddle, the result of COVID brain fog, and deserve the largest thank you possible. They've continued to provide knowledge, support, and suggestions with a large dose of humour and care. They show patience with the bloops in my manuscript, which at times have been bad enough to make them smile. I still attend Global Wordsmiths writing retreats and need the fun reminders of what I forget! I'm continuing to learn as I put Nicci and Victoria's words into practice. I still believe I could not do this without them.

My personal support bubble continues to be my safe space and gives me inspiration. Thank you, Gill, for being my author wife and all that entails...for the time we spend writing together, discussing plot and our stories alongside life in general. In particular, thank you for making me laugh.

Thank you, readers, for believing in me and downloading and reading my previous two books. It makes my life as an author rewarding and gives me energy to write more stories.

As always, I couldn't have done this without my wife. She still encourages me, gives words of sound advice, lots of cuddles and keeps me fed with all those vegetables she's grown. I love you.

Dedication

To G, as always.

And to the men and women who lost their lives
in Afghanistan. We shall remember them.

CHAPTER ONE

Jo Fitzgerald leaned against the shipping container to catch her breath. It was one of many in various colors scattered around the inner wall of the Army base, making it look more like a container port. They had many uses in Afghanistan, from storage to accommodation, and the troops were forever finding new ways of utilizing them.

One lap of the perimeter left. Her hands gripped her empty water bottle. Running sweat covered her body as she reached down and picked up the last bottle in her stash. She drew in a deep breath and moved. It was two o'clock in the morning and the coolest time of day, but it was still seventy-five degrees. Unusually there was no one out here enjoying the relative peace as she ran a few yards from the center of the operational base that never slept. Jo swigged heavily and loudly, losing a little water down the front of her running top. She enjoyed the moment's coolness over her breasts before she set off on her last lap through the velvet night that wrapped around her like a blanket.

The first few weeks of getting acclimatized to the Helmand province weather had been an absolute killer, but she'd been determined and could now complete ten laps. In those first days, she'd started running in the heat of the day, getting her body to cope with the temperature. The air she breathed took her breath away. It came to her lungs as if she were standing right in front of the sun. Her skin was fair, pink, and quick to burn, and it had done so a lot in those early days. When it eventually tanned, it looked good. Her body complained on a hot day in the UK, where it rarely rose above the high seventies, even in summer. Here, when it was in the hundreds nearly every day, she easily tired physically, and day-to-day living was an effort. She'd been in Afghanistan before and had learned that intense training was the quickest way to get used to the heat and to make herself tired enough to sleep.

But she was going to have to function in a job in these conditions. If she wanted to keep herself and her men safe, she would have to both give and carry out orders and ensure she was aware of every nuance of her environment. In this world, it wasn't possible to take chances. Jo hadn't been brought up like that anyway. She always gave it one hundred percent.

Relaxing into her body, the last few hundred yards became the final sprint as she increased her stride and speed. She crossed the mental finish line, slowed down, picked up her stash of empty water bottles, and ran to her tent to dump her stuff. She picked up her shower kit and clean clothes in one move and continued running to the shower tents. There was an empty cubicle, so she put the sign across the entrance. *Female showering*. The water was only lukewarm, but the soap helped remove the sweat and ever-present white-brown dust. It was over all too quickly.

As she dried herself, she remembered those showers she'd taken when she was working as an instructor at the training base in the UK. The water was hot and continuous and as never-ending as a waterfall in the spring melt. She could stand there and think through plans and ideas as long as she wanted to. What she wouldn't give for one of those showers right now. It would massage her whole body, take away all her aches and pains, and give her the sense of home she missed in those quiet moments out here alone in the dark.

She put on her clean clothes and made her way to her tent. As one of the few women on the base and the only officer, she had a two-person tent to herself. It meant that any visiting women would be bunked with her, privacy provided as needed by netting down the middle of the space. Not that Jo spent much time in hers; she slept, wrote her reports, and read the occasional book there. She tidied up and went to find breakfast before she bedded down to catch a few hours' sleep before work.

***

"Captain Fitzgerald, ma'am."

Jo awoke to a bright, melodic voice calling her name. She recognized it as belonging to Corporal Evans, a clerk from the company HQ of the Second Fizers.

"Ma'am, are you awake?"

Jo had been in Afghanistan for much of her career and the sound of a voice calling her name meant she was awake within moments, alert and ready to go. She was out of bed with her personal weapon in hand in seconds. She stepped to the front of the tent dressed in T-shirt and shorts, the informal clothing choice around the base when off duty. "Morning, corporal. What good news have you brought me this morning?"

He stood in front of her, keeping his eyes on hers, and she could see the effort he was making so that he didn't look below her neck.

"Lieutenant Graves sent me, ma'am. Brigadier McQueen wants to see you at Camp Fortress. There's a Chinook chopper coming in on a supply run in about an hour. The lieutenant says if you can be ready, there's a seat available for you on the return flight."

"Thanks, corporal. Tell the lieutenant I'll be there," Jo said. Evans disappeared, and she turned back into her tent, grimacing. Damn. Her free day had just evaporated. They were few and far between as it was. She patrolled on random days and at random times to keep any Taliban from guessing the pattern of her visits to villages. When she wasn't on patrol, she was planning the next operation for herself and her escort troops as well as exercising with them. Today, she'd been planning to spend an hour exercising with her troops, followed by a leisurely lunch and an hour or two with a book that had been calling ever since she arrived at the base. Though it seemed whenever she planned to read it, some emergency always arose.

Jo looked at her watch when she left her tent. 0835. It was already hot, and she gave a small, internal sigh at the sweat quickly forming on her back. She was dressed in her everyday battle gear including her armor and helmet, along with a SA80 Mk II semi-automatic machine gun. Her kit also included as much ammunition as she could carry, including six pints of water in a CamelBak and two more pints in bottles, as well as rations weighing about forty pounds. She had a PRC-354 commander's radio and Osprey body armor weighing in at a further thirty-four pounds. She wasn't as fully loaded as she might be if she went out on patrol but what she carried was still heavy enough.

As she walked, she wondered what the brigadier wanted. Her job as a Female Engagement Officer was relatively new—she was concerned something had gone wrong at a high level, and she was going to be removed before she could do any good. The Afghan women in the villages needed someone like her, and she hadn't had a chance to do enough in the few weeks she'd had so far.

Jo made her way to the landing pad and poked her head into the transport office to wave to the Buzzard, the air traffic controller. She put on her protective glasses and stepped into the dip behind a hesco wall, a specialized defensive wall made from large, lined wire cages filled with sand or gravel. They were all over the British military bases, offering easily constructed blast-proof walls. She stood with the other passengers as she waited for the incoming Chinook to be offloaded. Scanning the area, she looked for the unusual because even here in the base, it was possible for any kind of raid. It could be a rocket attack or a suicide bomber, and Jo was taking no chances. The wind picked up, and the dust started to swirl. After the unloading was complete, she and the other passenger troops left their relative security and ran over to the helo. She jumped on board, having put her neck scarf around her face to protect from the dust though it would do little good.

Jo didn't envy the men who had unloaded the supplies. They lay on top of the crates and pallets to protect them from the upward swirl of the Chinook's motion, which was a small version of Dorothy's tornado in *The Wizard of Oz*. There was no conversation once they were airborne. It was too loud, and no one looked interested in their fellow passengers anyway. Fine with her.

Camp Fortress was such a large base that it took her nearly fifteen minutes to walk to the HQ complex in the middle of the camp. She kept her weapon loaded and ready, because there was a high risk of attack by Afghan police, soldiers, or workers. Jo pondered the irony of her situation. She was going out to help the villagers in Helmand to become self-sufficient and not to have to rely on the Taliban. Meanwhile, the long arm of the Taliban reached inside the base and put fear into the troops. It wasn't going to work on her, for sure.

The brigadier was at the far side of the busy operations center which held some thirty people, mostly working away behind screens. She was looking at one of several wall-mounted maps which appeared to show troop deployments around the region. The room was quiet with a low buzz as many of the staff were speaking into headsets. Margaret McQueen was one of the first women to reach the rank of brigadier, and Jo admired her for having such a successful career in a man's world. Jo loved that world and wanted to get to that rank herself, maybe even get promoted higher as a full general. There weren't any female full generals yet, but she hoped she would change that. The brigadier saw her across the busy room, indicated the coffee machine in the corner and gestured to Jo to get two coffees. "Black?" Jo mouthed. The brigadier nodded and held up three fingers for three sugars.

Jo made the coffee and by the time she'd finished, the brigadier was behind her. She took the coffees from Jo, who had her hands full with all her gear.

"Follow me," she said.

The brigadier led her out of the semi-darkened room and along a couple of heavily fortified corridors to a small, private office. "Not many of us get one of these," she said. "I share it with two other officers. Please have a seat."

Jo sat and placed her kit and weapon on the floor, releasing a flash of dust into the air. A ray of sunshine from a small high opening at the top of the wall of the office made the dust shine as if in one of those children's snow globes.

The brigadier opened a folder in front of her. "So how are things going, Jo? I wanted to check in with you."

"It's been slow progress, but I've been learning as I go along. Have you read my reports, ma'am?" Jo asked.

The Brigadier pulled out one of the papers from the folder. "Yes, that's one of the reasons I wanted to chat to you. In your last report, you suggested that the journey time to the villages further out precluded you visiting them unless you stayed at one of the patrol bases for a few weeks. I'd like to discuss exactly what that would mean."

Jo nodded. "As part of current ops, I go on patrol from the Forward Operating Base to the surrounding villages with a platoon from the Second Fizers as my security guards. They're now used to the routine, and I get to meet with the female villagers in relative safety."

"How does that work?" the brigadier asked.

"I'm with the men of one squad as they clear the way in. We're careful, and although the Afghans know me well enough now and they're expecting me, we don't take any chances. The rest of the troop cover the village and our exit. We've had the odd stray shot around us but luckily nothing serious so far," Jo said.

"Any ideas about the shots?"

"We wondered if it was perhaps a Taliban sympathizer flexing their muscle, showing that we don't frighten them," Jo said. She leaned back in her chair. "The women believed it was random, with no idea who it might've been. Honestly, I think there's a much more pressing need in the villages further up the valley, and I can't get to them. The Taliban are leaving the area, and the women need help to get themselves organized, particularly with their own midwives and nurses to help with childbirth. They'll need supplies and perhaps medic visits."

"Hence your suggestion about the patrol base," the brigadier said, nodding.

"Yes. The road journey up there is far too dangerous to do often, and it's the same with the air support. I can't justify tying up a helo every couple of days and putting them at risk when they're needed operationally, and it would need to be able to transport twenty-five men," Jo said.

"I like your train of thought there. Looking at the problem from a strategic point of view. Good."

Jo was pleased that her logic was getting full marks. She needed to keep getting this kind of feedback if she were to make major anytime soon. "The answer would be to send me with a platoon to a patrol base or checkpoint and we travel from there by foot or vehicle," Jo said. She was trying to make a good case and although she was simply repeating what she'd said in her report, it was good to get the brigadier's point of view.

"What would it mean in terms of manpower and operations?"

"Well, if we travel up the valley in vehicles and we base ourselves at one of the checkpoints or patrol bases, we can use that as a strategic center of operations. If, for example, it was patrol base Top Hat, we'd get access to eight villages either on foot or in vehicles. Or if we had access to vehicles at the patrol base, we could be flown in. The word is that the Taliban visit some of the villages, so we'd have to be careful where we consider going and listen to what the villagers are telling us."

"Or, going from your last report, what they're *not* telling you. It's interesting that when you passed by Omar village, some of the male villagers you knew didn't wave as usual, which struck you as strange. On the way back, you said the same villagers were there and waved. You stopped to speak to them, and they said that the

Taliban had been there earlier, and they hoped if you thought there was something wrong, you wouldn't enter the village. They used the only warning they could think of," the brigadier said.

"We're getting to know them well, and the fact that I can talk to their women and give them help is important. The issue of removing the Taliban for good is vital. They want their children to have an education and that isn't possible, whether they're male or female. The Army has traditionally asked solely about Taliban movements, and me asking about families and schools is making them realize that someone can see them."

"So you think the word is spreading up the valley?"

"I know it is. The problem is that the word may be spreading to the Taliban too, which could put us at risk as well as the women we're trying to help. However, I believe they're on the back foot lower down the valley. As the International Security Assistance Force operations increase further up the valley, I'm hopeful that they'll retreat into the mountains and give up on the area as being too difficult. The Taliban have had heavy casualties in the last year," Jo said. This was ground she knew like the back of her hand, and she needed it to show.

"Hmm. We've had heavy casualties too. I think your idea is good in principle, and it marries up well with our ideas on improving the hearts and minds of the population and offering them support." The brigadier shifted forward in her seat. "I'm going to recommend that we do as you suggest, but I want to make sure that we've moved a little further forward in clearing the Taliban from some of the villages first. I'll send you orders, but it may not be for several weeks."

The living conditions were basic, and it was likely to be more dangerous, but this was going to work. Jo resisted pumping the air with her fist. "Thank you, ma'am," Jo said, trying to stay serious and keep the smile from her face.

"In return, I want you to do something for me. You've got a safe pair of hands. The Ministry of Defence want to send an embedded journalist from Global News to cover the Second Fizers, and I think it would be good to get her alongside you for the rest of your tour."

Jo's delight deflated like a popped balloon. Some damn reporter following her when she was such a private person. "Ma'am, I worry that she'll be in a dangerous place and at significant risk. Perhaps somewhere safer would be better?" Jo squirmed in her seat, but she didn't need some hack following her around. What if the reporter caught mistakes that could cost her a promotion?

"I see what you're doing Jo." The brigadier laughed. "It won't work. She's the daughter of Diane James, and I'd like her to get the full experience."

"Diane James? Is she the woman who carried on reporting even when Beirut was being bombed around her?" Jo had a vision of a woman in armor and a helmet with the sky behind her popping lights and the rumble of gunfire. She'd never met her but by all accounts, she was a hellcat.

"She's a legend in her own lifetime. She's a freelance reporter now and doesn't need a newspaper or TV station for accreditation. She can travel anywhere. Her daughter is a different matter. This is her first chance, and I'd like to be able to give her a good experience and keep her mother happy too."

"I get it; keep the Ministry of Defence happy, keep HQ happy, keep mother happy," Jo said, grimacing. Politics were part of the job, but it didn't mean she had to like it.

Brigadier McQueen stood and came around the table. Few women in the military were as tall as Jo but the brigadier was over six feet. Jo loved being taller than a lot of their male counterparts. It felt like it evened the playing field just a little.

"I'm bribing you, I know." The brigadier laughed. "I get a reporter placed, and you get to go to the patrol base that you want. Then we're both happy. It's the game we play."

"When is she due to arrive, ma'am?" Jo asked as she lifted her kit.

"She'll be here in a few weeks. I'll send your CO the info. I'd like you to meet her from the plane and bring her to see me for a welcome chat before you head off. It won't do us any harm to get people at home to understand the risks our soldiers take every day out here, while they're tucked up safe and sound in bed," the brigadier said. "We also need some morale boosting for the soldiers. We've been hammered by the Taliban in some areas for the last two years, and we've had to send too many soldiers home either injured or in coffins. This could be good for us if it's done properly. By that I mean we focus on the lives of the soldiers here and how they live and work. What a patrol is and why it matters. It will make the soldiers stand out as being ordinary in many ways but committed to an ideal. A soldier is something more than the contents of a body bag. He had a life, and we should show that it's so much more than just some vague idea of service. Of course, it will be good for morale for the soldiers to see their lives represented as well."

Jo understood then what she was being asked to do. The bosses wanted her to make sure that everything the journalist reported was good for the Army, and the Fizers in particular. It was this sort of thing that could make or break a career. A reporter on her first embedded assignment was likely to be a loose cannon, and Jo was about to stand in front of it.

CHAPTER TWO

"You'll agree that since I arrived a year ago, I've done every job you've given me and done it well." Toni James stood in front of Mike's desk, arms crossed, foot tapping.

"Yes," he said.

She took a deep breath. "And you'll agree I've done extra whenever you've asked, even if it meant staying late and coming in early."

"Yeeees. So, what d'ya want?" He tapped a pencil on his desk.

"I want a chance to show you how good I can be. Let me have the story on baby deaths in Northern England. I know the inquiry is about to end, and I know I can get some good interviews. I'm a digital specialist, so I know what you need to go on the web and how to ensure that it's a full spread for the paper."

There was an agonizing silence and more pencil-tapping. Rushing him never did any good but she really, really wanted to.

"I s'pose it's about time I let you loose. As you said, you've done everything we've needed since you arrived. Okay. You've got the story. Cheap hotels and low expenses. You're only starting out. Understand?"

Toni almost leapt into the air with joy. "Thank you, Mike. I'll do a good job."

"Yes, you will. Keep me in the loop as to what you'll be submitting and when. Now go." His head was turned toward his computer before she'd gotten up to leave.

Toni closed the door, her heart pounding. This was her moment to show them all how good she was. By biding her time and waiting for the right moment and the right story, she'd been able to get this chance. Now she had to produce the goods. She'd managed to get this job through the interview process and not because her mother knew the editor. Now she had this story through her own efforts. She'd show her mother she was a good journalist and that she didn't need any outside influence to make it in this world.

She decided to stay in Chester to give herself a central point in the area. She entered the address into her car's GPS and set off. She'd started this journey with the feeling that she was on an adventure, and it still felt that way six years after moving to the country.

The houses were so close together, and one town became another without city limit signs in a lot of places. She hadn't travelled as much as she'd have liked and, except for the motorways, the road system seemed narrow, winding, and complicated. She'd gotten herself a car with automatic transmission. Driving these cluttered roads with a stick shift was too much to expect from an Oklahoma girl. Those wide grass prairies of her youth seemed like something from a dream.

She turned onto a side road and stopped when her phone rang. "Hello, Daddy. How are you?" She'd spent most of her life living with her father in the US but had come to live with her English mother and attend university in London. She missed him and their life together terribly, but she wanted independence and had never regretted the move. Although the weeks of English gray skies and endless rain always made her briefly reconsider.

"I'm good, darlin'. Just calling to see how you're getting along."

Her father's familiar southern drawl made her eyes water. She missed him more than she could say. "It's good to hear your voice, Daddy. I'm on my way to a real story." Toni sat straight in her seat waiting for his response and, if she were honest, his congratulations. His approval still mattered more than it probably should at her age. "Mike, the digital editor, is giving me a chance."

"You show them guys those James genes you have. Give 'em something special. I know you can do it."

"I hope so. I'll do my best."

"How's your mother? Seen her recently?"

Her mother had a residence in London but was there less than two months a year. She was a world-famous international journalist who'd made her name reporting on wars and areas of unrest before embedding reporters had become something usual. It was now time for Toni to show that she could shine on her own and move out of the shadow that was the immense presence of Diane James, ace reporter. "Oh, you know. The usual. I saw she was in the Congo last month, but where she is now, I don't know. She hasn't called, as usual."

"Oh. Darlin', darlin', don't expect her to. She's not made like you and me."

"I know, but I keep hoping." She swallowed the emotion that always rose with the knowledge she was always a second or even third thought when it came to her mother. "I should get going. I'll call once I'm settled."

"Bye, darlin'."

"Bye, Daddy. Thanks for calling." She headed out on the road to Chester still missing the warmth of the physical presence of her father but happy about his belief in her. She could do this. Her first big solo job would ensure not only that her mother noticed her, but that she was worth noticing.

***

The story took a month and a bit more effort than luck. She'd worked hard to get contacts and to fashion the story into a number of informative articles. She'd managed to do significant research and in-depth interviews with the people whose lives had been impacted. She was proud of the articles she produced and headed to London both tired and buzzed by her efforts.

When Toni returned to the office from her time up north, her confidence had grown by a mile. She completed a follow-up article for the website and had uploaded it when she heard a familiar voice floating down the hallway like a storm cloud.

"It's all right, I know the way. Been here enough times. Tell Joshua I'm here. Diane James. Come to see my daughter. Ask him if he's got anything for me."

Toni's heart thumped. She'd been here over a year and had hardly seen her mother at home, let alone in the office. Her mother must have seen her articles about the baby deaths. She'd finally recognized that she could write.

"Ah, there you are." Her mother walked over, moved things across Toni's desk and leaned against it as if it were hers.

"Hello, Mother. How are you?" Toni rolled her chair back to look up at her.

"Just back from Denmark. Off to Paris for a break later today. Did you see my work from the Congo?"

Okay. So, they'd start with her mother's work first. "Yes, it was interesting. I was amazed you got to interview the colonel too. It must have taken some intense contacts to line that up." Toni stood to get on a level with her mother and remind her she was no longer a child. She could take an equal part in this conversation. "Did you see my articles about the baby deaths?"

"The colonel was a real scoop, and I knew if I could get my name in front of him, he'd let me interview him. Another Diane James special." Her mother stopped leaning and stood to face her. "Yes, I saw your articles. A step up from flower show reports, certainly, but you need to write a lot better." Her mother turned to leave. "Thought I'd pop in on my way to Joshua's office. I won't be home for a couple of weeks. Bye." With that, she left to see if the Features Editor had a good story for her.

Tears welled in Toni's eyes. She shouldn't expect anything different; this had always been her mother's way. She was never going to live up to the Diane James high standards and get a well done from her, let alone a hug or kiss. But she'd always had a little bit of hope that her mother might change, that somehow, Toni would do something right and earn the connection she'd always wanted. The tears slipped down her face, and she sat back in her chair quickly before her colleagues noticed her reaction. Her mother, international reporter, and the person they all wanted to be. But no one else had to be her daughter.

"Toni, Joshua wants to see you in his office," his secretary said as she walked past Toni with a tea tray ten minutes later.

Toni walked to his office and knocked. Was her mother still here? Oh god, she didn't want to know what her mother had cooked up now.

"Ah, Toni. Excellent work on the baby deaths. I've been impressed by your handling of it. Discreet, when necessary, informative, and pushing for outcomes when needed. Particularly when the police had to get involved, and you got their agreement for you to report on their involvement. I like your style. I told your mother, but she was on a visit to see if I have anything for her and left pretty quickly when I had nothing for her."

Toni sank into one of Joshua's chairs. "I think my mother wants a story to work on when she gets back from Paris. No doubt something will happen somewhere in the world, and she'll be gone again."

He looked at her for a moment. "I liked how you interviewed when we took you on. You aren't like her at all, are you?"

"Is that a good thing or a bad thing? No. Please don't answer that. I'm different, that's all. My daddy brought me up, so I take after him more." Toni hoped she didn't sound as defensive as she felt.

"As I said, I like your style, and your articles got a lot of reads and sold a lot of papers."

"Thank you. It was all good experience." Why did his approval not mean as much as her mother's directive to write better? He was the one who mattered, after all. She straightened. This was her world, not her mother's.

"Well, we've got something more for your experience. The UK is losing a lot of soldiers and marines in Helmand province in

Afghanistan. We've been using military press releases and Reuters for our coverage, but I want more in-depth reporting. I've gotten the Ministry of Defence to allow us to embed a reporter. After your success with the baby death interviews, I want you to go. It'll be for three months. Will you take it?"

"Is this something to do with my mother?" Toni was surprised. This was unexpected, and she suspected her mother had put her fingers into her life again.

His eyebrows rose, but his expression suggested he understood what she was really asking. "Actually, no. I'll admit I was going to tell her, but she didn't stay long enough. When I saw the first of your interviews, I knew that you could produce something worthwhile if you went to Helmand, something with both heart and details. You got this job on your own merits."

Her heart beat so loudly she wondered if it might burst. Compliments from the Features Editor and the offer of a job she could only dream about. In fact, it was a job her mother probably would have jumped at. But they'd offered it to Toni. "I'll take it."

***

Becoming an embedded journalist wasn't as simple as Toni had first thought. There was paperwork galore, medical tests and inoculations, and then more paperwork. Luckily, she had a helpful colleague who'd been embedded in the Iraq war and was an expert. She offered to buy Charlie a beer at her favorite bar, her local pub ever since she'd moved to London. It was a little bit out of the city in Wapping Wall and overlooked the Thames. A pub had been on that site since 1520, and Toni delighted that she was sitting in a bar that had been there when Henry VIII had been on the throne. A pub nearly two hundred years older than the creation of her country. The history here never ceased to amaze her.

The bar had wood floors and walls, but the varnish had seen better days and was slightly worn and scuffed. There were lots of darkly painted small tables and stools, giving the place a comfortable feel. This was what being in a pub in the UK was all about to Toni—historic, warming, and a place that encouraged her inner self to think about origins and what home meant. Charlie just liked the beer.

When they got to a small table to one side, they each pulled up a stool. Charlie took a big swig of his beer and left a mustache of fine froth on his upper lip. "Honestly, Toni, this is going to be a big change for you. I ain't saying that you won't cope, but you do need to get your head in the right place before you go. Otherwise, it'll be days before you can do or think much because you'll be in culture shock."

"Right, so what do I need to think about?" Toni readied her pen over the blank notepad, determined not to miss a thing.

"I'd say there are three things that you need to make sure you understand." He held up his finger. "The first and most important is the fact that you may not come back. This ain't something that's abstract or something that could happen to someone else. It could be you. When lady luck pulls the carpet out from under you, then it's time to go. So be prepared and take precautions."

"Precautions?"

He looked at her intently. "Make a will and leave letters for loved ones."

Toni's stomach dropped, and her heart started beating loudly in time with her breathing. "My God! Dying is so...well...final, isn't it? And I hadn't even thought about it."

Charlie took another swig of his beer, and Toni sipped her Corona, giving herself a moment to steady herself. Why hadn't she considered it? Plenty of reporters had been killed in combat zones. Charlie was right; it could be her.

He raised another finger. "The second thing you need to think about is the heat. You'll be arriving in May. It'll be in the thirties and forties during the day and in the high twenties even at night. June and July will be hotter, a *lot* hotter. So make sure you get advice about what you'll need and how to deal with the heat."

"The heat is the one thing that worries me. I mean, back home, it's in the eighties and nineties for most of summer, but we rarely hit higher than that." They got the odd day over a hundred in Oklahoma, but it wasn't prolonged, desert heat. That heat with no AC is what she would struggle with. "I'll get advice." She wrote it down, along with a few things to think about. Did she need her own water bottles? What kind of clothes should she get?

He held up a third finger. "My last point is to think about the dust. From the time you set down in Helmand until you come home, you'll be dealing with dust that gets into every nook and cranny. July is the windy month, so think about hot dust swirling everywhere. Make sure you're expecting it, and you're dressed for it as best you can. The Ministry of Defence has a Green Book. It's a handbook of what you'll need to do, so get yourself a copy, and it should all start to make sense."

"Right. So to summarize your advice; prepare to die, do some work in a sunbed to get used to the heat, and think about dust baths. Finally, get a book on how do all those things." Toni took a big drink from her glass as Charlie roared with laughter and everyone in the pub turned their way. The one thing he didn't really know much about was embedded life not only as a woman but a woman in Afghanistan. His advice was to understand she might be one of only a few women if she was on the front line, and facilities could be basic. She could be treated differently than a male reporter, but she should stand up for herself and ensure she got the story. Good advice, but she had a feeling there'd be more to it than that. She spent the rest of the evening enjoying Charlie's company as he told her stories about his time in Iraq, giving her a much better sense of the life of an embedded journalist. She took plenty of notes and had a lot to think about. This wasn't a story where she'd be staying in a hotel and would be able to grab a quick bite to eat before taking an evening bath. This was real.

Once she had a copy of the Ministry of Defence's Green Book, her life became exponentially busier. Going to Afghanistan had created a flurry of activity that had her lying in bed at night mentally working her way down lists of clothes, lists of military requirements and training, medical checklists, and more lists of things she still had to do.

Making trips to her office to get the latest updates on her status and when she'd be flying out to Afghanistan seemed like the easy part. She'd had to visit her doctor and get a completed medical checklist showing every illness and injury she'd ever had, and she signed a release to say that she didn't have any conditions that would affect her in the heat. Similarly with her dentist, although she wasn't sure what her teeth had to do with the desert or reporting. She had to undergo fitness training close to her home at a local Army base so that she could run a mile and a half in less than twenty-two minutes carrying eight pounds of weight in a backpack. She was in good shape and ran most days but carrying that amount of weight was new and left her a little more breathless than usual. Finally, she went to the Ministry of Defence to complete paperwork and hand over the various lists and signed papers to get accreditation as a War Correspondent.

She wrote a letter for her father and left it with Mike just in case she didn't come back. She told him how much she loved him and how he had both encouraged her and set her free. She didn't bother with her mother. She did start a letter then realized she had nothing to say. She had no partner or lover to leave a letter with, no close friends, which made her think about how alone she really was. But that was the price of the work she did, right? And maybe one day that would change.

When she was finally ready, she spent the following days on a major high. She went to sleep dreaming of what life would be like and how this would help her succeed in her career. Deep beneath the optimism was a twinge of fear, but she ruthlessly shoved it down a little further. There was no time for emotions. The story was all that mattered, and she'd get it done no matter the cost.

***

LESS THAN TWO WEEKS later, she was at Brize Norton Airbase waiting for a flight to Kandahar. She had all her belongings in or attached to a huge backpack that she had to be able to carry herself. Her navy-colored press helmet and navy body armor with the word PRESS emblazoned in white letters on the back and front was attached to the outside of the backpack, giving her a sense of pride. She also had a smaller pouch that she used for her electronic equipment, including her laptop, two phones, batteries, chargers, plus her personal paperwork, money, and toiletries. It was heavy and cumbersome, and she'd had to pack and repack a million times, arguing with herself about the necessity of a hairdryer before she managed to trim everything down to true necessities. She reminded herself that she didn't have to carry all her belongings all the time. She'd get to leave most of them on base while she was out reporting. The smaller pack was no problem.

This was the single most important day of her life so far, and she trembled with anticipation. If she was successful, she would become someone. Someone worth paying attention to. Someone with something to say. She walked across the tarmac and joined a line of soldiers waiting to board the plane. The early summer air cut through the distant smell of aviation fuel, and Toni savored the moment. The air reminded her of the days she'd spent walking in the New Forest national park last summer. She never did find the time to go back, and now her future called to her.

CHAPTER THREE

THE MORNING WAS GOING wrong in every way Jo could imagine. It was one of those days when she was glad she wasn't going out on patrol because her luck had seriously run out. There hadn't been enough water for her shower, so she was half clean. She went to eat breakfast and her favorite cereal had run out but more worryingly, they had none of her favorite strong coffee. Everyone assured her supplies were arriving within the hour but trying to do a day's work on a cup of coffee that tasted like weak dirty water just wasn't going to work. In the end, she settled for a glass of milk and some shortbread.

As she was finishing her substandard breakfast, Corporal Evans appeared at her side. "Ma'am, the colonel wants to see you in his office ASAP."

"Okay, I'll be there in ten minutes," Jo said, wondering what she'd done wrong. When she'd first arrived, the colonel of the Second Fizers Battle Group had made it clear that having a woman attached to his group was something he'd hoped would never happen and yet, here she was. She finished her breakfast and made her way to his office, her heart thumping and her stomach regretting the glass of milk. The day simply wasn't getting any better.

During her first interview, he'd questioned her closely about her ambitions. Despite her discussing her path as an engineer and her desire to get promoted, he'd decided that she was only there to snap up one of his "fine officers" as a husband. Then followed a ten-minute lecture on her behavior around the men and how she was expected to set an example and not encourage lascivious looks or actions. As she listened, rage had rushed through her, and she imagined punching him or retorting with something sarcastic. It was a toss-up between "I'll try not to run through Camp Fortress naked then," or to tell him truthfully "I'm a lesbian." But it wasn't the time or the place for either and both would likely ruin her career plans.

She'd stayed out of his way, and today was the first time he'd summoned her since. She drew in a deep breath and knocked on his door.

"Enter," the colonel said.

Jo opened the door, marched in, and stood to attention. She saluted. He said nothing and left her standing there. *Bastard*.

"At ease." He didn't look away from the file in front of him. "Brigade have given me a set of orders for you, and I can't decide if I'm pleased or not. I'm told you and your platoon will be sent to patrol base Top Hat in a few weeks along with an embedded female reporter. She's to accompany you for the rest of your tour. That should keep you out of trouble and will keep the press out of my hair as well. You'd better make sure that the news reports are all good and keep the Fizers' reputation intact." He finally glanced up at her, his frown deep.

"Yes, sir." Jo had nothing else to say. He was a misogynistic jerk who didn't deserve her time. This assignment meant she'd be far away, and that was perfect.

"Report to brigade for midday today and meet the flight incoming from Kandahar. The brigadier wants to see you at 1500 hours with the reporter. The brigadier will give you the rest of your orders."

"Yes, sir," Jo said.

"Dismissed."

When she moved to attention, he was already continuing to work from the file on his desk. She was nothing more than a moment's annoyance in his day.

She sighed. It had been weeks since Brigadier McQueen

had spoken to her about these orders, so she'd put it out of her mind and got on with the job at hand. Now, not only had it been approved, but also the reporter was about to descend on her too. She rolled her shoulders. So be it. She went back to her tent and collected her gear to catch a flight to Camp Fortress. Maybe getting a decent cup of coffee somewhere was the best she could hope for.

***

A few hours later she was standing in the heat of the midday sun watching the flight from Kandahar taxi across the runway. The passengers disembarked quickly and enabled Jo to get her first look at the reporter, who stood out from the rest of the thirty soldiers with her press armor and helmet and the general look of a flower dropped into the desert. She'd stopped moving, causing the other soldiers to move around her. She was looking at the scenery and smiling as if she were a tourist visiting the Costa Del Sol. *Fan-bloody-tastic.*

Jo ran over to her. "Toni James?" She didn't wait for a reply. "Quickly. You need to get under cover. You can easily be shot. You don't have time to look at the view here. Follow the person in front of you."

"Sorry, I was just—"

Jo didn't wait for her explanation and pulled her forward. It wasn't an easy maneuver with Toni's large pack and Jo's smaller daypack. Once they were in the shelter of a hesco wall, Jo pulled Toni to a stop. "I'll do the introductions shortly, but we'll head to the officers' mess for some food. I expect you're hungry, and it'll give you time to get your bearings," Jo said and marched quickly.

"Hey. *Stop.*" Toni's face was red, and her eyes flashed. "I need the bathroom first. *If* you can fit it into your busy schedule. I've been on a plane forever."

"Mm. We'll go around that way." Jo barely stopped and headed for the latrine block. "Leave me with your kit. These toilets are top of the range for out here, which just means that they flush. Enjoy the luxury while you can; you'll soon only have the basics."

Jo stood and thought about her day so far, while staring at the navy-blue bag with two giant yellow daisies stenciled into it. The kitbag also had a flowery fragrance which, along with the daisies, struck her as so out of place in this world of war.

"Peace," the reporter said as she came out and picked up her kit. "I understand you don't want to be here with me. Take me to wherever I need to be, and you can leave me there and return to wherever your work is. I'm sorry to have messed up your day."

Perhaps Jo had been overzealous with enforcing the rules, but there was no re-do. "Okay. Come on. We need to find food and then we have to see the brigadier."

Once they got to the officers' mess, Jo helped the reporter navigate the menu choices. She remembered how overwhelming it could be when first arriving from the UK. This officers' mess and attached food hall, along with three others, served over five thousand meals a day, a number that seemed to be difficult to comprehend in a war setting.

They were sitting at a table with their food trays when Jo slowed down. "So, introductions. I'm Captain Jo Fitzgerald with the Second Fizers' Battle Group. I'm an engineer by trade, but I'm attached to the Fizers working out of a Forward Operating Base, which is FOB Sherwood, as part of the International Security Assistance Force's Female Engagement program." Jo watched the reporter carefully and was glad she could follow at least that much information.

"I'm Toni James, reporter for Global News, both digital and written word. I'm American by birth but have spent the last few years studying and working in London, and as you've realized, I've never been in a conflict situation before." Toni's face turned red as she spoke. She took a drink of water from her tray as if to hide behind her paper cup.

Jo wasn't prepared for the tiny surge of protectiveness that touched her at Toni's obvious unease. It was misplaced, and she shoved it away. "In response to your peace comment, I'm afraid you aren't going to lose me that quickly, however much we both might want that to be the case. I'm your liaison. What that means is that after your appointment to meet the brigadier, you and I become inseparable for the rest of your time out here. You're going to live, breathe, and sleep life on the front line in Afghanistan," Jo said. When she finished speaking, she sighed, and Toni did the exact same thing but with a very different inflection.

"I'm sorry you can't get rid of me. I'm excited to have this post," Toni said. "I know I'm going to make lots of mistakes to start with, but I'm a quick study, and I'll try not to let you down."

Let her down? Jo didn't expect anything but irritation, so how would she let her down? "We'll do our best to make sure you're prepared. First off though, we need to prepare you so that you've a vague understanding of my role here and what you can expect. The brigadier wants you off to a good start," Jo said. "What do you know about what I'm doing here?"

"Nothing except what you've just told me. I'm afraid I was provided very few details, and there's very little online about you. There are the usual PR pics, like the one of you kneeling while talking to some children in a village, which I assume is out here. I noticed you because you're the only woman I'd seen. I was only told I'd be with the Second Fizers, so that was what most of my research was about. Before we start, I'm going to take notes, pictures, and video wherever we are in order to document what's going on. Is that acceptable to you?"

Jo stopped with the fork of food halfway to her mouth. She gulped. This was what was meant by washing your dirty laundry in public. She was going to be subject to this woman's scrutiny wherever she went for the rest of her time there, which was slated to be three full months. She couldn't move for a moment. All she could hear was her heart beating. She put down her fork and looked at Toni. "No, it's not really. But I've been ordered to accept it, so that's okay." She was a private person, and the idea of opening herself up to examination just became very real. She'd always understood the reporter was likely to do this, but to find herself chatting about it made her decide to be honest.

"I'm going to have to trust that what you share doesn't include too many personal moments or views. We're going to be living in close quarters, and you'll probably see more of me and my troops than is good for any of the public to see," Jo said. "And you're going to have to earn that trust to start with. You can talk to me as we go along about what you want to do. Will that work?"

Toni bit her lip and toyed with her water cup. "I think so, but I reserve the right to change my mind. If I have a story that I feel needs to be told, I will tell it, whatever you might think. That's why I'm here." Toni leaned forward, and her eyes sparkled as she gave Jo a pretty, open smile. "I'll try not to show you naked though."

This whole journalist saga was going to be worse than Jo had imagined it. Not only was Toni James likely to go her own way with her reporting, but she was going to shine like a diamond among coal around her troops. Jo wouldn't fall for it but some of her troops would. She could envision spending time admonishing them for trying to get intimate with the reporter. *Just what I needed. Why couldn't she look like someone's ancient grandmother?*

"Anyway, about my job." Jo forced herself to look away from Toni's soft skin. "I'm out here as part of the ISAF efforts to remove outlying villages in Afghanistan from Taliban control and allow the country to start recovering. There are a multitude of infrastructure projects in motion, like building bridges and roads and even a dam, so that the population can see what's possible when life starts to become stable." Jo got more comfortable now that she was in familiar territory. "The women in the country are basically unseen and rely totally on their husbands, fathers, or family. ISAF want to encourage them to be more independent. Military women are necessary to liaise with them because of the Muslim rules about women not being allowed to be seen by men. I've been trained to speak Pashto, though I'm by no means fluent. My job is to visit women in the villages and work out what will help them to become more independent. The Taliban have taken everything away from them, and I'm exploring what they can use to help them move forward. Medicine is a top priority. But education for both boys and girls is something they consider vital."

"Is there a problem with the schools and education?" Toni scribbled furiously in her notepad.

"It's something the Taliban don't agree with. Especially for girls. But one of the villages did have a school for boys running a couple of years ago. Eventually the Taliban came and frightened the teacher, so the school closed." Jo remembered the frustration she'd felt on hearing the news.

"Where's the teacher now? Is he still living in the village?" Toni asked.

"Yes, he works in the fields with the other laborers." It left a bitter taste in her mouth thinking about the waste of talent and the knowledge that the only way out of the villages was to have an education. To be able to read and write. Without it, children were forever condemned to village life.

"What a waste," Toni said. "Is it only the UK doing this work?"

"No, it's many countries. We each have different areas. In this camp, we have Denmark, Estonia, the US, and the UK. We each have an area that we're responsible for, although we often overlap."

"So when we go to FOB Sherwood, it'll be just the UK Army?"

"Yes, although we've had one or two Danes with us. The FOB is mostly made up of the Second Battalion of the Fizers. There are about six hundred troops working out of the base, many of them patrolling the surrounding countryside."

"Is that what you do? Patrol the surrounding countryside?"

At least she was asking good questions so far. Jo's shoulders dropped a little. "Yes and no. The platoon has twenty-eight soldiers in four squads. We go to a village and two squads guard the village from the outside to keep me safe. Another squad positions itself around the main entrance against any attack, and the final squad follows me into the village. Once there, I talk to the villagers. I have to start with the men and if I'm lucky, I get to talk to the women."

"This sounds exactly the sort of item I want to send back. You know, about the patrol and the villages you visit and not just the stories of the dead and wounded on both sides." Toni glanced up quickly and smiled, then looked back at her notepad.

"I'll be able to show you what we do in detail once we get you out on patrol with us. There are men and women in the villages who were qualified under the Soviets as teachers and doctors, but they've gone to ground since the Taliban took over. The word has started to spread from the work I've done so far, and we're being welcomed a little more openly. We need to keep the momentum going."

"Once we've seen the brigadier, we leave here?" Toni asked.

"Yes. We go to FOB Sherwood. I expect us to continue to work from there. We'll get you acclimatized and briefed before we take you out. Most troops do that here in Fortress, but I want you to learn how to patrol with us and get to know our different patrol positions before we get to the villages. There's no easier way to understand it than to do it."

"If we go out from Sherwood, where will we go?" Toni asked. "Is there a friendly village really close?"

"No, we'll patrol close to the base and use a couple of derelict buildings to show you what we do. I need to make sure you're safe and that the troops aren't jeopardized." Jo knew she was probably scowling, but the only way to prevent this novice from risking all their lives was to train her well. "Once you're ready, we'll head out into the villages. Later, we'll spend a few weeks at a patrol base and visit some villages further up the valley."

"What's a patrol base?" Toni asked.

"Good question. It's all UK forces. It's a small base and often only has about twenty soldiers working there, and we'll double their numbers. It really is the front line. The patrol base troops don't often go out on patrol but provide security for the villages near them by manning a sanger, which is the Army term for a watch tower. We'll take my platoon and visit the outlying villages from the patrol base."

"That sounds like a boring way of life for the soldiers," Toni said.

Jo breathed in deeply. This woman had no idea. She hadn't been in any dangerous situation over here yet. She hadn't lived on the front line of a war where you could be killed lying in your bed. Jo was going to have to be careful, because Toni could ruin her career talking about the *boring* life on the front line. "You may think it boring, but it's what they're trained for. Time on their hands one moment and difficult situations the next, both physical and mental for days on end. But it's also one of the more dangerous postings. If the Taliban come down out of the mountains, it's one of the first places they hit." Jo tried to hold her temper. Her stomach clenched, and she fought off nausea as she thought of the lives that had been lost fighting over a dusty outpost and piece of road. "The Army has lost many good soldiers from that patrol base. It's safer now, due to their hard work, however, we're never complacent. The Taliban want to cause us as much pain as possible and show us that we're still intruders in their country and that they have the upper hand." That bit wasn't clear or understood by the general public, she got that, but it was a little surreal trying to explain the suddenness of serious injury or death.

They finished their meals while Jo explained the basics of her role and the outline of the bases. "We're at the cutting edge of strategy; we're still trying to remove the Taliban from some areas, and they tend to slide back in if they can and frighten the villagers. I'll get us a drink. Tea or coffee?"

"Coffee, please. Milk, two sugars. It's going to be dangerous then, going out from base?" Toni asked.

"We call that NATO standard coffee. And yes, it'll be frightening and threatening at times, but that's true of most of Helmand province. Back with coffee shortly." While she was gathering their drinks, Jo gathered herself too. There were so many other things she could be doing today instead of explaining their world to an outsider.

As they drank their coffee, Jo thought through what else she needed to say. "You'll need an open mind for the first few days. There are people everywhere, privacy is difficult, and the jargon will leave you floundering at times."

"That's helpful, thanks. I expect to spend the first couple of weeks finding my feet, and I'm not expecting to upload copy or video for several days. I hope that works for you and your team."

Toni looked so hopeful, so sweet. So very, very naïve.

Jo looked up and was surprised to see Brigadier McQueen walking toward their table with a cup in her hand. Jo stood to attention. "Ma'am."

Toni looked from Jo to the brigadier and then stood.

"Brigadier Margaret McQueen. And you must be Toni James." She held out her hand, and Toni shook it.

"Yes, ma'am."

"How are you finding things?"

"I've only been here long enough to wash up briefly and eat. Jo has talked to me about some of her work too," Toni said. "To be honest, half of me is still traveling."

"We all have the same problem with the journey, but you'll get up in a couple of days and feel as if you've always been here. Please sit. I thought I'd grab you both over a cuppa rather than sit in my office. I wanted to meet you more informally. You're American, correct?"

"Yes. I was brought up by my father in Tulsa, Oklahoma and came to the UK to go to City University in London to get my degree and masters. I was taken on by Global News as a junior digital reporter before being given a major story. I covered the baby deaths in Northern England." Her pride in that was obvious.

"Oh, yes. Was that all your work?" McQueen asked.

Toni nodded. "I enjoy getting into a story and finding out what's happening. I have an insatiable curiosity, much to my father's despair when I was younger. I was always asking why."

"Those interviews of the families were some of the best reports I've seen. They were moving to watch, and somehow you managed to get their anger across without any of them raising their voices," McQueen said.

"I did what seemed right at the time." Toni's cheeks flushed, and her eyes were alight with the praise.

"I'm pleased we have you with us. It'll be good for someone to show the world what happens out here in our forgotten corner." McQueen stared ahead of her but didn't appear to be looking at anything. She sighed. "They only ever get reports of bodies, people dying, and coffins covered with flags. I'd like to showcase the villages and all the different viewpoints, from our troops to the men, women, and children in the villages."

"Thank you. I hope I don't let you down out here."

McQueen stood, and Jo and Toni followed, smiling like a kid about to go on an adventure.

"Let me know how it goes, Jo. I'll read your reports and Toni's news articles and hope for some good results. Be safe." McQueen left, nodding at the soldiers who stopped to salute as she passed.

Jo cleared their table as Toni collected her belongings. Jo looked at Toni and was aware that she'd completed her first step successfully. She'd recovered from her earlier lost situation and managed to do an okay briefing, but she wasn't convinced that Toni understood the situation at all. Jo was struggling not to look at Toni's sexy backside as she lifted her rucksack. Life was complicated enough without adding any difficult and wayward personal emotions. She'd ensure things stayed simple. Simple had always been Jo's best friend.

CHAPTER FOUR

Toni looked at her watch, and the luminous dial lit up the whole room. She giggled; there was little about this tent that was reminiscent of a room. Canvas brown walls and a canvas roof. In bed, she could shout to the men in the next tent. It was a good thing she liked Coldplay and Adele, although personal earphones would've been better.

She had a single bed and a wooden crate as a locker. The crate was a useful place for the gear that she would use regularly. Most of her belongings lived in her backpack, which most of the soldiers called a bergen, and she realized how her natural tidiness was a bonus. Jo had said the space would be sparse, but this was beyond what Toni had anticipated.

But then, there was nothing about the last twenty-four hours that she *had* anticipated. As she settled in her bed, she replayed the moments leading to her finally getting to lie down and put her head on her pillow. She couldn't help but feel she'd taken missteps all the way to this point, and her original plan to impress her liaison definitely hadn't gone to plan.

The ride to FOB Sherwood had gone all right, although there was little she could do wrong when she was sitting in the back of a helicopter with so much noise and no windows. She sat silently as if she were back in London on a bus with a lot of strangers. She didn't miss the looks from the soldiers though. Most just looked curious. One or two looked disdainful. Fortunately, no one looked outright hostile. They'd run from the bird and into shelter quickly, then Jo had taken her to their shared tent. She only had time to dump her bergen before they were summoned.

The colonel called them into his office. Jo warned her that he was officious in his outlook and demeanor, so she was surprised when he shook her hand and invited them to take a seat. He was a tall, gaunt man and gave the impression he was looking down his long, pointed nose at them. He had gray hair and a ruddy complexion that could be from the sun or alcohol. Maybe both.

"Ms. James, welcome to 2 Fizers. We have great confidence in our ability to complete the tasks we've been given to return this area to the Afghan people. We are a proud and famous Infantry battalion that has had success in numerous battles since our formation before the Crimean War."

Toni smiled at the colonel. A standard smile that said nothing, to counter his introduction, which said nothing. He was giving his standard PR chat, and she wondered why he couldn't see how unrealistic it was to be giving it to her. Because of her extensive research, she could tell him which wars and battles they'd been in, which soldiers had been given medals like the Victoria Cross, and even which school the colonel had gone to.

"Many of our infantrymen are part of a long family line of Fizers. I'm a fourth generation Fizer, and both my son and nephew are in the Regiment. Our men are both caring and heroic, and I'm looking forward to reading your reports about the fine, upstanding soldiers they are."

"I have no doubt I'll get to meet lots of great soldiers, sir. I'll most certainly do my best to report honestly and fairly," Toni said. *Two of us can play the PR line.*

"I've decided that the women in the villages further up the valley need Captain Fitzgerald's expertise, so I'm sending you to patrol base Top Hat in a few weeks, once the area is clear of Taliban. I hope you get some good material for your stories. The captain has been tasked with your safety and ensuring you see the best of us. If she can't get you what you need, please feel free to come and see me."

"I will. Thank you." Toni could feel Jo stiffen, though she barely moved and her expression remained neutral. The guy was typical, but clearly, he got under Jo's skin.

"It's been a pleasure meeting you. Enjoy your time with us."

They were dismissed, without him having so much as said a word to Jo.

Jo said little afterwards, but Toni was sure that things weren't good between the colonel and her. She'd keep her eyes and ears open and try to learn more. Thinking through the conversations of the day, she could see the colonel was a credit-taker. He'd said their moving further out to the patrol base was his idea when the brigadier said that it was all down to Jo.

After a quiet supper, where Toni failed to get Jo to talk about anything of substance, they returned to their tent.

"Tomorrow we'll be up at 0500 and have a quick meal, then we'll take you on a practice patrol around the outside of the base to get you used to working with us. Let's look at what you expect to have to take with you. I want to ensure that you have the electronics you think you'll need and enough personal water to last for our patrols."

She put her kit out on her bed to show Jo. "So, I have my phone and a video recorder, both have reasonable battery life. I have two digital cameras, some lenses, and filters. I've bought a supply of paper notebooks of different sizes and pens for everyday note-taking plus some larger journals that I'll need to map out my ideas for longer stories and features." Toni laughed as she pointed to a pile of Ziploc bags of varying sizes. "They're the most important thing. Dust and sand protection."

"It's bad, even in here. It seems to get everywhere. You've been given good advice. I'm impressed," Jo said.

Toni flushed under the faint praise. At least she hadn't screwed that part up. "My laptop. It's powerful, and I'll use it to piggyback on the military network if I'm in the bigger bases. In case there are problems with power, this pack contains spare batteries and a solar charger. I also have a BGAN data transmitter for satellite access if I'm not close to a military connection. I needed to be sure if we didn't have power or easy access to a satellite that I could still connect up."

Jo nodded approvingly as she scanned the pile. "You can carry it on your own and do what you need to do. We just need to load up your water as well."

Toni packed her bag with the things she expected to carry and three water bottles. Jo watched her every move, and Toni was determined not to be self-conscious. She packed the way she'd practiced at home and put a small camera and a notebook on the pockets of her waist webbing for easy access. She then put on her body armor and then the backpack.

Jo nodded. "Good. Be ready to leave the tent at 0500. If you shower tonight, you may decide to forgo the shower in the morning. I'll take you over there now. We wear shorts and a T-shirt and flip-flops or trainers around the camp, and you need to bring your wash kit. We do have running water here, but each shower is only a few minutes long, enough to wash fast with no extras. Shout when you're ready." Jo disappeared into her half of the tent.

Toni could hear her moving around on the other side of the blanket wall as she sorted out her kit. She hadn't packed her clothing in any particular order and was having trouble finding her flip-flops. She decided to unpack completely, put things on her bed, and repack after her shower. She changed into her shorts and T-shirt and picked up her wash kit. She didn't want to keep Jo waiting. "I'm ready."

The shower cubicles were four walls of hessian around a shower head with running water. They each took a wooden *Female Showering* notice and hung it on the outer flap. Toni moved into the shower, removed her clothes, and got into the warm water quickly. She started soaping, wondering when the water would run out, so she did a small area and rinsed, determined not to get caught all soaped up, which Charlie had told her about.

It was surreal to be standing here in the desert in a potato sack cubicle surrounded by hundreds of troops. Only forty-eight hours ago, she'd been on a London street drinking coffee outside a café looking forward to her new position. She had the same excitement now, but it was tempered with a slight anxiety that she would fuck it up. She managed to get out of the shower a moment before Jo. She returned the notice to its hook, and they made their way back to their tent.

Toni stared at the ceiling, listening to the unfamiliar noises just beyond the thin flap of material that separated her from a zillion other people on base. She was so exhausted she felt ill, and as she turned over on the thin mattress, she hoped that tomorrow would be better.

***

Her phone alarm went off at 0500, and she felt surprisingly refreshed. The excitement was still there, and today, she was going to show the military that she wouldn't be a burden. Yesterday's doubts were in the past. The only way was forward.

She put on her press uniform and gathered everything the way she had the day before. She'd heard Jo moving around but hadn't said anything, not wanting to disturb whatever morning routine she had. She was still sorting out her clothing from the night before, trying to work out what should go where in her bergen. She didn't need it today, but it still seemed to be a little blizzard of cloth chaos.

"You're not ready yet," Jo said when she moved the curtain. She looked at her watch then over at Toni's bed and the clothing on it. "You can do that later. We'll be late. Let's head out as soon as you have your rucksack."

"I have it. I'm ready." She *was* ready, but apparently she was already running behind. She picked her backpack up and followed Jo to what she hoped would be breakfast.

They were in the mess hall less than twenty minutes after her alarm had sounded, and it was packed. It was a shock to see the large tent filled to capacity at such an early hour. It was noisy and busy with troops queuing for plates loaded with a huge breakfast. Toni wanted to get her notebook out to find out where they were all going or whether they were all up so early just to miss the worst of the heat. Questions she'd have to explore later since she had to keep up with her temporary babysitter. She followed Jo into the officers' area, which was a little more sedate.

"Morning, ma'am." The duty server smiled. "Your usual?"

Jo nodded, and the server handed her scrambled eggs and two slices of toast.

"Thank you," Jo said. "This is Toni James, a reporter with Global News who'll be with us for the next few months."

The server nodded. "Pleased to meet you, ma'am. What would you like for breakfast?"

Toni looked along the counter and realized there was no way she'd manage to eat much today. She was far too nervous. "A couple of pieces of toast would be good."

Several of the other officers had nodded at Jo and smiled at them both as they stood in the queue.

The guy in front, whose label said PRITCHARD, turned to Jo. "Are you going out?"

"Yes. We're getting Toni used to patrolling. Toni, meet Jed." Jo stood back to allow Toni into the conversation.

"Hello, Jed."

Jed held out his hand. "I've got to be on my best behavior. Jo told me."

Toni smiled and took Jed's hand. "I'm sure that'll soon wear off. What do you do around here?"

"I run a platoon like Jo's, so we're often patrolling different areas at the same time. Or like today, she's going out, and I've not long been in."

"Perhaps we can meet up in the next few weeks so that I can get an idea of what you do that's different to what Jo does." Toni's natural nosiness was working. This was going to make some good reporting, she just knew it.

"Good idea. I can tell you how it should really be done." Jed winked and turned to get his breakfast.

She put her food on a table next to Jo and went to find herself coffee. It looked and smelled strong. This was what she needed, as long as she could add plenty of sugar.

Jo ate her food mostly in silence. "Is your food okay?" she finally asked, trying to find some topic of conversation.

Toni raised her eyebrow at the lame question and motioned with her toast, and then looked around the room. Several officers looked at her briefly. It was going to take a while to get used to being stared at. Hopefully the officers' curiosity would settle once she'd been around a week or two and she'd gotten to know them. Toni thought it was like being the new girl at school, with all that entailed.

She got herself a second coffee to settle her nerves.

Jo looked at her watch as Toni sat. "I need to brief you on army time. We're always early and ready to go at the time stated. So, when we're coming to breakfast, you need to be ready five minutes earlier. We have to be ready to leave for our patrol five minutes before the time stated. That means we always set off on time. There's no room for being late."

"Got it." Toni breathed out slowly. Jo's peremptory tone and somewhat abrasive way of communicating was going to take some getting used to. Timing hadn't always been her strong suit, sure, but she'd get used to it. Jo's irritation at being saddled with her though was going to be a little more difficult to get around.

It was 0600 by the time they'd eaten, and it was already getting hot. In London, the day began with a rising soundwave which got louder as the morning progressed. Sherwood was no different. Sometimes you could be somewhere completely different and some things were just the same.

They were shortly at the gates and about to go outside the wire for the first time. The noise of the base was behind her, and the quiet of the world in front of the gates and into the distance was a contrast she hadn't expected. Although she really had no idea what to expect. Jo had made her put a scarf across her face to keep out the dust, and with sunglasses and her helmet, she was protected as well as she could be. It was stifling. Before they'd left the base, her scarf was already damp with sweat. Her clothes underneath her armor and backpack were also wet, and her backpack seemed to have doubled in weight since they'd set off less than ten minutes ago. That flash of doubt from the day before hit her again. Could she do this? Was she capable? She straightened her shoulders. Dammed if she'd give in this early.

She was quickly introduced to the regulars of the Female Engagement Squad, or FEZ as they called it. Remembering their names over the next couple of days would be difficult. Jo referred to them with their rank and last name. The squaddies mostly just used their nicknames.

"This is Private Dance." Jo nodded toward one guy whose face was as invisible as Toni's. "He's one of the three soldiers I've put in charge of your safety."

He shook her hand. "I'm Dance, but they call me Flash. We all have nicknames we've got by doing something mad or bad. And no, I didn't flash anyone. It's in the look, see?" Flash looked at Toni, and his eyes twinkled. "This here's Wiffy, who uses too much strong aftershave," he said, indicating a serious-looking young man who nodded her way. "And last but not least, this is Sprint, known officially as Private Rush. He moves *fast*." Sprint looked at her and ran on the spot. The others jeered and teased him.

Jo held up her hand to stop the banter. "When we set off, I want you to stick to me like glue. Do what I do and go where I go. It'll seem awkward at first, but I want to see how you cope. We'll be out for about four hours, and we'll stay local, sticking to routes that I know have been cleared of Improvised Explosive Devices overnight."

Toni nodded, wishing they could go back to the banter. But

the somber intensity returned the moment the gate opened, and her heart hammered against her chest. They were outside the wire and into the silence. Inside the base, Toni knew safety. She thought she did anyway. Despite knowing all things were relative, it seemed safe. Here, though, it wasn't safe at all. She felt it in the air: the expectation of violence, the imminent possibility of attack. Her vision swam, and she gripped her camera harder, forcing herself to calm down. She slowed her breaths down by counting. Slow. Deep. *Someone could be holding a phone and waiting to set off an IED in the road. There could be Taliban in the hillside waiting for the right unit to pass their way to set it off. No. Stop.* This was what she'd signed up for. She could do this.

She set off behind Jo, focusing on her external world instead of her internal one. Jo wore her load on her back with rounds of ammunition, an anti-personnel mine, a dozen high-explosive grenades, a first aid kit with morphine, three quarts of water, a lightweight stretcher, flares, and camera. She also had a notebook and treats for the children in the villages. When she'd shown her load to Toni as she packed it up, it seemed an impossible amount for a person to carry, but Jo assured her she could handle it just fine.

Copying Jo was easier said than done. As the platoon set off, Toni could see they moved in a way that was some kind of choreographed dance across the landscape. Each soldier moved forward, turning and watching the horizon down the sights of their rifle with a vigilance she could scarcely comprehend. Jo was fully participating in part of this dance and if Toni treated it as some mapped-out way of covering ground, she could take part competently. It was apparent that Jo was normally in a squad in the middle of the platoon, and she asked Flash to take point at the front of it.

They hadn't covered much distance, perhaps only a few hundred yards, when Toni's legs started to burn. She was a long-distance runner, played sports, and considered herself reasonably fit, but this was something beyond her experience. Her electronics bag felt impossibly heavy, and the pressure chafed her shoulders through her body armor. The continual twisting, moving down to one knee and turning, then rising and then down to the other knee made her legs burn. Searching the horizon and being aware of the possibility they were being watched created tension in her shoulders that made her want to scream. She watched the two squads in front of them covering the ground in a similar way and couldn't help but be impressed as they moved over the barren ground.

She tried telling herself to relax a little. But the most difficult thing to cope with was the heat that sapped her body. As she followed the steps of the troops and looked to the horizon, her mind was working out the adjectives that would describe this heat. Draining, sapping, wet, exhausting, and boiling. The landscape was varying shades of brown and beige behind a curtain of heat waves that moved over the sand like water. Her squad shifted behind a crumbling adobe wall that looked as if it once belonged to a small building, and while Flash and the soldier she thought was Wiffy kept watch, Jo pulled her scarf down and drank a bottle of water. The other soldier—maybe Rush—gestured to Toni, and they did the same. The water was warm, but Toni swallowed it like it was the elixir of life, and it breathed new energy into her body.

Jo moved across to her. "How are you feeling?"

"I'm okay. I needed the drink, and my body knows it's done something different today, but I'm good." Toni ignored her aching legs and sore shoulders. There was no way she would say that she was anything but okay.

"Good. We'll relieve our guard so they can drink, then we'll be on our way." Jo looked her over as though checking to make sure she wasn't lying, then turned away.

Toni breathed out and rolled her shoulders and neck. She noticed they were being guarded by one of the other squads. There was a lot she was going to have to get used to. She made mental notes of colors and smells, the way her skin felt and the way the soldiers' eyes never seemed to stay still. It would paint the story in a way she never could if she wasn't right there in the middle of it all.

When they were on their way again, Jo talked to her about things she should be watching for, both close and farther away. Things like unexplained movements and lights and shadows that jumped. She talked about Flash and his instincts for knowing when trouble was ahead.

Exhaustion set in. Her feet were moving but the constant kneeling, ducking, and rising combined with the heat and the weight began to take their toll. Her vision continued to swim occasionally, and several times she grew dizzy enough that she stumbled. They stopped a couple more times for water breaks, and then she saw relief in the form of the gate they'd left behind four hours ago. It was such a welcome sight that she could have wept. She wouldn't, of course, until she was alone in her bunk. She wanted to throw off all this weight, take a cold shower, and fall into bed.

"We'd normally have a full debrief, but I'll let everyone off today," Jo said. There was a whoop from the men, and she rolled her eyes. "Tomorrow is for normal fitness drills and the inter-company volleyball match for those of you in it. We need to be ready for 1800 on Tuesday to take Ms. James on another practice patrol. Check company orders for details."

The men dispersed, and Toni followed Jo back to their quarters.

"I'd like to talk to you about how it went today. Once you've had a shower, we can debrief over some lunch. You're free for the rest of today and tomorrow, so you can recover."

Toni wondered just how bad she looked when she took in Jo's look of pity. "Thank you. I'm starving."

"That's what being out here does. You get hungry and you eat, and there's always food available because you're expending a lot of energy," Jo said. "Let's regroup here in thirty minutes."

Toni let her body armor drop to the floor in a wet, sweaty

heap. As she stripped down to her underwear, she realized she'd have to do a lot of laundry out here. She'd need to ask Jo how to wash clothes and where.

Toni didn't have time to lie down and let her body dissolve into the mattress. She forced herself up and to the showers and noticed the sign marking a female in the shower. For the briefest second, she thought of Jo in the shower, right there next to her. *Naked.* She scrubbed fast, trying to get the image out of her head. But there was no denying the allure of a strong, powerful woman in charge. *Stop it. This is work. Be professional.* The water went cold, and she shivered, but she wasn't sorry for the chill when she walked back out into the heat.

Once they were both clean and dressed, she and Jo went to get food and drink. They ate in silence. Jo had been professional but distant, and Toni wondered if there was any way to break down that impersonal wall. Not only would it help with her story, but it would also make this less of a trial if she could have a friend.

Jo cleared their plates. Toni would have gotten up to get them both a drink, but her body was so stiff and tired, she could barely move.

"How do you feel now that you're clean and have some food in you?" Jo set down two mugs on their table.

How honest should she be? She didn't want Jo to think she was weak, that she would be a burden. "I was hot and uncomfortable before we'd gone fifty yards, and I'm a little sore. I need more practice, and then I'll be fine."

"Good. I have to say you coped much better than I could've hoped. You're obviously fit."

"Fit for a journalist, you mean?" Toni raised her eyebrow.

Jo froze and frowned. "I wasn't being rude, I swear."

Toni laughed. "I know you weren't. I was teasing."

"Oh," said Jo. "Did you understand the way we worked together and how we signaled each other?"

So much for getting Jo to lighten up and let her walls down.

"I'll need more time to understand it fully, but I got a good idea of what's happening. "What do you do for fitness?" Toni turned back to something a little more personal.

"I tend to run around the base late at night when it's a little cooler, and we have a well-equipped gym. Running in the heat when I started out here got me acclimatized much more quickly though," Jo said.

"Can I run with you a couple of times to work out the route?"

Jo didn't answer for a while. "Well, er, yes. Of course. We can go tonight." Jo stared past her, her jaw clenched slightly.

Toni had put her foot in it again. *Remember, Jo doesn't want to be my friend.*

"Back to work matters. You'll need to be on top of your first aid while you're on patrol, just in case. I've asked the medics to give you a demo about how to deal with casualties should we have problems out on patrol. You'll find it useful. I've set it up for 1100 tomorrow, and it should last about three or four hours. Once you've completed it, you'll be free until Tuesday 1800, when we'll go for a dusk patrol."

"Great, that sounds good. I need to talk to the comms team about jumping on their network to send my email, and how to access the internet on base to update the web pages of the newspaper. I thought I might go now."

"I'll come with you and introduce you. I suspect you'll need their advice particularly when we're at the patrol base," Jo said.

Jo took her to the right area, made cursory introductions, and left. Toni faced the group with a smile, hoping she didn't look as lost as she felt without Jo there as a guide. It didn't take long before they were talking tech though, and she was more at ease. She got names and titles, and she started asking questions. When had they joined? Why? What was it like out here? What did they miss from back home?

It was exhilarating and a great reminder of why she was there in the first place. She needed to remember that she wasn't a soldier.

Yes, she needed to do all this training, so she could be out with them, but she was here to talk to people, and that's exactly what she was going to do.

Having completed another exhausting day in Afghanistan, Toni became more positive about her time with the Fizers. She'd survived her first patrol and hadn't messed it up, even though it felt like she'd been in a boxing match and lost. Jo told her she'd done better than expected, and while there was definitely a negative slant to that, she decided to see the positive in it. She could hear Jo on the other side of the blanket humming a tune briefly as she got into bed. So intimate, yet at the same time, so distant. And why should that matter?

CHAPTER FIVE

IT WAS NEARLY 0100 when Jo and Toni walked from their tent out toward the base perimeter. They met soldiers with towels and wash kits on their way to the showers, others in uniform obviously on their way out to patrol, and those on their way to get some food or drink. The base that never closed was still awake.

"You think I'll need five pints of water?" Toni had been incredulous when she'd suggested a bottle per lap.

Jo knew that dehydration was their worst enemy while trying to keep fit, and she didn't want to have to stop to take Toni to the med tent because she hadn't drunk enough. "You'll thank me in an hour or so. Come on, let's get moving."

They each carried a bag of water bottles to replace the water they sweated out. Jo started jogging as they left the tented area behind, and Toni followed. Jo showed Toni where she put her stash to mark out the laps and set out running. She'd never had anyone run with her in the daytime, let alone late at night. Although Toni said she was fit and that she jogged, Jo didn't know what pace to set, so she ran at her normal speed without pushing herself. Having another person would ruin her alone time, those nightly quiet moments when she could be inside her head with no worries. But Toni was silent and apart from her heavy breathing, the only noises she heard as they moved around the camp were those of the base. The sounds were accompanied by smells of showers, toilets, and food as they made their way around the track. She noticed these things as she tried her best to empty her mind of thought, but she couldn't really, not with Toni beside her. How could a woman getting ready to go jogging at one in the morning still look so beautiful? Why did her running top have to fit her breasts so perfectly? And why, oh why, did the shorts not cover a hell of a lot more of her long, slim legs? Jo focused on the pounding of her feet on the ground, trying to stomp out the attraction that had no place here.

They stopped for water after each lap, and Jo noticed after four laps that Toni's breathing was jagged as she bent double with her hands on her knees. "Are you okay? Maybe you should stop now."

"No, I'm good. I'm just not used to the heat," Toni said.

When they set out again, Jo wasn't so sure. She understood that Toni would keep going, that she was stubborn and wouldn't admit defeat. Jo slowed, just a little, and hoped that Toni wouldn't notice. She didn't want to break her.

"I know what you're doing, and I'm not giving in. Keep going." Toni continued at her original speed.

When they got to the end of the run, only half her usual laps, although she didn't tell Toni that, Jo had developed a little new admiration for her. The way she'd stuck to it and pushed herself was commendable, if not entirely sensible.

Toni leaned against the container and looked exhausted, but her eyes were bright. "Thank you. I really had to push to do that, and the last couple of laps were torture."

Jo could see the sense of achievement it had given her. "If you want company any time, you only need to ask," she said before she could stop herself. She tried to ignore the way Toni's shirt clung to her sweaty body. Tried not to stare at her skin glistening in the moonlight as they walked to the showers together. She tried to ignore the fact that she was trying so bloody hard to ignore these facts. There was no room for them in her life or mind. She hurried out of the shower, back to the tent, and got ready quickly enough that she was already in bed by the time Toni was coming in.

The following morning, Jo went off to sort out their next operation and deal with her day-to-day admin, leaving Toni to her own devices. Once she'd finished the visits to the ops center and the company clerk, she went to get a cup of tea. She could see her men playing volleyball in the distance and smiled. It was good to see them having fun. The volleyball was loud and the joshing back and forth was the good part of everyday life as a squaddie.

"Go, Jim, go! Yes! Good shot."

The cacophony of cheering and clapping grew louder as she approached. *Jim?* They didn't have a Jim amongst her men. She squinted and saw that *Jim* was a woman with brown hair. *Jim* was Toni.

Jo stayed where she was with her tea and watched the game progress. Toni was an excellent blocker and outside hitter with lots of spring as she jumped up at the net. Jo could see how athletic Toni was and looked forward to coming up against her in the opposing team. She looked at Toni's lithe body, her broad shoulders, and slim hips. If she ran a hand across those shoulders and down her back... God, what was she thinking? She shouldn't be having these feelings for a colleague she hardly knew and who was undoubtedly straight. She had a career to focus on and couldn't handle any diversions, however beautiful they may be. She walked back to her tent and shifted her focus to their trip the next day.

Toni came back to the tent. "I thought I was hot before, now I'm roasted. I'm going for a shower."

Jo's hormones immediately reacted to the sheen of sweat covering Toni's body, and they had her core doing somersaults. She became overheated with a strange mixture of lust and anger. She swallowed and took control, trying not to act as if she were a teenager with a crush. "How did the team do? Did you win?"

"We came close but lost in the quarter finals to HQ. Who would've thought that clerks and stores guys would be so good? It was a tough match. I thought you might join us at some point."

"I enjoy playing and would have loved to take part. I did watch a little, and I wondered who *Jim* was," Jo said.

"I went over to watch, and they asked me to play in a later round. They called me Ms. James before we played because that was how you referred to me. I told them it was Toni, but it was already too late. I was Jim."

"I had to deal with a couple of admin matters that wouldn't wait. It was happenstance that you were there and could take my place. Thank you." Jo was happy that Toni had enjoyed the tournament, and it had obviously given her time to get to know the troops without her being there. Maybe things with the reporter were going to be all right. Just so long as she could bury the irksome attraction trying to get her attention, everything would be fine.

***

The platoon was standing at the gates ready to start the second practice patrol for Toni's benefit and chatting amongst themselves. Jo looked at her watch for the third time. She'd explained to Toni that army time was five minutes before time, but even allowing for that, Toni was late. She hadn't been in their tent when Jo came out for the patrol, so she'd wrongly assumed she was already on her way here.

There was a commotion at the back of the platoon. "I'm sorry, I'm sorry. I forgot the time. I was interviewing one of the chefs and got carried away. I'm here now and ready to go."

Toni was breathless as she spoke. She'd obviously run all the way. Jo banged her fists against her thighs. *Damn reporter.* "Okay, platoon. We're ready." Her voice was steady as she looked toward the now open gates. The sun was low in the sky, giving the landscape a golden hue that was somehow magical. She breathed in the calm it gave her and breathed out her irritation at Toni, then turned around. "Toni, I want you to follow Private Rush, just like you did with me on Sunday. Where he goes, you go. Dance, you're on point. I'll follow behind. Just remember that as the sun gets lower and disappears, the light and shadows will affect your vision. You'll need to be doubly careful."

The platoon headed out, and Jo focused solely on their patrol.

After about an hour, the squad stopped for a water break. She ensured they had a squad protecting them as they dropped and lay in a shallow ditch. As she took off her helmet and poured a little water over her head and drank, she became aware of Toni joshing with the rest of the squad about the dust on their faces. Toni stood, completely unaware of her surroundings and a sliver of fear moved into Jo's stomach. Dance and Rush moved out of cover to pull her down. *This* was the reason she didn't want a reporter on patrol with them. Either she'd be killed or someone with her would when they tried to protect her.

Jo raised her chin and sweat dripped down her back, compounded by the flare of fear at Toni's disregard for safety. She had to stop herself from shouting. *Stay calm.* "Squad. We'll speak about this at debrief. Let's give the others a break before we continue."

The patrol was uneventful after that. Jo briefed Toni on the things she should notice when patrolling in the dusk, like how visibility was reduced as darkness falls, and it became difficult to read the terrain. It meant that it was easy for soldiers to lose their bearings, particularly if there was gunfire flashing in the distance. Toni's squad was very quiet, and Jo knew the soldiers were already dreading the debrief.

They entered the base at the end of the patrol, everyone tired and ready for a shower and food. "Good work, men. I only want to debrief Ms. James and her squad. Tomorrow is fitness drills. Be ready to go to the villages on Thursday. There'll be an O group tomorrow at 1800. Dismissed." Jo had already turned toward the small square inside the gate and was waiting for Toni and her squad.

"Normally I would speak to you separately from Ms. James, but I want her to hear this. What were you men doing? You're professional soldiers, specifically tasked with protecting Ms. James. What did you do wrong? Someone tell me." Jo took in Toni's look of surprise and mentally shook her head. She didn't even know something had gone wrong.

"Ma'am, we lost concentration and let Ms. James stand up without us noticing," Wiffy said.

Jo waited. "And what else?"

"We had to leave cover to get her to safety," Wiffy said.

"Ms. James, perhaps you can tell me what your actions would mean to the soldiers." Jo kept her face like stone with no hint of emotion. Showing how angry she was wouldn't help the situation.

"I'm so sorry." Toni was turned toward the soldiers as she spoke but was looking at the ground. Her lip quivered. "I've let you all down. I wasn't thinking. I put you all at risk. There's no excuse." She turned toward Jo. "It won't happen again." She put her arms around herself and slumped her shoulders.

"I think you all are now clear as to the mistakes you made. You need to be one hundred percent vigilant and focused. We have a civilian with us, which means we have to be extra aware of her lack of training and discipline. Dismissed." Jo ran to the shower block and changed quickly, hoping to avoid Toni. She was obviously still talking to the squad or avoiding returning to their tent, so Jo headed to the admin offices, deciding that a little bit of paperwork and ops planning might help her calm down.

When she returned to the tent, Toni's side was dark. Jo had finally calmed down. Hopefully they'd all learned a lesson. They couldn't expect a civilian to know what they were doing; they'd had months of training and years of experience. They were going to have to have eyes like hawks to keep Toni and themselves safe. And she had to admit to a twinge of real fear at the idea of Toni getting hurt out there, all that beauty and sweetness snuffed out in the blink of an eye before Jo could get to know her any better. That was an aside, of course, and she didn't *need* to get to know Toni. She just needed to keep her alive.

***

By the following afternoon, it was clear that Toni had been avoiding her. "Once you're showered, I'd like to talk about the village before we go tomorrow. I need you to have a full background of what's happened there. It'll help give you a better sense of the people."

"Sure. I won't be long."

Jo leaned back on her bed and rested her eyes whilst she prepared her facts, deftly and defiantly ignoring thoughts of Toni in the shower.

"Knock, knock. Are you awake?" It seemed only a moment later that Toni appeared in the entranceway with two mugs.

"Always, if you're going to bring me tea," Jo said, wiping the sleep out of her eyes.

"And cake," Toni said. "I'm trying to get my account in credit, for those times when I get it wrong."

Jo didn't know how to respond. She was doing her best to keep out of trouble, but Jo was sure that Toni was going to get out of hand and things would be difficult to control yet again. Tomorrow was their first proper patrol, and Jo wasn't certain it was a good idea. In fact, her gut told her it was a bad one. "We're going to the village up the valley closest to the base. It's the first village I went to with this platoon when we were all new. One of the intelligence officers from the Royal Dundees that we took over from came with us. He was in charge, as he'd been to the village before." Jo took a big swig of tea as she considered how much more information to impart. She couldn't forget, even for a second, that Toni was a reporter. "I learned a lot. There was no conversation between him and any of the villagers as such. He needed information, so when he spoke to the old man who was the village leader, he interviewed him. He only wanted to know about Taliban movements, and there was no day-to-day chat about the village or its inhabitants. There were no women or children present. I looked at the village leader, an elderly man with white hair and a beard surrounding a face rendered walnut brown by the sun, and the two younger men standing protectively with him. I took a chance and introduced myself. I asked if they were his sons. It was lovely to see the old man smile. It could have been because I was speaking Pashto. The other officer had spoken slowly in English with added hand signals."

"Did you expect him to speak with you?" Toni asked.

"I was hoping that it was unusual enough that he would talk. I understood that women didn't have this kind of place in Afghan society, so I was concerned. I needn't have worried. He introduced me to his sons. Khava, his eldest son's name, means hero and his second son's name, PurDel, means courageous. He told me he'd given all his sons strong names. He said that he had two more sons and a wife and daughters."

"Do you know why strong names were important to him?" Toni asked.

"I have to guess, but names are usually given to children that have tribal or village significance if they're not from the Qur'an. So I expect the chief needs his sons to give strength to his leadership and perhaps take over from him."

"Seems sensible. I'll look it up later."

A sudden chill hit Jo's stomach. "You can't print their names. That would be a death warrant."

Toni flushed. "No, of course I wouldn't." She sat upright and went rigid. "I'm sorry you think I'd do that. I need to learn all I can about the culture so that I can show their lives in more detail, but I'd never put anyone in danger."

"I'm just making sure. I wasn't accusing you of anything. You're new, and I have to protect everyone until you find your feet," Jo said.

Toni nodded, and her body relaxed. "Do they have a school?"

"No, he told me that the Taliban haven't allowed any education. One or two of the villages further up the valley have informal classes, and we'll visit them as part of our patrols. But they risk their lives trying to give their children an education," Jo said.

Toni made notes in one of her bigger notebooks. "How did you manage to speak to the women?"

"I asked the leader. He thought for a moment and nodded. He spoke to one of his sons, and they gestured me forward. He stopped the rest of the squad from following me though." Jo relived the moment in her mind. Walking off into the unknown, alone. But that was what she'd signed up for, life as service to the sovereign and country. Grandiose large claims often whittled down into a risky solo walk.

"How did that make you feel?" Toni asked.

There was no doubt in her mind that Toni was a good reporter. She was getting Jo to tell her what had happened almost without her realizing that she was about to spill her inner thoughts. She smiled. "I see what you're doing."

Toni laughed. "I wondered if you'd notice me slipping something personal in there."

"I just wanted to explain how things started a few weeks ago so that you're aware of the fact that it was only a few weeks ago. You'll be able to see how my relationship with the women has blossomed." She didn't need to say that she didn't want to answer questions about feelings. They weren't relevant. At least not in relation to a reporter's questions.

"Why do we always go out on foot?" Toni asked. "Isn't it quicker to use vehicles?"

"Good question. We don't always walk. It depends where we go. We decide based on the village, the roads to them, how often IEDs have been used on the road to kill us, and things like that. Tomorrow's village is relatively close. It's not on a main road and can be reached along a number of different paths which gives us freedom to choose a path at the last moment, so we don't become predictable."

"That makes sense. It's about safety as much as anything, even though it's a lot harder physically," Toni said with a cute grimace.

"Yes, as well as keeping us in range of the big guns above us in the hills. The ditches and such provide safety as well. It's not just one thing that influences my decision."

Toni was still scribbling in her notebook as Jo stood. Wisps of hair had come loose from her ponytail and framed her face, making her look soft and sweet. When she looked up at Jo and smiled, the resulting flutter in Jo's stomach made her swallow hard. "Come on, I have a platoon briefing at 1800. We should leave." Maybe having Toni here would work out after all.

***

The next morning started hot and bright like nearly every other day since her tour had started. But today was different. It was Toni's first patrol into a village, and it had become a matter of pride for her that she got things right. Jo wanted her to be safe and to get information for her reports and articles. It reflected back on her, and she would be measured by Toni's results. She'd completed the two patrols around the grounds outside the base, but this was real, and there was no room for error. They were visiting a village that were happy to receive Jo's visits, but she shouldn't be complacent. It would only take one suicide bomber to forfeit the lives of many people.

Jo wanted Toni to see the work that ISAF was doing and the happiness amongst the women and children when they realized what change could bring. The project was about affecting long term change in the country. Too often in the past, the countries taking over in Afghanistan had promised support but they all left, taking their promises with them and leaving the villagers with nothing more than dirt and bombs.

The platoon set out from the base, and Jo moved into her usual central position and noticed that Toni went between Flash and Wiffy, just as she'd been told to do. Vallonman was leading the way. His name was Greg, but he was the operator of the Vallon IED detector and was always in front of the patrol. He was an absolute necessity to keep them safe, as these pathways were riddled with landmines and IEDs. They moved slowly and surely forward, checking the horizon and where they placed their feet. Their operation had been accepted by the HQ and as usual, there was backup in reserve if it was needed. There was also heavy artillery support available from the distant hills above them. But Jo knew full well that wouldn't do them a whole lot of good if they got caught in an ambush or hit an IED. Once again, she glanced at Toni. It would be a nightmare if things went sideways, but even more so with her in their midst. Jo set the thought aside and focused.

It took nearly two hours to get to the village. The platoon split into sections, and those entering the village marched forward with rifles at their shoulders, looking down the barrels and pivoting as they turned and checked it was all clear. Jo could see the village elder and his sons outside one of the houses and knew that it was safe. He wouldn't risk his children if there were likely problems.

"Salaam Alaikum," Jo said to the man and then to his sons. She checked that all around her was clear and that they'd received the okay from her external team. "Chetoor hasti?"

He nodded and smiled, but his gaze went to Toni before he focused on Jo for an explanation.

"This is Toni James, a journalist from London who is writing about our work here," Jo said, speaking in slow English so Toni could follow, although it would have been easier in Pashto. She motioned to the elder in charge. "This is Atal, and these are two of his sons, Khava and PurDel." Jo wasn't certain how the villagers would accept a journalist and she waited, her expression neutral but her heart pounding. If they turned them away, it could damage the relationship they'd built to this point.

"Do you have a photographer with you?" Atal asked, looking behind her. He looked sad when there was no one.

Toni looked at Jo for permission, then smiled and stepped forward. "No. I take my own. And I'd love to take shots of you and your sons." She opened her bag and took out one of her better cameras. "I'll have to go back to the base to print the pictures, but

I'll try and get them back to you if you'd like copies." The three men gathered around her as she showed them the camera and some of the photos she'd already taken. She seemed completely and utterly at ease.

Jo marveled at how Toni slipped into conversation and asked questions that were non-intrusive and yet yielded genuine answers. Some of her initial worry about how Toni would fit in with the villagers dissipated. She could see the women watching from behind a corner of the building and out of sight of many of the soldiers. They were careful about being seen with the men and would only allow the translator, who was always a man, outside any room or area they met in. In reality, she always met the women alone and only called the translator if there was genuinely something she didn't understand or couldn't communicate.

After asking if it was okay, she walked over to the women and beckoned Toni to follow. She was instantly surrounded by children hugging her legs and laughing. She introduced Toni as she removed her helmet and gestured for Toni to do the same. The women sat down on the ground in an area that was big enough for them all. There was some shade but not a lot.

Toni took some photographs and asked questions that Jo translated as well as she could. The women giggled at their words and gestures and joined in the fun. Toni's recorder sat unobtrusively in front of her feet, and she made notes without looking at the notebook, which was impressive. It also meant she didn't break the flow of conversation or eye contact, and the women clearly didn't feel threatened or like they weren't being heard.

"Does the Taliban know you've been talking to me over the last few weeks?" Jo asked the group when there was a pause. They looked at each other and Sahar, the self-elected leader, nodded. The banter stopped, and the mood turned somber.

"We think they have eyes and ears in the village and know what we're doing, but we have ways of dealing with things."

The other women all started talking at once, and it was

impossible to work out what anyone was saying. Sahar gestured to them to let her speak.

"We're expecting a visit from them any day," Sahar said. "As you know, our first teacher is too frightened, but we have two of his older students who are happy to take his place. We still don't have a school room or proper materials, but we have open air classes with lookouts in case we get a visit. Although we have no teaching materials, in some ways it's easier because we don't have to hide books or paper, and it's simple to close down a class if we get word that the Taliban are coming. It's going well."

Toni made notes while Jo asked questions about the school and how things were going with individual women. She could see Toni listening closely, occasionally sucking the end of her pencil before writing furiously again.

After an hour or so, Jo ended the visit. She'd created a list of things the women suggested would be useful to help them become more independent. The children popped in and out of the conversation, talking to them both. "Hello, we speak English" was mixed with short phrases like "Manchester United" and "Thank you, lady." One or two of the older ones begged Toni for a pencil and paper. She didn't have any to spare but told the children she'd try and get them some. When they ran out of treats for the children and said farewell, Jo radioed Travers, the lieutenant in charge of the external team, to say they were leaving the village. The sections joined together and moved back toward the base.

The hottest part of the day approached. The patrol back to the base would probably take around three hours as they navigated their way along the valley and around the fields and ruined compounds. The green belt was a system of irrigation ditches that made the whole area rich in crops of vegetables, fruit, and poppies. They were in their usual single file with Vallonman out in front wielding his IED detector when Jo sensed a problem and turned around.

The team slowed, and Jo could see Toni standing with her back to them as she videoed the village behind them. Her escort was covering her, but her actions still angered Jo. Toni was putting her men's lives at risk again. *For god's sake.* She fought to remain calm against the mounting pressure in her head. "Jim and escort, please make progress forward," she said into her radio. Toni continued to film as though she hadn't heard the command.

"Private Dance, move to Jim's position and push her forward. No excuses."

Jo watched as Flash moved across to Toni and tapped her shoulder. She started and looked around. He wordlessly pointed to Jo and marched them on. They'd only gone a few hundred paces when Jo heard a sharp crack that echoed through the air around them.

"Take cover! Incoming."

It was one shot, but the platoon reacted as one man, and they were all face down on the ground in an instant. They couldn't go anywhere off the path as it was likely to be mined. Jo had a small mound between her and where she guessed the shot had come from. It wasn't enough cover. Her heart hammered in her chest, and everything went in slow motion, defined by the tension in the air around them. Two further shots sounded, then there was silence. "Charlie Two from Charlie Two delta. We have contact from around GR641316. Request air support."

Her men readied their weapons, and more shots sounded in the distance. Her platoon engaged and returned fire, but she still needed to get them away from open ground and into better cover. She ordered two soldiers to provide cover fire, allowing the two sections to move into cover. Their heavy machine guns started pouring fire toward the insurgent positions. "Move. Quickly. Move. Move. Faster!" she shouted as they headed into an irrigation ditch ahead. Jo could see Toni keeping her head down as she ran beside the men, and there was no question about the fear in her eyes, even as she kept her phone in a death grip, focusing on the area around her.

Once the troops were concealed, there was the sound of planes in the distance. "Cease fire." There was still sporadic fire from the insurgents. She listened as the fighter jets flew overhead and dropped their load. It was some distance away, but the explosions were loud and the ground vibrated.

Toni gasped slightly. She had her eyes shut tightly, her hands over her ears, and her phone in the dust beside her. At least she wasn't standing up and videoing the damn situation. Despite knowing it was coming and having experienced the sound before, it still twisted inside Jo's body. Someone out there was losing their life. They waited until the noise of the planes disappeared.

"Fire sporadic shots. Let's see if we still have company," Jo said. It was all quiet. Time to get her troops home safely. "Point, start moving west toward the base, taking your squad forward. Dance, follow behind with Jim. The rest of you stick with me and engage the enemy as necessary." She needed to ensure Toni was safe and given how pale and shaky she looked, she needed someone beside her. If Flash's experienced nose didn't keep her out of trouble, then it probably wasn't possible.

They waited for fifteen minutes behind the point, who was now ahead in relative safety along with Toni. She called HQ and told them they were standing down. They moved out and returned to the base slowly and carefully, keeping their eyes open for any further contact. The moment they were back inside the base gates, everyone breathed easier as they stripped off their gear quickly. Toni slumped onto a bench and dropped her bag beside her, her eyes on the ground. She looked haunted. *Good.* Maybe she finally understood the gravity of the situation.

Jo debriefed her men quickly. There'd been heavier fire than they'd expected. Whether it was an attempt at disrupting their visit to the village or whether it was a last gasp attack by the Taliban, it was a serious event.

"Toni. We'll debrief privately later in our quarters. I'll let you know when I'm back." The extra time would give Jo longer to calm down. She didn't want to shout at Toni despite the fact that she deserved it. Toni nodded, picked up her gear, and started toward the tent.

Jo visited the ops center and debriefed the regimental intelligence and operations team before setting out to return to her tent. She retained her professional and stoic façade and didn't say anything at all about Toni's presence or stupidity. This whole embedded reporter thing was a bad idea. Toni had put her men in danger on the very first patrol. She didn't belong here, and the PR from it wasn't worth people's lives. For fuck's sake. What if Toni had died out there?

Jo stopped in the shade and gathered herself. It wouldn't do to lose her temper, but there was no way in hell she would let Toni off the hook. She'd have to learn, or she'd have to leave. Those were the only options.

CHAPTER SIX

TONI SAT ON HER bed in her shorts and tank top, still damp from a shower, her wet hair cooling in the afternoon heat. She was still smarting at getting caught up in the moment, trying to show her audience the wonder of what she could see. Trying to best capture the light and what little shadow there was in the noon sun had been her primary thought. But still...she'd been doing her job. Granted, Toni was new to all this and was going to make mistakes, big and small. Jo had to accept that she was on a learning journey, and that they had different agendas. She was trying to record events and get a good story. Jo should make allowances. Toni would learn, but she needed some space to do what she needed to do. Right?

She sighed and plucked at the blanket. Okay, it wasn't a good time to film, but she needed the practice, and it wasn't like there was ever going to be a *good* time out here. Capturing events on camera was new to her. She'd learned the how and practiced at university but never needed to film anything on her own. In truth, she probably couldn't use the footage anyway because it might give away the village's location. She'd taken some excellent video of the platoon coming under fire and firing back before the noise and fear had gotten through and she'd dropped her phone. That footage was irreplaceable and after all, she was her mother's daughter. Gunfire was something she shouldn't be frightened of. No one ever needed to know that she'd been so scared she felt paradoxically frozen and like she wanted to run as fast as she'd ever run in her life.

She could hear Jo moving around next door and took a deep breath, deciding to face the inevitable. "Jo, I need to speak to you.

Are you up to a visitor?"

"Yes, come on over. I've taken my boots off and haven't showered yet, so it might be a little smelly over here."

Toni entered Jo's bedspace. Jo sat on her bed, her face was smeared with dust and sweat, and Toni had to concentrate and not think about how sexy Jo looked. Her thoughts strayed to sweat running over Jo's body as they lay together. *Stop.*

Jo sighed. "You ignored my orders and put my men at risk yet again, and I'm still working out how to deal with that. I have no problem with you doing your job, but you need to do it within the rules. Honestly, I'm not sure you're capable of that, and I won't jeopardize other people's lives just so you can look at how pretty something is."

Jo's stare was icy, and Toni wished she'd been given the friendlier impersonal stare that was Jo's usual look. This look was cold and officious. Defaulting to a position she'd heard her mother use, she lifted her chin. "But to do my job, I need to be able to cover the work *you're* doing. I get that shots were fired but that *cannot* stop me taking video of the men. I need to show more than just troops playing volleyball and drinking tea." Toni needed to stand up for herself, otherwise she was going to end up sitting in the base writing stuff that barely made it into the paper at all, let alone hit the front page.

Jo's jaw clenched, and she crossed her arms. "But you cannot do that if you're injured or dead or if you cause the injury or death of my men. There's a thin line between getting out there and getting a good story and getting shot. You need to be aware of that. You're making my life very difficult and to be honest, it's rather pissing me off. I'm seriously considering telling the brigadier this isn't working."

Toni's heart lurched. Things had to work between them. If she didn't make the most of this opportunity, she'd be sent back home in disgrace. She'd eat humble pie to get in Jo's good graces again. "Before we go out next time, we can discuss what I can do and when, and I promise I'll obey all your orders." There was a small part of her that was furious that she'd given in. But the other part of her understood that she had to play the game. And this game was serious. It had rules that meant she couldn't do things the way she wanted to without consequence. So be it. "I'm really sorry."

Jo studied her for a long moment, her eyes narrowed. Finally, she gave a sharp nod. "Good. Just know if you disobey my orders, I'll send you home. I need to get cleaned up. We can discuss this later if you have anything more to say."

When Toni looked closely at Jo, she could see dark shadows below her eyes. She was ready to start making good on her apology. "I've already apologized to Flash and Wiffy. As penance, can I buy you a pizza when you're ready?"

"You don't need to do that." Jo had her back turned and was already sorting out her gear.

Toni stood her ground, knowing that if she left now, she'd probably struggle to recover any ground. "I know I don't need to; I'd like to."

Jo turned and stared at her, and Toni didn't miss the way Jo quickly looked her over before meeting her gaze again. Toni tried not to look away in the face of Jo's intensity, and then breathed easier when Jo shrugged.

"Okay. I'll come find you when I'm done."

"I'm going to be sorting out some words and pictures for my first upload, so there's no hurry." She went back to her side of the tent, relieved. Okay, so this wasn't going to be easy, but it didn't need to be. Toni just had to play Jo's game or she'd get sent back to the UK, proving to her mother that she wasn't good enough. She couldn't take that kind of humiliation.

Jo reappeared forty-five minutes later looking a little more relaxed. Her dark hair was wet from the shower, and Toni detected patchouli, the soap scent that Jo preferred. She tried to lean toward Jo inconspicuously to get a little more of the perfume as it gave her a lightness in her chest, and she wanted more.

"I want to show you what I'm working on," Toni said. "Pull up a seat for a moment." She patted the end of her bed, which felt a little intimate, but there were no other options. She held out her laptop. "This is the Daily Globe website, and I've uploaded a couple of images and some copy to start things rolling. My headline is *The Life of an Embedded Reporter in Afghanistan*, and I've added 'Toni James reporting from 2 Fizer in Helmand province.' I then go on to show that I needed some training and how we went on a teaching patrol so I could learn. I've added some pics of us in full gear."

Jo scanned the screen and smiled. "These are impressive. I wasn't expecting that it would look so...well...so professional."

"What do you mean?" Toni crossed her arms, irritation flaring. "I'm a multimedia journalist employed by one of the top papers in the UK. Did you expect me to be a hobbyist hack?"

Jo held up her hands. "I'm sorry. I didn't know what to expect. I'm not on top of multimedia like you obviously are, and it leaves me feeling a little inadequate. Let me try again. This is impressive, and you're already showing us to the public in a good way. I like it."

Toni took pity on her. "I accept your apology. I have some off-duty pics of the squad playing volleyball, and you running in the dark that I'd like to add next before going into some detail about the patrols and things." She didn't say that some of the pictures of Jo running had taken her breath away, and that the intensity of Jo's usual expression had softened under the moonlight, making Toni want to caress her cheek and tell her she was gorgeous. Those pictures would be her private stash for nights when she felt particularly alone.

Toni stood and started clearing her bed as she wrapped her laptop, phone, and cameras in their dustcovers. She picked up her notebook and pen. "I'm hungry. Let's get pizza, and we can work out what I can and cannot show the public about the villages, and how I can get to work on some footage of patrols out on the ground without killing us all."

Jo raised her eyebrow but said nothing. Baby steps, Toni thought. She would win Jo over eventually.

***

A couple of days later, Toni took her place in the squad as they headed toward another village. She was more on edge this time, a little more wary but more focused. None of those were a bad thing, and she knew full well that Jo would be glad that was the case. They'd traveled most of the way in two Mastiff troop carriers with a weapons-mounted Land Rover providing fire support. As in all their travels, the road had been recently cleared of IEDs, which allowed them to travel without a mine clearance squad.

The inside of the Mastiff felt like a hot, metal box, and Toni struggled to relax. The smell of hot bodies with a mixture of various shower gels, aftershaves, and farts was overpowering. She would be glad of the outside air but more than that, she'd be grateful to get away from the feeling of being in a cage. She couldn't shake the thought of being a sitting duck, like in a fairground sideshow, just waiting for a shot to knock you into the tank of water. With no windows, she felt like she was traveling blind through the dark directly toward danger.

Toni was with her protectors in the second of the three-vehicle convoy. Apparently, the Taliban liked to play Russian roulette with the vehicles, deciding which one to set off the IED under at random. The guys didn't talk about it, but there was a lot of joshing as they made progress, hiding any darker thoughts they had with humor and bravado. Toni kept the recording going on her phone and shot a few photos but in the dark, the flash was blinding and without it, the soldiers were vague shapes.

Toni's nerves had literally been shot to hell, and she beat herself up for her fear. This was why she was here. She asked some questions and recorded some great answers, and the ground steadied even with her uncertainty.

When they arrived at the village, she could see that they knew Jo and were pleased to see her. The women made space for both of them just the way they had last time, and Jo spoke with them in her halting Pashto. They talked about families, and their children, and their lives. Toni took a lot of film but didn't catch the faces of the women, and she was aware of avoiding any defining features the village had. She took plenty of Jo hunkered down among the women and children, and her heart warmed as Jo listened carefully, so they knew they were really being heard.

Jo talked to the women about setting up a school; one of the women had been a teacher under the Russian regime some years before. She wanted to train some of the other women as teachers. Four villages surrounded them with good road links, and they would probably send their children too. But it needed the help of the provincial government and the military to get things off the ground. The hearts and minds program of the ISAF was clearly now in full swing, and the forces pushing the Taliban back were trying to give the Afghan people more electricity and water by protecting and then upgrading a dam of the Helmand river. The Taliban had mostly moved further north and away from this village complex, but the villagers' fear and concern about Taliban reprisals was evident from the discussions. It needed the stronger-willed women to push things forward even at the risk to themselves and their families.

Toni was desperate to capture the discussions, so she made notes and recorded what she could. She also wanted to get Jo speaking Pashto to the women and then explaining in English so that Toni could understand. Sometimes she got muddled and spoke English to the women and then spoke Pashto to Toni. They laughed and teased her. Toni wanted to give an honest representation of the fear but also the joy and happiness that the women felt to have a voice in the future.

***

Life on the base had become normal and despite it being completely alien when she arrived, Toni settled in and made herself at home. They visited villages every few days. One evening, she managed to call her father. At the sound of his voice, her eyes welled up. He was a reminder of home, which felt so far away.

"Hey, darlin', lovely to hear you. How's life treating you?"

"It's going well. It's hard with the heat and the dust, but we manage," Toni said.

"Is the dust bad?"

"It covers *everything*. I have to be careful about my electronics. I'm always cleaning and dusting." Toni laughed loudly, and her father joined in.

"We both know that you and cleaning don't go together in the same sentence," he said, still laughing. "I've been reading your articles on the web and enjoying them. My clever girl. I didn't ever think about the heat and how it would affect people until you showed all the bottled water and empty bottles."

"I don't think I'll ever drink water again without thinking about the undying heat of Afghanistan." Toni took a swig from her water bottle. Her father laughed again when he saw what she was doing. Toni felt warm inside. He loved her and was always there for her.

"I've loved the volleyball pics and videos too. There's a handsome woman playing for one team that you seem to have taken quite a few shots of."

She flushed, well aware of how many photos she'd taken of Jo. "That's Jo. She's the captain I work with. She's incredibly professional, and I really admire her bravery." Toni didn't say that she also admired how great she looked in a tank top and combat pants. "The whole regiment is following my work, which is pretty cool." She grinned. "And you're right. Lots of the comments are about wanting more pics of Jo."

"You two get along okay?"

"I created a few problems for her at the start. Me being stupid and risking my life and the lives of people around me. Damn. She was *pissed*."

"What happened?"

"I took too many risks taking video of the platoon one time when we were under fire. I have a job to do, and she wants to keep me safe. I get that, but I'm not going to get a story unless I take a few chances. We talked it out, but I know she's still not happy about having me around. So, it's been a difficult couple of weeks." There was silence for a moment.

"Sometimes you sound just like your mother. You may not want to hear that, but chasing the story is your reason for being a journalist, and you're growing into your mother's world."

"Please, Daddy. I'm not my mother, you know that," Toni said. How could he think she was?

"I know that. But that doesn't mean you don't live in her world and need to fight for what you want to do."

"People the world over think that it's life and death out here, and it can take you in a minute. That's true, but I want to get them to understand that the soldiers risking their lives are just ordinary people like you and me. They have families and loved ones, and at the same time they're risking their lives." She was fully aware that she'd skated over his comment about her living in her mother's world. Once again, she was being told her world wasn't hers: it was one her mother controlled and which Toni was a ghost in. That wasn't a conversation she wanted to have. Ever.

"I'm sure you'll get that message across. Stay safe," he said when their connection began to warp. "Keep being my brilliant girl and be happy. I love you."

"I love you too, Daddy," Toni said. When he was gone, an emptiness overtook her that was hard to explain. Her moment with home, that familiarity and warmth, was irreplaceable. But being like her mother? The thought made her skin crawl like she was wearing wool in the summer. Surely she was just being a good journalist. Granted, she'd learned a lot from watching her mother, but that didn't mean she'd treat people like they were replaceable or unimportant. Did it?

***

Toni lay in bed each night, conscious of Jo lying only a few feet away. She could hear Jo's breathing as she slept and wondered what she was dreaming about. She had this barrier around her, as strong and impenetrable as the wall around the base. It was fascinating how Jo was close to her men and the villagers but that no one really seemed to know her. She shared very little of herself even as she got other people to open up. Toni wasn't certain that anyone else was aware of that. But through her lens, and via her questions, she saw it was definitely true.

"Are you all right? Are you ill?" a hoarse, sleep-filled voice asked. "Your breathing is uneven, and you must have turned over twenty times."

"I can't sleep. I'm hot, and my head is full of stories and feelings I want to get into words. I can't switch my brain off."

"I get that sometimes. It can help to start over," Jo said. "Go to the loo, remake your bed, have a cool drink, and get back into bed."

"I've tried that. It didn't work. Will you talk to me? Maybe if I can think of something else, I'll sleep."

Jo's bed creaked, and there was silence for a few minutes. "I don't think I can do this."

Toni's pulse raced a little at the huskiness of Jo's tone. "You can't talk to me? You can in the daylight. What makes the dark different?"

More silence. "It's a different place." Jo's voice was low and strained as if she were pushing out each word.

"You sound...frightened?" Toni wasn't sure that was the right word, but she wasn't about to let up if she could get Jo talking.

There was a long moment of silence. "I am."

Toni stiffened. The brave and heroic soldier was frightened. Not of the dark, but of sharing time with Toni in this intimate way.

"But it's only me, and we talk all the time in the light. I won't hurt you."

"Maybe. But this is my safe space, and I've never shared it," Jo said softly. "The darkness of the tent is like a warm cocoon for me, and I don't have the worries I have in the daylight."

Toni wanted to hold this courageous woman in her arms. "I know you have lots of responsibilities and pressures, but you always appear confident, and you're popular with your troops. What do you mean exactly?"

More silence. "I've never found personal communication easy. I have to work at what to say and how to say it."

Toni's intrigue and excitement ramped up at Jo opening the door, even just an inch. "Tell me about you as a child."

"That's easy. I'm an only child of service parents, and we moved every two years. I've been all over but nowhere for long," Jo said.

Which must make a life in the services easier since it was all Jo had ever known. It was an interesting insight. "It must have been hard getting to know people if you were always on the move," Toni said. "I've always been in the same spot in Oklahoma and then in London, I've been in the same place for six years."

"In some ways, I envy that. I was always the new girl in class, and after my mother died, I was always away at school. That was hard," Jo said. "I used to have a silly dream that I'd get my mother back somehow and go to a normal school like everyone else. Then I'd wake up, and I'd still be at boarding school."

Toni wasn't sure what to say to that. She'd had plenty of her own dreams about having a normal mom, but saying so when hers was still alive would be insensitive.

"Why did we start this conversation?" Jo asked.

"To help me sleep, I think." Toni couldn't help but sigh. "I didn't mean to make you unhappy or uncomfortable. How old were you when your mother died?" she asked anyway, desperate to keep the conversation going on this deeper level.

"Ten. Just the right age for boarding school, according to my father. Get a bit of backbone and learn to be independent," Jo said, adopting a lower voice.

"Was it hard being away at school?" Toni couldn't imagine it. Being home with her father had been everything to her.

"In a way. I was always that odd girl. I only had a few...friends. Actually, no friends. Just people I knew," Jo said. "I guess that's still the way things are. I'm surrounded by people, and I like them, but I'm not close to anyone, not really." She sighed deeply. "It gets lonely sometimes. I still feel like that kid on the playground watching from the sidelines... Why am I telling you this stuff?"

"Because it's what friends do, and *we're* friends. Or we will be, in time, if you want." Toni grinned, picturing Jo rolling her eyes. "If it were daylight, I'd come over and hold your hand and thank you for sharing. You'd get embarrassed and push me away both physically and verbally. Then pretend you'd said nothing."

Jo laughed. "You're right."

Toni wanted to keep her talking. "This is a conversation for the darkness, and it can stay in the dark. We don't need to acknowledge it in the daylight if it makes you feel better."

"Do you have a conversation for the darkness? Something that I can keep safe?" Jo asked.

There was something in the way she said it, something subtle, that made Toni shiver.

"Let me think." Toni fluffed up her pancake-flat pillow. "There are two things. When I was growing up, my daddy was my everything because my mother travelled the world. He's always loved her deeply and wouldn't ever ask her not to go. He once said to me, 'It would be like caging a bird. Her feathers would fall out, and she'd lose her gloss.' That means that all my life, my mother has either been going away or coming back. She was never simply *there*. Whenever she came home, she was attached to my father like a new lover, and there was no room for me. It was hard." Toni took a deep breath. Maybe sharing was overrated after all. Did she sound ungrateful, given Jo's loss?

"I can't imagine having them there but not when it counts. At least I had my mum until I was ten. I can remember her giving me one hundred percent before she got sick," Jo said. "Are they still together?"

"Technically. But he still lives in Oklahoma, and she has a house in London. It works for them, as weird as it seems to everyone else. I still struggle with the situation though. I've never said that to anyone, though I think Daddy understands. I live in my mother's house in London, but I rarely see her." Toni's eyes filled with tears. She wasn't going down this route, feeling sorry for herself. It was a dead end. She'd made that journey too many times in her life.

"I can feel your sadness. Most people in the services have stories to tell about difficult lives. Sometimes it's good to remember you're not alone when it comes to feeling a little lost," Jo said.

"For someone who worries about how well they communicate, you're doing great." Toni needed to shut down this line of discussion that would only lead to her brick wall of crumbling emotions.

"I'm safe, and it's dark. Nothing more, nothing less." Jo yawned loudly. "I'm sorry. I can't hear your second thing tonight. I need to sleep. Maybe we can return to this another night."

"Thank you for talking to me. I think I'll be able to sleep now." Toni turned and pondered the surprise that was Jo Fitzgerald. The frightened child in the dark, and the handsome and sexy woman in the light. It was an intoxicating combination and as she fell asleep, she thought about crossing the flimsy divide that led to Jo's bed.

CHAPTER SEVEN

"Captain Fitzgerald and Ms. James, ma'ams."

Jo awoke with a start to the voice of Corporal Evans. She was out of bed and at the front of the tent in seconds.

"Morning, corporal. This is an early call," Toni said as she yawned, obviously still in bed.

"The colonel has visitors and wants you both in his office in the next ten minutes in working kit," Evans said.

"Okay, we'll be there as ordered." Jo was already turning to sort out her hair and find some clothes. "See you shortly." She spoke a little louder. "Are you up yet, Toni? No going back to sleep."

"I'm upright, if not awake. I'll get moving, don't worry," Toni said. In moments there was a lot of scrabbling, and several swear words. "Do we really have to miss coffee?"

Jo smiled at the slight pleading in Toni's voice. "Let's get it over with and then we can make it a two-coffee morning."

They were both in front of the tent in minutes, water bottles in hand, Jo in her regular Army green and Toni in her navy-blue shirt and cargo pants that she'd adopted as a uniform. Jo liked and appreciated the fact that Toni made an effort to blend in. Not to mention, she looked awfully good in it. Last night's conversation had left her a little raw, and there was a tension between them that hadn't been there before. She hoped it would fade like the mist at dawn and ignored it for now.

They arrived at the HQ offices and waited for the colonel. The door opened, and he ushered them in. Toni stopped, and Jo nearly crashed into her. Something was wrong.

"Come in, Ms. James," the colonel said. "Obviously, no

introductions are necessary."

As Toni slowly recovered from her paralysis, Jo managed to get into the room. Sitting in the colonel's armchair was a woman in her fifties who looked familiar. Standing at the side of the chair was a tanned, sandy-haired younger man wearing brown cargo shorts, a white shirt, and trainers.

There was silence in the room. Jo decided to take matters in her own hands. The woman in the chair was obviously someone important, since she'd been given pride of place in the colonel's armchair. Jo offered her hand but before she could speak, the woman stood.

"I know who you are. The colonel has invited me out on patrol with you to one of the villages today," she said.

"I'm sorry, but that won't be possible. You'll need to attend two days of acclimatization and practice patrols with my team before I'll allow you to come out with me." Jo wasn't going to let this stranger browbeat her into cutting corners.

The woman almost stamped her feet, and her face reddened. She straightened her body, almost imperiously. The man with her looked at the floor, his eyebrows raised.

"Don't you know who I am?" she asked.

"No. I don't know who you are since you didn't introduce yourself. But I'm not risking the lives of my men to take you out to the villages on a whim, whoever you are." Jo turned to the colonel. "Sir, this is standard operating procedure. What's going on?"

The woman raised her chin. "I've been here before, and I know all about protocols. I've been to more war zones and dangerous situations than you are aware of. I would not endanger anyone."

Jo shrugged, puzzled at the colonel's silence. "You may have been. But I don't know that you won't disappear off when you get the whiff of something interesting and endanger us all. I want to see you out on patrol where no one will be hurt. Hence the protocol."

Before the colonel could reply, the woman turned to him. "You invited me here, and now your proposal is being turned down by a mere captain. I need to speak to your superior."

"Mrs. James, please don't be so hasty. There are plenty of other places you could go," the colonel said, clearly on the back foot. "There are other groups for you to work with."

Clarity hit like a brick. *Toni's mother.* Maybe that was why she looked familiar. Now that Jo looked carefully, she could see those flashing gray eyes that her daughter had inherited.

"Get me Brigadier McQueen on the phone, colonel. She's an old acquaintance, and I'm sure we can sort this out," Mrs. James said.

The colonel turned to pick up the phone, red-faced and sweating profusely. Jo didn't like him, but Toni's mother had made him look small in front of one of his troops, and that was a pretty major faux pas. He wasn't going to forget this in a hurry, and Jo was sure she'd end up with the blame. Toni was pale, her hands shoved in her pockets, her jaw clenched tightly. Still, she didn't say anything.

"Ah, ma'am, good morning. It's Colonel Musgrove. Yes, ma'am, it's another hot one. I have Diane James in my office. I think she must have passed straight through Fortress, which is why you didn't know she was here. No. She's not visiting her. She wants to go and visit the women in the villages with Captain Fitzgerald. Yes, exactly what Toni James is already doing. The captain is insisting on Standard Operating Procedures before she'll take the journalist and her photographer out on patrol." His face grew even redder. "Yes, ma'am, but I promised her. No, ma'am. I'll ask her to return to you so that you can brief her. You'll send her by helo? Yes, ma'am, I'll tell her. No, ma'am. I'm due to visit in forty-eight hours."

The colonel wiped his hands on the sides of his trousers and shifted restlessly as he turned to the group watching him. "The brigadier would like to see you back at Fortress. She has a job which she believes is something you'll enjoy. One of the components for the dam is about to be sent up to Kajacki. It's a huge operation and is vitally important for the success of the construction. She'll brief you fully once you get there."

Mrs. James didn't hide her disdain or irritation. "I won't forget this, colonel. I was quite looking forward to this, and now you've changed the parameters. Come on, Wilf. Let's get our stuff and get back to Fortress. Bye, Toni, dear. I'll catch up with you when you get home."

And with that, Diane James was gone.

"Why did you invite Diane James here when Toni is already covering the story, sir?"

"There are several strategic reasons. None of them you need to know."

Toni was still frozen in place, and Jo could hear her stealing each breath. The colonel looked first at Toni and then rounded on Jo.

"And you clearly wanted to embarrass me with your little stunt. Be sure I will take this further. Dismissed."

When Toni didn't move, Jo took her by the arm and walked her out. The colonel was going to get her, there was no doubt in that. She obviously didn't get the reasoning or the plans he had, but she needed to stay squeaky clean so that he had nothing to use against her.

They went back to their tent, and Jo sat Toni on her bed. She handed her a bottle of water, which Toni drank heavily from.

"And now you see what I was talking about last night," she said, her gaze unfocused.

Jo struggled with how to be diplomatic. Diane James was a bitch. "There's nothing I can say to make you feel better. Between the colonel and your mother, we've both been kicked sideways. What would happen if we put them in the back of a Mastiff together? How long would they last before they started yelling at one another about things not being done right?" Jo asked, trying to pull Toni from her shell. "You look as if coffee and breakfast might help. Let's go and refuel."

Toni remained still. Some moments later, she shook her head.

"When will I ever learn? I expected her to be pleased I was out here and doing well. But she isn't impressed by what I've done, and she felt the need to do it herself. I'm never good enough." Toni blinked hard and took a deep, shaky breath. "Sorry, I know this is a darkness chat, but I'm promoting it to daytime." Her eyes filled with tears. "Daddy says she'll never change and that I should put my expectations away. She's only ever been about herself. But I can't help it. And now, she's come here and completely undermined my ability to do the job." She wiped at her falling tears.

Jo couldn't help but wonder why Toni's father stayed with her mother. But thinking about how other people's relationships worked was fraught with questions that never had answers. Much safer not to think about any of it. "It's no good worrying about her. She's heading off to get her story somewhere else and pictures of the dam, thanks to the brigadier. That leaves us free to do what we want to do today and for you to keep going with the great job you're already doing. Breakfast? Coffee?"

Toni brightened, and Jo was pleased to see the beginnings of a smile return to Toni's face. She wasn't going to overthink her reaction to Toni's tears or the way she wanted to pull her into an embrace to console her for the damage her mother had done.

"Good idea. I need coffee. There's nothing like a visit from my mother to induce the need for something strong."

Jo couldn't help but reflect on the last hour and hope that it didn't have too many lasting consequences. She'd managed to upset Diane James, one of the world's top reporters as well as her colonel, who already didn't like her. She sighed. Upsetting the colonel was something she'd managed to do solely by being posted to the regiment in the first place, so actually *doing* something to upset him would be an even bigger deal. If Brigadier McQueen hadn't rescued her, she'd have been in severe trouble. She hoped she could stay out of any more trouble, otherwise she'd never get the promotion she was working so hard for.

She glanced at Toni. This wasn't in her plan. Getting close to someone who could upset the apple cart was a bad idea. A few weeks away from Sherwood would help. They'd both be focused on other things, and conversations in the dark that opened Jo to emotions she didn't have time for would be impossible.

So why was that prospect a little disappointing?

CHAPTER EIGHT

WHILE TONI WAS PORING over the news, looking for one of her mother's exclusives, she thought about how much her mother's visit had unsettled her. She was doing well, but still her mother had showed up and tried to muscle in on *her* story. She wished she could understand what her mother was thinking. Her mother didn't think that Toni was a worthy reporter and could write good stories, but she hadn't expected her to try and take over the story she was already covering. She needed to speak to her father to help put things into perspective.

"Hi, Daddy. Sorry to call you again so soon."

"Hello, darlin'. How is the embedding going? Are you still having fun?"

Fun wasn't really the word for what she was doing there, but she knew what he meant. "Yep, I'm still having a good time."

He cleared his throat. "How are you getting on with that officer?"

"Daddy, stop! I know what you're doing. Yes, Jo's handsome; yes, I think she's crazy attractive; and yes, we're getting along. But that's all there is to it." There was no need to mention the after dark conversation or the desire she had to be more than midnight confidantes. "She also put Mother in her place today too."

"Your mother? What's she doing on the telephone or internet or whatever that would upset the captain?" he asked.

"She came out *here* at the colonel's invitation. She insisted that Jo take her out on patrol into the villages," Toni said. "I was speechless. We were called in to see the colonel, and I was plain shocked. I mean, I don't understand."

"I hope she didn't cause you problems," he said, his concern crystal clear.

"Jo didn't know who she was and said she wouldn't take her out unless she did two days on safety patrol with her. It's standard operating procedure so that the Army can make sure you're not going to risk anyone's lives. Jo didn't back down when Mother demanded to talk to a superior." Toni smiled at the memory of her mother's incandescent rage and Jo being so calm and totally professional.

"Huh, was it a light the match and wait moment?"

"The brigadier managed to persuade her to write a story about parts for a dam that's being built." Tears started to flood down her face as the emotion of the moment came back to her. "But, Daddy, it was awful. I stood there just like a little kid with nothing to say. She didn't even acknowledge me until she left, like I was just a random acquaintance. Could she really have no idea how it would make me feel?"

"I'm sorry I'm not closer. I'd give you a big hug."

"That's exactly what I need. I so miss your hugs." The solid feeling of home and safety was difficult to keep alive when she was a zillion miles away. "I'm coming home as soon as I can get away."

"I'm here for you as always. Now you have a pissed off mother and a humiliated colonel," he said. "Is that going to make life difficult for you?"

"It might, and Jo is definitely in the colonel's crosshairs. Mother will no doubt calm down and move on to the next story. But why did she come out here? She must know this is my chance to really do something big."

He sighed. "Oh, baby. Your mother is still the mixed-up kid I met thirty-three years ago. She's never known how to deal with you, which is why you and I have such a strong relationship. If I spoke to her, she'd tell me she wanted to make sure you were okay, but the rest of her can't help sniffing out a story. That's who she is. Not a wife, not a mother, but a story hound and a superb lover."

Toni grimaced. "Yuck. I did *not* need to know that."

"Still, that's why we're together. I let the story hound go free. She comes back on her way to somewhere else. But I'm sorry that she did that to you. It wasn't fair."

It was good to know that Toni wasn't being irrational. If she'd said anything directly to her mother, that would have been the accusation. "She unsettled me. And now I'm worried that it's going to affect Jo's career. She's a good officer, and Mother put her in a terrible position."

"Well, it sounds like the colonel put her there first, and your mother probably didn't even think about Jo. I'm sure she'll be on to the next thing and will have forgotten your friend before she leaves Afghanistan. She's been talking about coming home to recharge for a while."

Even with his explanation, Toni didn't know why he put up with it. She couldn't help but feel sorry for him. "It's good to talk it over with you. I needed a sounding board." She hesitated. "Her showing up here made me feel inadequate. Just like she always does."

"It isn't right," he said, sounding tired and washed out. "I'm sorry she makes you feel that way. I've tried talking to her, but you know how she is. So I'll just say this. You're damn good at what you do. You're enjoying it, so don't let anyone take that away from you. Okay?"

She smiled through her tears. "Okay. Thanks, Daddy."

"Bye, darlin'. Love you."

Toni began to add her report from the last patrol and the latest pictures of Sherwood base. She had a great photograph of Jo on the volleyball court blocking a shot at the net. It was sure to increase the numbers in Jo's fan club. It showed the gray of the mountains blurred in the background with a hesco wall in front and the sandy dust in the foreground. She'd managed to capture the heat too, with the sweat on Jo's skin. She looked at the picture more closely and followed the defined muscles in Jo's legs up her body. She shouldn't be looking at Jo like that. Nothing was going to happen between them. Jo wanted a career; she didn't have time for emotional entanglement. At least, that's what Toni believed. She didn't actually know anything about Jo's dating life. It hadn't come up yet, though she hoped it might.

But what about casual sex? That didn't have to mean anything, and in the middle of the night, Jo wasn't working on her career, right? It would no doubt be delicious. *Stop.*

Toni needed sex even if Jo didn't. She'd been here six weeks and with the rush to get her life together before she left the UK, it had been nearly three months since she'd felt the warmth of a woman's body. She'd always had regular lovers and enjoyed every aspect of sex, from the anticipation to the quiet moments after. She never had a shortage of partners, nor did she take any of them seriously, despite her father trying to get her to think a little longer term.

She took one last lingering look at the photo of Jo and then set it aside. A brutal workout at the gym might help crush her libido for a while.

***

After her gym workout, she enjoyed dinner with the guys from her troop. There was a lot of talk about going to patrol base Top Hat, so she was able to ask a lot of questions. The most important being what a patrol base was and why it was different from where they were in Sherwood.

"If Camp Fortress is the Hilton and this is like an Ibis hotel, basic but with all the facilities, then Top Hat is what you Americans would call a roach motel," Sprint said and laughed. "There are *no* facilities. Whatever you need, you have to provide. That includes bags of water for washing and showering, pipes for piss, and bags for toilets." He stood and mimed the actions in turn.

Toni laughed along with the men. "Okay, I know about washing with bags in the showers and having to leave them in the sun to warm. So how do I pee into a pipe? And toilets in bags? Please tell me you're joking."

"Nope, sorry. You'll have to pee into a bag. You don't have the right bits to go into a pipe." Sprint mimed a woman trying to pee into one of the stand-up pipes, fueling more raucous laughter amongst the men. "The pipes take the piss out of the base, for hygiene and smell. You'll use WAG bags: Waste Alleviation and Gelling bags. You do your business in a wooden shed or toilet with canvas walls. You get toilet paper and a wet wipe. The bag is full of powder which covers the contents and starts to decompose it. You seal the bag, put it into a Ziploc, and add it to a dump which is then disposed of. Clean and no smell," he said. "I heard a story about a soldier who said that when he got home, he kept flushing his toilet continuously so that he could watch the water going round and round the basin."

"Sounds good to me. Clean and no smell is what I'd be looking for. So where do we sleep?" Toni wasn't about to let on that she was both horrified and disgusted, and had no idea how she was going to manage. She already felt like she was roughing it here. But this was a whole new level of tough.

Flash hopped over the legs of the rest of the lads and pulled up a chair in front of Toni. "I expect you'll have some private ladies only place with the boss, somewhere away from us. We'll end up wherever there's enough room," he said. "The place is an old Afghan compound with a couple of sangers that are heavily fortified watchtowers. The troops patrol close to the base to keep the area between their patrol base and the next one in the line clear of sight. They watch the surrounding countryside from the sangers and look out for passing Taliban transiting through the area."

"They stand in a tower and watch the countryside all day long?" Toni couldn't take the boredom of standing watching the same area for hours on end.

"Yeah, it's not a popular job. Luckily, the troops are only there for a few weeks before they trade out with another group. It's hard to maintain your concentration when there's not much happening, and there's nothing to look at, especially in the heat. But if you miss something, they could either attack you or the troops on patrol. I expect we'll have to do a few duties in the sangers. Usually, visitors are co-opted to give the patrol base troops a little break from the endless routine, so you'll get the chance to see us in action."

"It'll be interesting to see another type of base and the life there," Toni said, "even if the action is all Sprint's." The laughter continued, and Toni felt totally accepted by the guys, despite her mistakes. She was fascinated to learn how the guys joked and laughed about their own mistakes when they first arrived, and that led to stories from their training and their home lives. She left her phone recording on the bench next to her, only checking it occasionally to make sure it hadn't stopped. Being part of the conversation kept it informal, and that always led to more interesting, deeper information. Connecting with people this way made her heart sing. It might be a world her mother inhabited, but it was hers too, and she loved it. Nothing could take this moment away from her.

When the conversation waned and it got late, everyone made their way back to their tents. The troop waved her off, and she returned to her tent to get packed up and ready to leave in the morning. Jo was already doing the same thing. Other people would move into their tent temporarily because accommodations were always short, especially for visitors and guests.

"I've been given the lowdown on patrol base life from the guys. They had great fun telling me the ins and outs," Toni said.

"I expect the chat was around toilets, food, and where you'll sleep." Jo grinned and shook her head. "Out here, that's the usual stuff."

"You're not wrong. Food wasn't mentioned though. They made me smile and answered any questions I had about life in the patrol base." Toni groaned and tossed her notebook onto the bed. "I know all this stuff came out of this bergen and I don't have any extra, so why won't it fit? I'll have to start again." Toni was exasperated that something so simple should be so difficult. She needed to get on with planning out her next report as well. She was tired and cranky and really just wanted to go to bed.

"Can I help?"

"No, it's all right. I'm regrouping." Toni took a deep breath. She could do this.

"Don't forget all those outside pockets were full when you left the UK. Bet you haven't filled those," Jo said.

"Oh, damn. I'd forgotten. I probably didn't need to restart," Toni said.

"Here. Let me help." Jo scanned the assortment of things on Toni's bunk.

Toni breathed in Jo's woodsy scent and drew strength from the feeling of her shoulder pressed against her. She desperately wanted to rest her head on that shoulder, to let her guard down and admit that she was overwhelmed and overtired. But Jo began expertly putting things in the bag, folding clothing into tiny cubes and fitting things together as though it was a puzzle.

When she'd finished, she turned to Toni. They were only inches apart, and their gaze locked. The moment was filled with potential, but Jo took a step back. Toni took a shaky breath. *So close.*

"I've got an extra Coke. Want one?" Jo turned back to her bunk.

"Sure, thanks. And thanks for packing me up. It's way better than it was when I did it." She gave Jo a quick smile and then settled on the bunk with her soda. Jo talked about the next base, about other bases, and about the places she had been. Toni set her recorder going but didn't take any notes, allowing the conversation to go wherever it needed to. She liked the glimpses she was getting of the woman she was liking more every day.

When it was dark, Toni lay down to sleep, but it was another of those nights when she tossed and turned. How different would things be? How would things change for her? She'd gotten used to her life in Sherwood; the charged atmosphere had become part of her everyday life, as had the routines and basic level of safety. That was likely to change, and a frisson of fear sat beneath the challenge of being somewhere new. Adrenaline raced through her body. She turned over again.

"I'm not asleep either. Shall I pop out and get us a cuppa?" Jo asked from the other side of the divider.

Toni sat up, relieved to get away from her thoughts. "I'll take a tea and perhaps a cookie or two?"

Jo left and returned quickly with tea and cookies. "I'm going to get into bed so I'm nice and relaxed when I finish and will fall asleep. Well, that's the idea anyway. I'm usually too worked up to sleep before we go out on a mission like this one."

Toni waited for her tea to cool a little. "I spoke to my dad and told him about Mother's visit and how you stood up to her."

"What did he say?"

"He thinks Mother will forget about it. He thinks that she came here to make sure I was okay. But that's obviously to make me feel better, since she came at the colonel's invitation and barely even acknowledged me. But it was good to speak to my dad. I miss him." Toni had always been independent, but her daddy was important to her, and she wished he were a little closer.

"When did you last see him?" Jo asked.

"About a year ago. I need to recharge my Oklahoma batteries once this tour is over." Toni wanted to show Jo her home state and some of the beautiful architecture in places like Tulsa. *Where did that idea come from?* They were quiet for a moment, and Toni wasn't sure what to say that wouldn't be her asking how they could continue their friendship outside the military.

"I spoke briefly with my uncle today. When my father died, his younger brother looked out for me. Like my father, he was Army all his life. They were both colonels in the Royal Engineers. He follows my career and thinks that this tour will be good for it. But he's conscious of the risks of this place. He said that the fatality and injury numbers have skyrocketed in the last few months. Said I should keep my head down," Jo said, her tone thoughtful.

"I don't think irritating the colonel is keeping your head down, although I'm not sure that was what he meant." Toni didn't want to think about death stats on the night before they were heading deep into bandit territory.

"No, he wouldn't think that was a good idea at all." The smile was obvious in Jo's voice. "Reminding me of the danger is his way of telling me he loves me and he's proud of me," Jo said. "I'm going to try to sleep now."

"Thank you for the tea. Let's dream about loving family and how the way they care for us is sometimes absurdly complicated," Toni said, laughing a little. She turned onto her side and pulled her pillow into a comfy shape before closing her eyes. She drifted to sleep, and her dreams were filled with the sound of gunshots and the feel of Jo right beside her, her arm around her as she pulled her close...

CHAPTER NINE

Travel arrangements for the troop were changed at the last minute, and they flew to Top Hat in a chinook. The only sight that Jo had of the Afghan countryside was through the open door around a gunner protecting them. Jo loved being in the aircraft, one of the defining sights and sounds of military operations. The Chinook moved troops and supplies all over Helmand and could get an injured soldier to the hospital in Camp Fortress in minutes.

The armored underbelly gave her a sense of safety. The Chinook helicopter was the workhorse of the forces in Afghanistan and had completed numerous missions with few incidents. The noise of the engine was like sitting under the bonnet of the biggest truck in the world. It was *loud*. The inside of the aircraft was basic, with belts and hooks visible and hanging from every available space.

Jo looked over to Toni and saw she was looking at her. She smiled. "Are you okay?" she shouted.

"Okay," Toni mouthed, nodding.

She didn't look okay. Her slightly green skin pallor and the way she was white-knuckling her pack made her look like she was going to vomit. There wasn't anything Jo could do about it though.

The combined smell of recently washed men, their aftershave, and the overriding odor of sweat alongside the stench of avgas and engine oil was somehow comforting. This was what being in the Army meant to her: venturing off into the unknown with men who trusted her with their lives. This time, she also had Toni in her care.

Toni's moments of not concentrating had dwindled since the attack incident, but Jo wondered if she could still be a loose cannon. The image of her standing out in the open, a target for anyone in range, still haunted her dreams. Toni still had to earn her complete trust. Perhaps that was impossible. Maybe she needed to be Army-trained for Jo to trust her professionally. Outsiders didn't have the same values.

Jo was starting to trust her a little more personally, however. She was holding several of Jo's secrets. Toni was sweet, kind, and determined. She often said she was okay when she wasn't, and Jo admired her tenacity. For a civilian, she was doing her best, and Jo appreciated that, even if it drove her crazy sometimes. Toni's beauty was distracting, and it hadn't been helping Jo sleep, that was for sure.

Once more, thinking about Toni James had taken her mind from her number one task of keeping them all safe. She needed to get her head into the right space and start considering the landing and getting them under cover quickly. She'd briefed the troop before they set off, and they all had tasks to get them away from possible attack and to ensure they were covered in case of ambush. Everyone knew their place.

Her team sat on both sides of the aircraft, wearing full kit including helmets, rifles, and daypacks. The rest of their gear-filled bergens were under nets, piled high between the rows of soldiers. Because they were ready for action, they would clear the aircraft in minutes when it landed. The rear of the Chinook was filled with supplies for the patrol base, netted and strapped down. There was little space to fit anything else.

When the Chinook landed, its engines continued to run and the rotors continued to turn, ready to lift off the moment it was clear. The rear door opened, and patrol base troops appeared to unload the supplies. The invasion of hot air and helicopter exhaust fumes into the aircraft almost took Jo's breath away. The noise of the engine was much louder, and her ears throbbed at the noise and the change in air pressure. Toni winced so Jo gave her an encouraging smile.

They removed their safety belts, and Jo jumped out of the door, with her troops following in line. Toni and her protection squad were behind her and quickly formed a protective cordon. The rest of the platoon formed an outer boundary. Bergens started coming out of the door and each soldier picked up his own bergen as it arrived, ensuring there was still a good protective perimeter. After the last bergen came out of the aircraft, the whole platoon moved into the barrier of the patrol base.

Jo had only ever seen this patrol base when she was passing through, putting together the plan for her team to move out here. Due to changes in troop availability and the need for changes to the strategic plan, there was now a manpower shortage. Nothing unusual for any deployment. The need for troops in different areas to thwart the latest insurgency meant that troops were often moved at a moment's notice, and the workforce was spread thin. She'd therefore had to make do with her operation to patrol base Top Hat being shortened to three weeks. She couldn't let herself get angry about it. It wasn't long enough to make real changes in the area, but Jo forced herself to be pragmatic. It was what she had, and she'd make the best of it.

Captain Evan Goldsmith, the officer in charge of the troops at Top Hat was waiting inside to greet them. "Hello, Jo. Good to see you. The space we discussed is all clear for you and your men," he said, waving to his right.

"Thanks, Evan. We'll catch up with you when we've set up," Jo said, already on her way with the rest of the soldiers.

There was an empty section of the compound which she'd negotiated for her platoon. She was lucky that the patrol base was working on smaller numbers since the Taliban had started to leave the valley and the patrols were no longer at such a risk. But the patrols working here had lost eleven soldiers over the last year, so they still had to keep their guard up.

One thing the Army was good at was making the best of a situation and within minutes, her men were setting up camp, banter and laughter filling the air around them. Within a couple of hours, it was as if they'd always been there. The two tents along the wall were for the men, and the small room in the compound was big enough for Jo and Toni. A sign naming the area around the troops as Fizer Champagne Corner was the final touch. Jo couldn't have been prouder of the way they sorted their camp, including making a partition across the doorway into her and Toni's quarters, now lovingly named the Powder Room. Jo didn't mind their teasing about her gender. They respected her, no matter what, and that really mattered. Toni seemed to find it cute too, though there was no question she looked underwhelmed by the blank, crumbling walls and bunk that had seen better days.

There were enough troops at the patrol base that they still had a small cookhouse, so they wouldn't have to cook their food individually from one-man ration packs, but the shower block and the toilets were basic. Jo and Toni were scheduled to take their showers at six p.m. every day, along with any other women. Jo had her notice up to remind people.

"As of now, entering the shower's block at women's time and ignoring the notice will put you on extra duty sorting out WAG bags," Jo said. There were plenty of laughs and bets being taken as to who would forget first.

Jo had already introduced herself and Toni, and several of the troops from the patrol base had read Toni's writing and had seen some of her photos and short videos.

"We've loved your work and it's been good to see the background to patrols in the media. It's a new approach," Evan said. "Can you do some articles about us and our patrols? We're here for four weeks, and it would be good to let our families see what we're doing." He gave Toni a charming smile.

Jo's stomach clenched. She'd worked around these guys long enough to know when interest wasn't just professional, and the way he was looking at Toni made her want to deck him. The fact that she had no claim on Toni and that Evan was a nice guy didn't matter. It should, but it didn't.

Jo took a step closer to Toni, her mouth dry as she sucked in a breath through clenched teeth. She opened her mouth to speak, but Toni beat her to it.

"I've been going out with Captain Fitzgerald's platoon, and we all know where we should be. I feel safe and well-protected with the three guys who look after me. We're here to do a specific job in the villages, and I have to follow that through. I'll certainly give you some coverage in between though, of course. Perhaps we can work together to give me some time to cover your men." Toni turned to Jo, a question in her eyes that didn't seem solely to do with planning.

Jo forced a smile. Toni had made it clear her troop was the priority, and that was good enough for now. "That'll be fine. We can have a chat after supper and sort out something that will work for us all." Jo briefed them about what her troops were hoping to achieve in visiting the six villages near the patrol base. "Local intelligence has said that the Taliban has left the area and moved further north," Jo said. "Would you agree?"

There were a few shakes of the head. "It's been too quiet while we've been here so far. And we've seen nothing," Evan said. "But we think that this is the calm before the storm. The fact that we're seeing *nothing* is suspicious. You'll need to be aware; we think something is happening. There's the feeling on the air, you know?" He glanced at his men, who nodded.

Jo ran her hand through her hair. "The villages need some support, so we'll go out to see what we can do, but we'll keep our eyes and ears open for trouble. If things go well, a team will be sent here to add to the work that we start, so it will be down to us to figure out what's needed both now and, in the future," Jo said. "That means other teams will follow down the line."

There were nods amongst the patrol base troops.

"We'll all be grateful for the support from your sangers. It'll be good to have your eyes and ears on us as we set out and come back," Jo said. "Our first op will be tomorrow and we're heading for Gubar Kheyll. Leaving at 0500."

Conversation continued with plenty of lighthearted banter mixed in with operational information, and Jo watched as Toni took it all in. She wasn't as pale as she'd been in the chopper, and it was good to see her laughing and asking questions the way she usually did. Her eyes lit up when she got excited, and it was easy to see how she put everyone around her at ease with her interest in who they were beyond the uniform.

The more time she spent with Toni, the more time she wanted. And that was bad news indeed.

***

Later, Jo lay on her bed. She breathed out slowly and closed her eyes. She couldn't stop thinking about her reaction to Evan wanting to spend time with Toni. Jo never wanted more than a night of sex, more to scratch an itch than anything deeper. She'd spent time earlier in her career visiting bars and lesbian events and enjoyed herself. But as her career took off, she curtailed her dating life to focus on her professional one. Soldiers who were openly gay were being held back as they got to the higher ranks. Even in this era, it remained true, though no one really wanted to acknowledge it.

She hadn't given it much thought over the last few years, content with the decision she'd made. So it was particularly unsettling when a shock of anger blasted through her like a gust of wind tearing up trees from the ground. She'd been *jealous*.

She stared up at the dirt-encrusted ceiling. There was no denying she had feelings for Toni that went well beyond the professional. They were more than an itch. She *wanted* Toni. She wanted to kiss her senseless. Wanted to protect her. She wanted to hear Toni whisper her name in the dark. Jo wanted to make her laugh and wipe away her tears. *Shit fuck damn.* She had to clamp down on her runaway mind and body, but she was thinking of

Toni's naked skin against her own before she had time to shut it down. Her astonishment battled with a small amount of guilt.

How had this happened? Spending a lot of time together and talking into the night about life and worries had been an eye-opener for her. Toni understood Jo well enough to work out that being close to people was difficult. She had a way of getting people to open up, to feel safe. But damn it all, she was also beautiful and sharp, feisty and determined. She was the kind of dream you woke up from, yearning for just a few more minutes.

"Penny for them."

Jo froze as the object of her thoughts spoke.

"I know it's not dark yet, and we haven't had supper, but we can pretend it's night and share more secrets," Toni said.

Jo couldn't speak. It was as if Toni were reading her mind.

"Come on. I can hear your brain whirring from three feet away. Share with me."

"I was going through the day and thinking how proud I was of the lads and getting the tents set up." That wasn't a lie, but it definitely wasn't the whole truth.

"It was like watching a well-oiled machine; I was impressed too. I took a lot of photos and video. I'll be writing some pieces once I get time to draw breath." She hesitated. "I think Evan was jealous of you."

"What? Evan jealous? Oh, no. It's the other way around." Jo clasped her hand over her mouth. What the hell had made her say that? Toni wasn't looking her way so maybe she'd got away with it. "What I'm trying to say is that I mean he's a handsome man. I expect you find him attractive, and he obviously likes you. You'd make a good couple. I'm sure if you—" Jo couldn't stop her mouth from uttering inane words to cover up her feelings.

"Seriously, Jo. You haven't worked it out yet, have you?" Toni laughed.

"What do I need to work out? Am I missing something?"

"I'm not into men at all. I'm gay." Toni giggled. She turned onto her side and looked at Jo with a smile.

Jo pressed her hand to the thin mattress to ground herself. Her thoughts had taken flight and left behind a vacuum.

"It's not a secret or anything, I've always been open about who I am. I've never said anything because it didn't come up. The guys like to talk about the people they're with, but no one has actually asked me," Toni said and laughed. "Anyway, I hope it doesn't bother you, since we're sharing a small space."

Jo wondered if Toni had worked out that she liked women too, or was she being ultra-careful? "Who you are doesn't worry me. But Evan making nice to you did worry me. I was trying to analyze why instead of napping," Jo said.

"What did you decide?"

There was a note in Toni's voice. Was it hope?

"I'm not sure I can explain it," Jo said, knowing exactly what she'd been thinking.

"Maybe you didn't like his interest in me. That was why I intervened," Toni said. "You seemed...protective, maybe."

"Oh, god. You don't think that's what he thought too?"

"No. We spend a lot of time together so I was conscious of you and what you might've been thinking. I'm sure he had no idea," Toni said.

"So...you think you may have understood where I was coming from?" Jo said. Her heartbeat pounded in her ears.

"I only need you to answer one question to confirm it. Do you like women?"

Jo stared at the ceiling. No one had ever asked her that so openly. Jo had always been careful about who knew she was gay; it was the way she'd been brought up. Her father didn't understand how anyone could be gay. After she told him, he never mentioned it again. She wanted a career as a senior officer, so she couldn't afford to be gay. Yes, it was accepted officially, but there were still barriers in some areas, and it was believed in the gay community that senior military officer promotion was one of them.

"You don't have to answer, you know? I'll tell you what I believe," Toni said before Jo could say anything. "I think that you didn't want him schmoozing with me, because you wanted it to be you. I think...I think maybe you like me."

There was a still silence in the room. Jo had a hundred thoughts running through her mind but could hold on to none of them. Toni was right, and now Jo was stuck. She had to admit it and be embarrassed or deny it and be embarrassed.

"If I'm wrong, and you want to ignore the conversation, all you have to do is say goodnight, and we'll start—"

"Yes," Jo said. "Yes, I like women and yes, I was jealous. It was a bit of a shock to work that out a few moments ago. You've obviously got under my skin." She sat up and put her feet on the floor. Blurting out her truth had been a release, but it also left her worried about what would come next.

Toni left her bunk and knelt in front of Jo. "You're under my skin too." Toni stroked Jo's cheek. "We're doing nothing wrong. We're both single, and if we're discreet, I'm sure it won't be a problem. We don't need to advertise it, and your career should be fine." Toni pulled Jo to her feet. "Is it being discreet if we kiss here where there are only the two of us?" Toni asked softly, her hands loose on Jo's arms, as though anticipating her pulling away.

Jo looked into Toni's gray eyes and then at the red of her lips. She looked down at the faint sheen of sweat covering Toni's body and inhaled the smell of her citrus shampoo. She took Toni in her arms and gave her a gentle kiss, the moment as fragile as a glass teetering on the edge of a canyon. Toni responded gently, and then Jo kissed her again with a little more urgency, and Toni pulled her tighter.

A moment like this was something she'd only dreamed about in the sacred quiet of the night. In contrast now, there was no quiet. Her heart was hammering its way out of her body as she pictured a kaleidoscope of images of Toni in her bed, and her legs grew weak. It was all she could have hoped for and more. She hadn't expected a kiss to feel like she was drowning and not need air.

"No lads! Too close! That would have been trouble. Nearly in the powder room, boys! Keep the ball over there, or we'll be doing some punishment the captain will dream up," a loud male voice said from too near the doorway.

They sprang apart as if a bolt of lightning had split them in two. Her attraction to Toni had given her a vacation moment, with no thought about work or any consequences of her actions. Jo's hands shook as she put them to her face and realization set in. This was her life and career that she was throwing around for a second of desire that wouldn't go anywhere.

"That was so close. Too close. And the reason we need to talk," Jo said as she gently pushed Toni to sit on her bed. She sat on her own so there was plenty of distance between them. "I love kissing you and believe me I want more, a lot more kisses and a lot *more* than kisses. I've never been in this position before."

"I want more too, but I get where you're coming from." Toni gave her a small, sad smile.

Jo gulped. This was the point where the bud of her relationship with Toni would wither and die. "My career is everything to me. As much as I'd like to explore this with you, I can't have this kind of distraction in my life right now. Not when I'm working so damn hard for a promotion."

Toni got up and sat next to her, taking Jo's hands in her own. "This is one of our conversations for the dark. Let's wait until then." She smiled.

"You're going to leave and go back to your own world. But this is my world, and it's where I'll stay." Jo looked at Toni, her face inches away. She was silent, and Jo could hear the volleyball match continuing noisily in the yard outside.

Toni's stomach gurgled, and they both laughed, breaking the tension.

"Let's go shower and find some food. We can let things take their course for the next hour or so." Jo did her utmost not to think of Toni in the shower, right beside her, naked and soapy.

They ate supper as usual with the soldiers from their troop. Once they were back in their area, Jo sat on her bed and got out her leather notebook to continue working up her plans for the rest of their time in the patrol base. She hoped that Toni would get the message that life had to continue as before the kiss.

Toni, however, seemed to have a different idea. "I want to have our nighttime chat now. Do you need to do that work before tomorrow?"

Jo looked up and folded her pen into her book, tying up the leather bindings to keep it safe. "I'm good." She pushed back on her bed and plumped up her pillows before lying on her side and looking at Toni, who sat on her bed cross-legged.

Toni cleared her throat. "I don't have many friends and my girlfriends are almost non-existent. I rarely see a woman more than once or twice."

Jo couldn't understand why women wouldn't want to spend all their time with Toni. She was friendly and attractive and so hot. "Is there a reason for that?"

"I haven't ever had anything in common with them except their need for a warm body and to have some fun. At the time, I could think of nothing worse than spending a lot of time with them."

Ah. So it wasn't the other women who made the decision, it was Toni. Jo understood that. She'd been in a similar place. "I only ever wanted women to scratch an itch. I travel well away from wherever I work to find some fun if I'm in a country where that's possible. I want to keep my work life really separate. But surely you have your pick of the London scene?"

Toni laughed. "Perhaps I do, but coming out here has taught me a lot about loneliness. I've never been short of acquaintances, but I don't have friends. I realized my dad doubles as my best friend, and I've always been on my own."

Jo ached at the sadness in Toni's voice and the way she hunched over slightly, as though warding off an attack. "I get lonely sometimes too, but it was a conscious decision to put up a wall and concentrate on my job. It's easy enough to do, particularly if I can find a plus one for the social outings that don't raise eyebrows."

"What does that mean?" Toni asked.

"It's just the same as lawyers becoming partners and appointments at director level in the US. Your face has to fit, and your partner's face has to fit too. I've been lucky. I've met a couple of men who have been only too happy to be my partner as they were in the promotion race too and couldn't afford to be seen with the wrong person." This almost felt like a dangerous conversation to be having, but she had to trust that no one would be close enough to overhear it.

Toni smiled. "I get it. You must be really dedicated. I mean, I've seen it in action. But deep down, you must want it. At least I can pick and choose where and when to have my fun. No one really cares if a journalist is gay."

Jo couldn't even fathom that kind of freedom. "If you want promotion, then it's hard to get the time to concentrate on a relationship even if you're straight. If you're gay and can't afford to take a chance, it becomes an even lonelier life." She wondered, for the first time, whether getting a promotion was worth the loss of a potential relationship and all that entailed: the feeling of being close to someone, having someone by her side when she needed warmth and support, and those times when she wanted to give it. She'd enjoyed the hours she and Toni had spent hanging out in their tent. But maybe that wasn't a good thing if it meant revisiting her life's decisions. "I suppose if you travel a lot then you have little time to build a relationship."

"I suppose so, and I've found I'm picky who I'm close to. I travel and get involved in stories at the expense of any time I might otherwise spend with a partner. I know when I get a lead, I concentrate one hundred percent." Toni's breath hitched. "Any partner I have will need to be understanding,"

"You thought of something?" Jo asked.

Toni put her hands to her face. "Just like my parents. Do I want to be like my mother? No way."

Jo tried to hide her laugh. Toni's sensitivity about her mother was crystal clear. "And on that note, I think we have a lot to think about. I have to consider my future. I don't want to go ahead if this is only sex to you. I haven't had a relationship before, but I feel like we have something that could be more than one night." She shrugged, confusion warring with desire. "But I'm not about to give up my career to suddenly settle down either. So maybe we're at an impasse."

"I want sex. That's obvious," Toni said. "You're tying my body in knots with want. But I think I want more with you too. We seem to have a connection, and it would be good to build on it." She smiled, her eyes soft. "But eventually our worlds will separate. So is sex on the table even if nothing long-lasting can come from it?"

They were both quiet for a long time. No answers were forthcoming except one. With the troops paces away, it wasn't the place to have sex unless it was a quickie. "I want you. I'd like to think that when we have sex, it'll be more than ten minutes of fumbling while hoping we don't make a noise," Jo said. "I believe we should have something a bit more than what we could have here. Perhaps when we get back to Sherwood. We can deal with the other questions later. Or never. The answers may be clear without us having to do anything about them." Jo grinned a little.

"I totally agree with that, but does that mean we can't kiss each other good night?"

"I'm ahead of you. Come sit with me, and we'll work out how much of a goodnight we want," Jo said, holding her arms out to Toni and waiting for her to fill them. It was sometime later that they split up to head to their own beds.

"A final goodnight," Jo said, wondering if she'd ever manage to sleep with her head and body whirling.

"Goodnight. Sweet dreams."

Jo heard Toni's bedclothes rustle and then there was loud

silence as Jo's thoughts raced, about the sacrifices she would have to make to get a promotion and how lying here with Toni made that seem an impossible decision to make.

****

Her alarm sounded, jerking her from a dream full of sensuality and desire. She'd fallen asleep despite her fears. It was 0430, and she switched on her battery-powered light. She opened her eyes to see Toni lying in her rumpled bed looking across at her. Jo wasn't sure what to do or say. The dreams left her bemused and throbbing, neither of which was good for morning conversation that didn't include sex.

"Good morning," Toni said with a smile that went from her lips to her eyes.

"Good morning," Jo said. "I was...er..." The heat rose up her neck and across her face before she could stop it. She was never tongue-tied. Toni was causing all kinds of chaos.

"Yesterday was full of emotions and questions, but now you need to be Captain Fitzgerald, and I need to concentrate so I don't put you all in danger." Toni nodded sharply and threw off the covers. "Let's get going and we can talk later."

Jo got out of bed and dressed without responding. Focus was paramount now and a perfect reminder of why she couldn't afford emotional turmoil. People's lives depended on her clear thinking. She grabbed her kit and headed out for some sustenance. Toni wasn't far behind her, and Jo handed her a cup of coffee and biscuit as she reminded herself of the route they'd be taking today. By 0500 they were all at the patrol base gates ready to head out.

The patrol to the first village was uneventful. It was large enough to be called a small town, which meant there were more hiding places to be aware of. Jo took Toni with her to introduce her to the village elders and initiated their first conversation. It was slow, painstaking work to make sure they understood Jo and her team were there to help. Luckily, the villagers had heard of Jo and her work near Sherwood and were ready to have open conversations. She was even permitted to speak with the women on her first visit, which she suspected was because Toni was with her and showed them some of her work in photograph and film. She would be unable to give them many pictures, but the women responded to her easy way positively. They also responded to Jo proactively. Maybe having Toni around wasn't such a bad thing.

One of the women, Simi, had been a doctor under the Russian regime and once the Taliban took over, she'd been forced to stop working but she continued to quietly look after the women as their gynecologist. She and her friend, Paksima, a teacher, were the women's leaders and both were strong characters, which they needed to be to stand up to the men. Most of them wanted help to start businesses and make money so they could contribute to village life.

Jo translated for Toni as they spoke. "They need all the things that most of the villages are short of, particularly medical equipment and medicine, which Simi finds hard to come by. She's a doctor and has nothing to help make their lives easier. No medicine for sick children is a difficult thing to deal with."

"Imagine if you're trained to save lives and then have to live a life where you watch children die because you can't treat them. People really must see this," Toni said.

"Paksima is teaching class outside and doing it in shifts so that she can teach more children. She has no materials. Anything will be a help." Jo nodded and listened as a couple of the women spoke to her. "They've heard about women in other villages having a small flock of chickens whose eggs earn them money. That would help them buy supplies if they were available at some point."

"That would be good. They can use it to improve their food as well. Do ISAF provide chickens?" Toni continued to smile and snap photos of the women, some of whom turned away, while others looked almost defiant as they let Toni capture their images.

"Well, it comes with risk as the men in the villages usually view chickens as luxury food and will kill them and present them as a gift to their wives to cook for supper if they're hungry," Jo said.

"It gives new meaning to the saying 'a bird in the hand.' I can't imagine having to scrape by and then having to fight my own husband as well."

"One of the women wants me to get her some cloth, because she could make small bags to sell to women here and in the surrounding villages. She's sure she could make a go of it. This is one she made from some scraps." Jo held up a small bag made of colored material squares.

Toni smiled at the woman as she looked it over. "It's really good. And I bet she's right, she could sell them elsewhere." She looked at Jo. "Can I buy it? Or would that be out of line?"

Jo shook her head. "It's hard to say. If you buy it, then the others will want you to buy the things they've made too. And they'll hope that happens every time we show up, which isn't tenable. So it's best if you don't, for now, anyway. Let's get them the things they need first."

Jo took a big swig of the tea made for them. It was hot work, and she was dry-mouthed with all the talking in the hot, dusty atmosphere. "Simi is keen to set something up with the women in other villages. She wants to have something official so they can show they're helping themselves. Somewhere where the men aren't making all the decisions for what the women are allowed to do."

"Can you help with that?" Toni asked.

"I'm going to speak to the brigadier to see what we can help put in place. My idea, which the brigadier and I discussed a while back, is that we help create a Women's Council area and hold a shura, the Afghan word for a meeting. It will take some time to organize as we need a local mayor with clout to let us use somewhere like his town hall. If we can give the women their own platform, we can help them much more easily. The added benefit is that it becomes self-sufficient, and the women can speak for themselves as a group. Simi is a godsend."

It was a fruitful visit, and Jo was pleased. They'd been well-received, despite the fact that the Taliban had not long evacuated the village. The women hadn't been worried about talking to them, and while that was unusual, it was a good sign.

On their return route, Jo noted there were no traveling Afghans along the roads and paths. They had Vallonman ahead of them, and she passed the message to the squad to look out for traps or ambushes. She took a relieved breath when the sangers from Top Hat came into view. Safety was in sight. Not that it was time to let down their defenses, but it was good to know there was help close by if anything went bad. Fortunately, they made it back into the base without trouble. Still, she couldn't shake the feeling that something was off.

Following her debrief of the lads and discussions with Evan about their worries of empty roads and paths, she headed to the powder room to write her report for the brigadier. Toni was already there with her electronics spread across her bed, her head bowed as she was obviously creating her next piece. She'd taken most of her outer clothing off and was sitting in a vest and shorts. She still had the grime of the day over her body and face. Jo enjoyed watching Toni, her shoulders bare and her legs under her laptop. It was a little glimpse into what she would look like back home, curled up on the sofa as she wrote.

She looked up as Jo entered and smiled before bowing her head again to continue her work. Her enthusiasm for her job was something Jo could understand. Before she started her own report, she got a drink and a bottle of water for each of them. She put Toni's drinks on the floor by her bed and then sat down to work.

Jo couldn't ever recall being so comfortable in such a small space with someone. They fit together somehow. Neither of them spoke; there was no need. Jo glanced at Toni as she searched for a word in her mind, only to find Toni staring at her. They smiled and simply continued with what they were doing. Eventually Jo finished her report and uploaded it. She still needed to plan their next mission for the day after tomorrow, but she couldn't concentrate any longer.

Sometimes life throws an unexpected curve ball, and Jo was working out how to deal with this one. She wanted to take Toni to bed and explore her body inch by inch. Once she'd done that, she wanted to do it again. And again. But she'd spent most of her life trying to get to the point she was at with her career. She was standing in exactly the right spot to be plucked out and given her greatest wish. The greatest wish she'd had until now. Now she wasn't so sure. There were one or two senior officers who had come out, but she wasn't yet aware of any who'd come out before they got there. But that didn't mean it didn't happen. Lots of people mixed their relationships and their careers, and there was no reason why she couldn't. Why was she holding back?

She wondered if her reasoning was flawed and she was just being cowardly. She was afraid. Afraid that she'd mess it up and hurt them both. She'd never had a relationship of any length and had always kept herself separate. Now that she had a chance, she could be taking the easy way out and not starting something that could be risky. If she was honest, she was fed up with being alone and having no one to share her life with. She wanted someone to come home to, to share small moments with, to laugh and cry with. She didn't want to leave the world knowing she hadn't loved and that she was unloved. Those thoughts hadn't even occurred to her before Toni had come onto the base, and now she couldn't get away from them. Almost as if to prove the point to herself, she knelt at the side of Toni's bed and looked at her working. "Are you nearly done?" She was impatient for a kiss, and the anticipation was killing her.

Toni looked up and laughed. "You're quite determined when you need to be, aren't you? I finished ages ago. I didn't want to disturb you, so I've been cataloguing pictures."

"Let's eat and shower, then we can get some kisses and sleep."

Toni leaned over and kissed her. Her world settled. Outside, the noise of Top Hat continued. Loud voices, music, the familiar sounds of pans from the cookhouse, and the inevitable game of volleyball became distant. This was here, in this room, and now. Jo decided to stop fighting with herself and for today, let things be. Kissing Toni tonight made her see how much she'd been missing.

CHAPTER TEN

IT HAD BEEN AN eventful three weeks at Top Hat, though the patrol side of things had been relatively uneventful. They'd heard about a medical charity mission further up the valley that had been ambushed, and everyone had been killed. Jo had known the English doctor in the mission, and it brought home to everyone that life out here hung by a thread. The other villages they'd been to seemed more subdued, a little less interested in talking, and a little more wary of the surrounding countryside. They'd made some progress, but Toni sensed Jo's frustration, and the rest of the group were on edge too.

The eventful part was all about her and Jo. She hadn't been this happy since being home in Oklahoma. Toni wanted Jo badly, more than she'd wanted anyone for a long time, perhaps ever. It might've been the conditions, making her conscious of the danger and the risk to life, but her body had lust, desire, and need permanently switched on. She and Jo had the beginnings of something, that was undeniable. But she was totally frustrated, and there was virtually nothing she could do about it.

And there were more problems to overcome than just her desire. Toni wondered if Jo realized the extent of the walls she'd put up around herself, and whether it was more than her need for promotion. Did Jo realize that she might be afraid of getting close to someone, something she'd never done? Her emotions were deeply buried, and Toni was digging through them every day. Toni was concerned that Jo would be pragmatic and think that this was too difficult, and that she would decide to end things. And what if she did? It wasn't like Toni was all about settling down and staying in one place either. Where did that leave them? In a whirlwind of desire and confusion, that's where.

The physical side had been especially hard in the heat. Neither of them wore much clothing, and bare skin was so tempting. Toni would be sitting on her bed, supposedly working and putting reports together with pictures, but she'd really keep looking at Jo. She couldn't stop herself. She wondered what her skin would feel like pressed to her, wet with sweat. Jo would glance up and she could see the same feelings reflected in her eyes. They'd both sigh and carry on working. More than once, she'd woken in the middle of the night with a burning need to take Jo where she lay. She'd had to stop herself from going over to her bed and climbing on top of her. But that wouldn't make things any easier in the long run, so she'd just turned over, punched her pillow, and drifted back into dreams that created even more longing.

Today was their last patrol before returning to Sherwood. They were revisiting the first village. Jo wanted to catch up with Simi and Paksima to update them on what she'd done so far and how she and the brigadier were going to move things forward. When they entered the village, the elder told Jo the Taliban had been there and taken one of the women, although no one had seen anything. And if they had, they certainly weren't saying anything. He appeared to accept this was their life, and the defeat in his expression said more than his words.

"How can this happen? How can he be so accepting?" Toni asked, her emotions building to tears. "To lose someone from the village must be so hard. How can you live here knowing that you could be grabbed in the middle of the night, and no one will try to help you?" Her stomach turned. She had to get a grip. This was no way for a reporter to behave. She clamped down on her gut reaction. *Record the facts. Nothing else. Show the truth, and people will understand.* She repeated it like a mantra.

Jo listened to Simi, the only woman who'd been allowed to come out to talk to them. Her eyes were puffy and red, and as she spoke, her eyes were always watchful of their surroundings.

Toni's legs went wobbly as she listened to Jo translate what had happened.

"Three days ago, Paksima didn't arrive for her classes. One of the women went looking for her, and her husband said the Taliban had taken her. He said they were concerned about her setting up a school in the village." Jo looked stricken as she continued to translate.

"They will have killed her. We won't see her again," Simi said, her hands clenched into fists at her side. "It's to give a message to the women here that we can't do anything with you because we'll be killed."

Toni put her hand in front of her mouth and shook her head. Paksima had been standing here a couple of weeks ago, ready to do what needed to be done, and Toni wished she could put back the clock and pretend she'd never met her. It would make all this easier. Jo and Simi both looked at her silently as tears slid down her cheeks, and she wiped them around the dust on her face, uncaring as to the effect.

Jo turned to Simi. "Where do we go from here?" she asked. "I'll understand if you want us to go. It's a lot to ask of you to put yourselves in such danger. You have enough in your lives to be frightened of without us making it worse."

Simi put her hand on her hips and looked to the village elder. "You may come with me to meet some of the women. They asked to see you again." She gestured Jo and Toni forward at a nod from the elder, and they went to the square where they'd met the women on their last visit. "The women will continue to try and move the health and education of our village along," Simi said. "We already discussed it. Paksima would have been proud that you cared about her. We still need and want your help," she said, sitting down. "But we need to move forward more quietly until we are sure the Taliban have left the valley."

The women began talking and offered them green tea and the

sweet treat jalebi as they discussed how to move forward. Their visit continued with Toni taking photos of the women and children using her Polaroid camera. She didn't use it often as it had been difficult getting film. This was likely to be their last visit though, and although Toni had only been there twice, the women felt like old friends, and she wanted to leave them with some pictures. She was going to miss getting to know these groups, learning about their lives, and the hopes and fears they had for their children. Tomorrow they'd be heading back to Sherwood, and this would be a memory for Toni to revisit. Nothing more.

While she was taking photos, Jo was having a long and quiet conversation with Simi, which Toni knew was about setting up the women's group among the villages and explaining how messages would be passed to her. They had a plan, which was good, but Toni was worried for Simi's safety, frightened that she'd succumb to the same fate as Paksima. But there was nothing she could do about it. Women here knew all the ways they could be betrayed, and they still tried to move forward. Their strength and courage were beyond impressive, and Toni promised herself she'd remember it when she was fretting about things that were largely inconsequential.

When it was time to leave, Jo picked up her gear and put her scarf and helmet back on. Her radio came alive as the troops checked in and signaled it was clear. Toni picked up her own gear and followed behind. As they got further into the village, they were picked up by their escort to head back toward the patrol base.

They traveled for a couple of hours. Their progress was, as always, painstakingly slow, and Toni guessed they'd only gone less than two miles. Toni's thoughts wandered, and she wondered when it had become less frightening to be doing this. The idea that she could be blown up instantly, that she'd no longer exist, and that her family would never see her again filled her head. And yet...it was just the way things were.

When they heard heavy gunfire somewhere ahead of them, Toni fell to the ground and lay flat, as she had a couple times before when they were on patrol. There didn't appear to be any shots coming their way.

Wiffy beckoned her forward. "Keep your head down, Jim. This is serious. That's a lot of gunfire, and we need to find out what's happening."

She made her way forward, following Wiffy toward a ditch a few yards ahead. She could hear Sprint slithering along behind her. Eventually, Wiffy stopped in the ditch that provided a small measure of cover. It had mud in the bottom and appeared to flow ahead in a long, straight line. Between them and the gunfire was the path they'd been traveling. On the other side of the ditch were the fields full of red and white poppies that made Helmand province famous for opium.

Toni had expected there to be some kind of odor lying so close to the opium plants, but the ditch they were in reeked of earth and excrement, and she could smell nothing else. She managed to take a couple of shots as she listened to the radio chatter around her. She didn't understand much of what was happening, but she was reassured as she heard Jo's calm tones every few minutes.

"There's a patrol from FOB Sherwood ahead in trouble. I expect the captain and lieutenant will offer to help. They're being fired on from that derelict building we saw on the way to the village. I think this ditch takes the dirty water out of a building much closer to us. We'll smell like shit for a while." Flash grinned, but it didn't reach his eyes.

"Do you know anything more?" Toni asked.

"It looks like a lot of insurgents, maybe fifty or more. Now we know why it's been so quiet; they've obviously been getting a large number together so they can take out as many of us as they can." Flash listened to his radio. "On our way," he said into it then turned to Toni. "We're moving slowly along this ditch. Keep your head down and stay between us. If we say down, move like shit off a shovel and bury yourself flat."

"This is echo two niner. We're less than two clicks away and can provide backup. We're making our way toward you and taking point at GR691423." Jo's voice came through the radio loud and clear and most importantly, calm.

Part of Toni was exhilarated. Her adrenaline peaked, and the rush it gave her helped her move forward, past the fear. She took her video camera out and filmed them moving forward. It was jerky and awkward, but that would only add to the authenticity of the piece. There was nothing to see except Flash in front of her and fragments of Wiffy in front of him. The noise of the fighting had gotten heavier and closer. Her heart thumped in time with the gunfire.

They got to an abandoned wreck of a building that was little more than an old animal enclosure and began the complicated operation of getting to it. Luckily, the firing was coming from some distance away on the other side of the building. Getting out of the ditch was difficult. They were wearing eighty pounds of gear and having to free themselves from the mud was made more difficult by it sucking at their boots. It was fantastic video footage, and the men groused with dark humor as they freed themselves. Then they were on the move, silently running toward the building in a line. They crawled through a hole in the side. As Toni went past the wall and into the baking sun, she could see the whole platoon had arrived and were drinking water. They were all still on alert, and everyone had their guns at the ready. Jo looked at her map and relayed messages to and from Corporal "Aerial" Taylor, the communications expert, as he talked to headquarters.

There was a set of open concrete steps that led onto a roof of sorts. Toni watched Jo walk up them in an almost crab-like movement. She bent over and became smaller the higher she went up the steps to keep her head from sticking out over the top.

"We need somewhere we can fire from that's close enough to the fight, but also that we can defend. This building looks good, but we need to be sure we have enough cover. It'll be no good without it. I don't want to take fire unprotected unless I have to." Her voice over the radio got quieter as she disappeared at the top of the stairs.

When she reappeared, Toni let out the breath she'd been holding. She'd have to think about this when she had a moment. What would it mean to fall for a woman who was always in this kind of danger?

"All good up here," Jo said as she came down. Her gaze flicked briefly to Toni then she looked away. "Let's get into place. I want all our firepower toward the north and the gun battle. We need to take some of the heat off the guys that are being held down. The Sherwood patrol has been separated, and there are bits of squads in a number of locations. We've been tasked with providing some cover so that they can reunite, and then we'll all wait for air and fire support."

Jo directed the different soldiers into position behind the small wall around the roof. She used others for cover fire looking for any infiltrators coming from behind or around the side. Toni didn't move, uncertain where to go so that she wouldn't be in the way but still get the footage she needed. She wanted her guards to do what they needed to instead of hanging around to babysit her.

"Are you all right?" Jo's expression was shuttered.

Goosebumps raised along Toni's neck. In the middle of enemy action, Jo had taken a moment to check on her, and Toni looked into her eyes. She was scared, thrilled, worried...but she wasn't about to put any of that on Jo. "Yes, I'm fine," she said. "I feel like I'm keeping Flash, Wiffy, and Sprint from doing a much more important job than protecting me."

"You're important to us too." Jo gave a quick smile. "You can't be on the roof with us though. It's too dangerous."

"I thought you might say that." Toni grimaced. "But I can't see anything down here. I'd be much more in the thick of it on the roof and could get what I need. And so starts another argument between us. I need to do my job and get the kind of footage I came here for."

"You won't get much if you're dead. Being on the roof is risky even when you're armed. I've seen soldiers talking one moment and gone the next in places like that. I'm not asking, Toni; I'm telling you to stay here."

Toni could see Jo already looking around and planning her next move. Damn it all. She had no choice but to back down. Jo couldn't argue with her when there were lives at stake. "What about the stairs?"

Jo let out a big breath, and Toni thought Jo wanted to punch her when her hands clenched.

"Fine. If you move up the stairway, please ensure you stay well below the top. Dance, Rush, Crawford—watch her back." She turned and took the stairs two at a time, disappearing from view.

"So, Jim, what do you need to do? We'll work out if it's possible and how we'll do it," Flash said.

Grateful for the reprieve from judgment, she looked around. "I'd love to get a view of the surrounding countryside and the building that the firing is coming from," she said. "Perhaps something that shows where some of the men are pinned down, and a few shots of the guys on the roof. I don't need much," she said. "But I want to show people the reality of what you're doing. It's important."

Flash nodded. "We should be able to help you do that. If Wiffy and I search out some good spots and Sprint stays with you, then we can see. So stay here for now. Okay?"

"I won't do anything silly, I promise." Toni didn't want to put these soldiers in any more danger than they were already in.

"There's a hole in the wall at the far end of this building, and we may get to see the firefight happening from there. Let me check."

Flash scooted over to the far end of the building and peered around the corner. He came back from the window and gave a thumbs up. Toni edged toward the space and slid her camera around the edge of the hole. Maybe she could pull her video camera out and take a scene or two. The noise from the firefight got louder, and there appeared to be heavier armaments being used on both sides.

"We need to be careful of the heavier guns. If they've got a grenade launcher, one grenade on target over here could take us out," Flash said.

"I'm hoping they only have a few, so they'll use them on certainties instead of possibilities," Sprint said.

The photos from this angle were hardly capturing anything. Video wouldn't work either. She looked around. "Can we go up the steps? I need a better angle from the rooftop where our guys are doing their thing." She knew it was risky, but Jo had said not to go on the rooftop, not the steps. She ducked as bullets hit the concrete, showering them with small debris.

"Okay. Let's head up the steps. Stop at six steps from the top and keep your head down. Hunch over like the captain did," Flash said.

Toni headed up the steps, and the anxiety hit her. She was exposed here, as were the men with her. She could hear her heart beating, and her breathing started to become erratic. Her vision started to dim...

Flash squeezed her arm hard enough to pull her attention back. "It's all good. Keep your head down, and I'll come alongside you. We can do it together."

She took a deep, shaky breath and reminded herself that she was strong enough. "This is paralyzing when you aren't used to it. The idea that a bullet can fly across here in the space of less than a second and take me out... I don't know how you do it," Toni said as she filmed their walk up the crumbling stairs toward the firefight.

"We do get anxious, but we're trained for it. You're doing fine." He patted her back. "Let's look on the roof carefully and see what's what."

They stopped a few stairs from the top. "That wall is taller than I expected." Toni went to stand to look over it, but Flash dragged her down again.

"It's still easy for a bullet to be on an arc or to ricochet. Let's be sensible. Got your cameras ready?"

She moved the camera around and hoped she could pick up the firefight in the distance without actually looking through the lens. Occasionally shots seemed to be close, but Flash and Sprint ensured she had her head down if anything came close. She panned over the area, sure to tilt the camera in various directions to get as much video footage as she could. Then she took more pictures with her camera.

She hoped she'd captured the atmosphere from the roof, especially the sense of complete concentration and soldiers demonstrating their expertise. She glanced at the screen, and her heart lurched as she saw a picture of Jo returning fire. She looked so strong, so courageous. But Toni's breath caught at the knowledge that she was in the middle of the fighting.

Following an order from Jo, there was silence. Firing stopped on the roof but continued elsewhere.

"We've been waiting for air support," Flash said, his gun still raised, and his gaze turned toward the sky.

"I thought I could hear an airplane coming in." Toni looked to the sky to see if she could see anything. "Can you see it, Flash?"

"No. I can hear it though." There was an explosion of gunfire in the distance. "That noise is the Taliban firing into the sky to see if they can shoot the plane down. Hopefully it's out of range."

There was a series of loud explosions followed by the sound of the airplane getting quieter as it moved away. There was still heavy firing coming from the enemy compound.

Jo's voice came over the radio, and they all listened.

Flash nodded. "We've called for more fire support. That's light artillery based in the hills above us. They have big guns that can fire from about twelve miles away. They tried to help earlier but were pinned down too."

There was a series of loud explosions as they bombed their target. The firing from the insurgents' compound stopped. The silence was punctuated by the sound of debris hitting the ground.

Soon the silence filled with radio chatter. Flash and Sprint held up their hands to stop Toni from speaking until the radio chatter stopped.

"Sounds like some of the Sherwood soldiers have been hit. They're calling for medevac," Sprint said.

There was silence as they all took that in. Toni could see the soldiers looking straight ahead. That could be any one of them on any given day. She swallowed hard, glad she could still hear Jo on the radio. Shortly, she appeared on the steps above them and seemed irritated at how close they were to the roof. She waved them down, and the rest of the platoon came down after her.

Jo turned to the group. "I need one of you checking each direction on the roof for the next thirty minutes. I'll relieve you as soon as we've had water." She motioned to the troops. "The rest of you, get some shade and rest. We could be here for a while."

Toni, Flash, and Wiffy settled in the shade with the rest of the platoon. Everyone got out their water bottles, and the only sound for the next few moments was the glugging of water as the thirsty soldiers rehydrated.

Toni took the opportunity to get more photos and thought about what she'd just been part of. It was difficult to take in and the fact that some troops had been injured underlined the worry that Jo had about her safety. She'd returned her empty water bottle to her day sack when Jo came and sat next to her.

"Are you okay?"

"I'm fine. Flash had to remind me to breathe when I got scared. Now I'm just exhausted." She gave Jo a brief smile and then looked away, not wanting to telegraph just how frightened she'd been not so much for her own safety, but for Jo's.

"All those emotions whirring in your head are enough to wear you out. You'll be tired for a day or two. We get tired too, but we're used to it. Rest while you can." Jo took a large swig from her water bottle.

"I was wondering how we get back to the patrol base," Toni

said.

"Same way we got here: walking. Do you think you'll be able to make it?"

"Of course. I won't let you down. I'm not made of cotton wool, you know. I'm tough." Toni could hear her heart beating loudly, and her tensed body was making a fool of her. This was part of the job. Her mother did this all the time. There was no way on earth she'd fail. And she didn't need Jo treating her like a precious doll.

Jo looked into her eyes. "I'm not questioning your ability; I'm making sure you're good to go. I'd be foolish to expect you to do something if you didn't think you were up to it."

"And what would you have done if I was too weak?" Toni knew she was goading Jo, but honestly, she hadn't been this physically vulnerable since she'd arrived in Afghanistan. She alternately wanted to pick a fight and to be gently held until they were safe again.

"Got you a ride from a WMIK Land Rover. I'm not going to fight over this. I'm doing my job and making sure everyone can make it back to base," Jo said. "We need to be super aware of what may be out there. Firstly, there may be insurgents who've escaped the bombing and are just waiting for us to come out of cover. Secondly, they may have had two groups. We've taken out the first, but there could be a second force waiting for us with a planned attack. We'll take our time and move carefully. Did you eat something?"

"No. Not yet. It's been all too much to think about food," Toni said, accepting the explanation and olive branch. She shouldn't be such an ass.

"Please eat a snack. As much as you can manage. It'll be several hours until we're back, and I need to make sure you don't faint from hunger." She patted Toni's shoulder awkwardly and then turned away.

Toni pulled out a granola bar and settled back against the wall to listen to the talk around her. The chat amongst the soldiers was about the casualties and what they'd managed to piece together about who they were and what had happened. Based on how they were talking, it was a conversation they'd had before. Toni thought about how strange it would be to have a commonplace conversation about dead and wounded friends and colleagues. It gave her a thought about an addition to the article, and she pulled out her notebook and wrote as she ate.

"Let's not start guessing, lads. It isn't good for us to worry about things that might not have happened. We know there've been injuries, but let's wait 'til we get back to base to find out what's gone down," Jo said.

Aeriel appeared and spoke quietly to Jo, who listened attentively before turning back to the troops.

"Charlie Charlie Two has messaged to thank us for our assistance. They weren't sure they were going to make it out. You've done a great job today, and I couldn't have asked for more. There are a number of lads in Foxtrot Company who were glad you had their backs." Jo made eye contact with everyone in the troop. "Orders are for us to return to the patrol base and debrief. We're detailed to head out to Sherwood in the morning so John and I can debrief command then. Let's head out. Be hyperaware as there could be some surprises along the way. Eyes and ears."

The journey back to Top Hat was exactly as Jo told them to expect. Long, slow, and difficult. The heat molded Toni's clothes to her, dust was stuck in every crevice and each footstep was like trudging through quicksand. When she saw the sanger in the distance, she was so pleased home was in sight that her knees went weak. She was going to have the coldest drink of Coke that she could find and wet her head with a bottle of water. She smiled inwardly. Some women's everyday items were another woman's luxuries.

Later, clean and relatively cooler, Toni sat on her bunk looking over footage and making notes. Try as she might, she couldn't completely focus. Jo and John Travers had been debriefing in the radio room for several hours. Toni was concerned that Jo hadn't managed to eat or shower or get her thoughts into place. But it wasn't her place to worry, was it? This was Jo's life; she was used to it and didn't expect anything different. Toni's perceptions and worry mattered about as much as a dust particle in the desert. But why did the idea that she had no part in Jo's world make her chest ache?

CHAPTER ELEVEN

JUST PUTTING ONE FOOT in front of the other took monumental effort. Jo decided to brief the platoon in the morning. Four soldiers were injured in the insurgent attack, two of them seriously. One soldier wasn't expected to survive the night. If they hadn't arrived to back up Foxtrot company, it would've been a hell of a lot worse. But she still felt the loss of any soldier; it was an absolute reminder of the danger they were in. Not that they really needed one.

She'd done her duty but now, as she sat outside the cookhouse in the dark, exhaustion swept over her. The heat was relentless. She rubbed her face; the dust from the day embedded in the sweat made it feel like sandpaper. She had the remains of a bowl of warmed stew on her lap which she'd eaten almost without chewing. She opened her eyes and smiled a little when Toni handed her a steaming mug of tea, complete with extra sugar.

Toni sat opposite her, not speaking, clearly understanding this was as much as she could cope with. When she'd finished her tea, Toni took her plate and mug and handed her some shower kit and clean clothes. "I've cleared the shower for you. Go. Then get back to the powder room and bed."

"I need to pack." Not only did she have to pack her kit since they were leaving the base at eight hundred hours, she also needed to leave the patrol base as pristine as it was when they arrived. She sighed and closed her eyes again.

"Your platoon has done most of the packing. Sometimes a sergeant is useful. He told me to tell you it was all in hand. They got it done."

"They're good lads," Jo said, eyes still closed. At least that was one thing off her plate. Strange, though, that they were using Toni as a go-between instead of talking to her directly. Although she'd been in briefings since they returned.

"And you're lucky you have me because I've done most of your personal packing, and you can finish it in the morning." Toni stood and hauled Jo to her feet. "Now go shower and get some sleep. If you get a move on, you'll get five hours."

When she got back to their area, Toni had already pulled back the covers.

Jo saw the remainder of her gear ready to be packed and sat on the bed. "Thank you." She swallowed hard and couldn't meet Toni's eyes. It had been a long, long time since someone had cared for her this way. She didn't want to get used to it. She couldn't. Toni would be gone soon, and Jo would have no one to depend on but herself. That was just the way things were.

But damn, what she wouldn't give to fall asleep with Toni pressed against her tonight.

***

The next morning, she briefed the platoon about the injured soldiers and promised to update them all again as soon as she was given names. Some of the injured might be their friends, and they'd want to know. Thankfully, they had an uneventful return journey to Sherwood. Toni was quiet, not that she had much choice with all the noise, but Jo thought she looked more contemplative than usual. More often than not, Toni was constantly on the lookout, noticing the things around her, asking questions, talking to this soldier or that one. Now though, she simply looked lost in thought. Jo tried her best not to stare. Toni had pulled her hair back and small wisps framed her face. Her tanned skin glowed, setting off her beautiful eyes. Jo shook her head a little and looked away.

Once the platoon was squared away back on base, she had a few hours before she needed to do anything. She undressed and flopped back onto her bed. She wasn't sure where Toni was, but hopefully they'd get a chance to talk some more before bed. Their nightly chats had become the highlight of her day as they spoke softly in the dark about things that would feel too sacred in the light of day. Her body grew warm as she reflected on Toni taking care of her.

Yesterday was a day like no other, and she needed some space to think about it. The loss of Paksima was part of the brutal and vicious way these women lived. But Jo still felt her loss deeply. No, she hadn't known her well. But she'd looked into her eyes, and they'd spoken about Paksima's dreams for the future. They'd held hands, and Jo had promised to help. And then...Paksima was gone, along with all her hopes and dreams. Jo turned over and punched her pillow. How was she supposed to make a difference fighting this kind of enemy? One who came out of the dark and ripped people from their homes.

The death of Paksima hadn't deterred the other women. Rather, it had provided a catalyst. The word would certainly spread and ensure that other villagers understood what sacrifice she'd made, willing or not. Their courage was something beyond understanding. Outsiders might expect them to buckle under the pressure, to give up the struggle, but it seemed to spur them on. Truly, it was inspiring.

Being catapulted into the insurgent incident had made her heart beat as quickly as it had when she first got reports of what was happening. She began reliving the whole thing to check that she'd done all the right things and looked after the men properly. They were the most important thing. She wanted to make sure she could correct any small issues for next time.

She drifted into an uneasy sleep, bombs and gunfire mixed with images of Toni, her eyes wide with fear even as she held her camera up to video everything. Jo saw the danger she was in but couldn't get to her...couldn't save her... She gave a silent scream as she leapt toward her, but she was too far away—

"The rumor is that the soldier was killed and the others were injured by the bombs that were supposed to be for the Taliban. Is that right?"

Yanked from the nightmare, Jo opened her eyes and looked toward Toni's bed. They'd dispensed with the central netting when they returned. After the closeness they'd developed while they were away, it seemed unnecessary now. Toni's bed was empty. She was standing at the entrance to the tent with her hands on her hips, legs braced. Her face was red, her expression one of rage.

"I can't believe it. How can we kill our own troops and not admit to it?" Toni asked.

"What?" Jo woke as if a grenade exploded. She sat bolt upright and frowned. "What are you talking about?"

"Those soldiers were hurt by *our* bombs," Toni said.

"Who said that?" Jo asked. "There was no mention of it in the meeting with the colonel." This was *not* good news. Soldiers loved nothing better than rumors to pass around and if this was true, it would spread like wildfire.

"Of course there won't be mention of it. The guys reckon they'll try and hide it from everyone. Especially from me," Toni said. "And because we share accommodation, that could include you."

Jo hoped Toni had got it wrong. Keeping Jo out of the loop was both embarrassing and likely to cause her problems. "Please don't jump to conclusions on a rumor or what the soldiers are saying. Let me find out what really happened."

"Every reporter knows that rumors start somewhere. Someone has an idea about what happened, and that means the rumor must have some basis. I'm going to follow it up," Toni said, her arms crossed and her eyes hard. "I need to speak to the injured soldiers."

"Please, Toni. Let me ask the ops staff what the word is and then we can take it from there. Please don't print anything yet." Jo hated that she had to beg, but she'd do whatever she needed to in order to handle this the right way.

"Why not?" Toni asked.

"Because the dead man's family in particular need to be told, and those men who are injured also have families. We try not to release news that we've got injured and dead soldiers until we've informed their families. Otherwise, every single family of every soldier serving out here will worry, and that isn't fair. Think about all the families worrying if it's their husbands, sons, wives, dads, lovers that are one of the dead or wounded. So just hold off until we've confirmed with the families, and until we have all the facts."

"How long will that take?" Toni asked.

She looked almost like she could stamp her feet with impatience. Clearly, she had inherited one or two of her mother's genes.

"As long as it takes. We have to make sure everyone knows who needs to know." Jo swung round on the bed and put her feet on the floor. "I'd also rather you didn't start writing about friendly fire until we know more details. To find out your son has died in one breath and then that he was killed by the British Forces in the next is not a good thing, especially if we don't know that happened for sure."

"Okay." Toni took a deep breath. "I won't report until I know things for certain. But you know I won't back down," she said.

Jo could understand Toni's impatience with the military casualty machine but wondered if Toni blamed her personally for the delay. "I know that. I need to find out what's going on. And as soon as I know, then you will." She could hear her voice rising as she became more wound up. Dammit. She didn't expect to spend her evening defending the Army. She should have known though. Toni was there as a reporter, one determined not to live in her mother's shadow. Jo had known better, but she'd still allowed herself to think that maybe, somehow, one day... Stupid. Illogical. Impractical. She swallowed the ball of anger and frustration.

"I'll accept that for now," Toni said. "And tomorrow, I'll listen to what you've found out, but meanwhile I'll carry on talking to the guys to see what they know. And I want to talk to the injured."

Jo's stomach sank. Toni wasn't going to sway on this, and Jo knew it would take a good argument to convince her to stay quiet. As far as she was aware, there wasn't anything unusual in the report, but if that wasn't true, then it meant they were keeping things from her. The promotion she'd been aiming for may well have been ripped out from under her without her even knowing. And Toni jumping the gun could only mean heartache for the soldiers' families.

She stood and faced Toni, channeling the diplomatic tone she'd used to get this far in her career. "I was told that embedded journalists always think they're independent and give their 'independent view' of what they see and hear whilst on deployment. But after living in close quarters with us, it means that they eventually lose their independence and will do nothing to hurt the battalion they've been embedded with. I'm hoping that rings true with you. Please don't hurt us," Jo said.

Toni's hard expression faltered a little. "I can't promise that. If there's a story that needs telling, expect me to tell it. You do your job, and you have to let me do mine." Her eyes glittered, and she had a determined look on her face, as if daring Jo to cross her.

Jo stared at Toni and all the feelings of surprise, anger, and indignation disappeared as she looked at the magnificent woman in front of her. She was red in the face, almost shaking with the knowledge of the possible cover-up and her eyes were bright. With her hands on her hips, her chin raised, and the glare in her eyes, she moved from beautiful to exquisite. "I haven't seen you this angry before," Jo said. She stepped closer to Toni. "It's glorious and quite takes my breath away." She stood as close as she could get without touching her, then leaned in and kissed her. Not gently this time. Not tentatively. But with the passion that had built over the last weeks to the point of an explosion.

Toni took hold of Jo's T-shirt and pulled Jo closer. Jo put as much feeling into her kiss as she could, crushing their lips together, her tongue demanding entrance. This was a bad, terrible, horrendous idea.

"You can't distract me with sex," Toni said between kisses.

Jo was still harboring hurt from their earlier discussion. If sex would have fixed things instead of making them infinitely more complicated, she would gladly have thrown Toni onto the bed and ravished her. But this aggravated feeling wasn't going to do their relationship any good. She wondered how to be honest without ruining things between them. She pulled away, holding Toni at arm's length and then pulled her over so they lay on her small bed facing each other. "I want you. In case that isn't clear, you're driving me fucking crazy. But there are a hell of a lot of walls between us, and frankly, I need to take some time to recover from the full-frontal assault that is Toni James when she smells a story." Jo decided that she would be honest, but lighthearted at the same time. Maybe that would take the sting out of it.

"Full-frontal assault? Are you using that term as an Army phrase? Of course, you are. Why would I think otherwise?" Toni nipped at Jo's bottom lip.

"Is there another way? It means a direct attack on enemy forces," Jo said. "Have I said something you don't understand?"

"In my world, it means grabbing a woman's breasts against her will. If I did that now, would you consider it a full-frontal assault?" Toni placed her hands over Jo's breasts and squeezed.

Jo looked into her eyes and could see an endless future in their depths. It was terrifying. "If you keep doing that, I won't be responsible for my actions," she said, breathless as Toni ran her thumbs over Jo's nipples.

"I hope not. I want to know you, really know you. Inside and out. We can be irresponsible right here, right now. We'll deal with the consequences in the morning."

Bad idea. Bad idea. The words melted away under the fire of Toni's touch. They both had a faint sheen of sweat over their skin, and Jo marveled that Toni could look so sexy in the half light. Toni's hands on her breasts were doing things to her insides and making it hard to breathe. She was going to embarrass herself by pleading if she didn't get Toni to move her hands somewhere else. She hadn't been touched in so, so long. She *needed* to feel Toni everywhere, all at once. She kissed her again, trying to communicate her desperation.

"Tell me," Toni murmured as she kissed Jo's neck.

"I'm on fire, and I need you." Jo dipped her head and nuzzled against Toni's neck. "Can we lose our clothes?" Within moments, they were both naked, and Toni continued her full-frontal assault. Jo moved her hands over Toni's body, needing to feel bare skin beneath her hands. But Toni held her wrists and stopped her.

"This is the Toni James show, and I'm going to enjoy you on my terms," she said. "I've been dreaming about this moment."

"But–" Jo wasn't one to take orders. And yet, there was something damn erotic about it too.

"You can have your own show later, but this one's mine," Toni said.

Jo had never been in this position before but decided she might quite like it. She was in control of her life, and she was in command all day long. But right now, it felt good to let go. She relaxed onto the bed and into Toni's touch.

Toni's hands continued their journey all over her body, never settling long, keeping her on edge.

"Touch me, please," Jo said, raising her hips. She wanted Toni inside her, not only at her core, but she wanted Toni to be inside her skin, totally enmeshed with her. They could be together and nothing from the outside world would invade their togetherness. Tomorrow, that would change. But for now...

Toni did as she asked and ran her fingers along the length of warmth and wetness between her legs. She did the same thing a couple more times before sliding off the bed and pulling Jo's legs over her shoulders. Jo wanted more; she *needed* her. Toni settled her lips on Jo's clit, and she jerked at the intensity of her touch. The feeling of Toni pulling and sucking was enough to push her to the edge. Before she could beg, Toni's fingers were inside her. With

Toni's lips on her and her fingers rhythmically moving in and out, Jo's body was taut. The release was total as all Jo's need was swept away on a tide that was Toni. She let the orgasm cascade through her, biting down on her lip to keep from making any noise. When she settled, she was nearly dizzy with the release.

Toni quickly moved up her body and with wet lips full of her scent, she kissed Jo. "You're so beautiful. That was beautiful," she said.

Jo couldn't move. Her legs didn't seem attached to her body, and she couldn't remember ever feeling so languid. She eventually clasped Toni close to her and moved her legs around to hold Toni between them. "Beautiful doesn't do it justice. It was a cool English morning, a hot summer's afternoon having a picnic by the river, and a combination of all the wonderful things that have happened in my life," Jo said. She gently put her hand on Toni's face. "Including meeting you and you getting under my skin." Jo kissed her harder this time. "And now I'm going to get all over your skin."

Toni stretched out along her body, and the heat between them began to rise once again. Jo slowly moved her hands down Toni's body, taking care to respond to her pleasure points. She eventually slid her hand between Toni's legs and was rewarded with wetness that made Jo feel powerful. It was a heady feeling, turning a woman on this way. She slid down the small bed so that her feet were on the floor. She took Toni's wetness into her mouth, caressed her clit and responded to Toni's movements. She continued to move her hands across Toni's breasts before moving them to her core. Jo entered Toni and within moments, Toni moaned quietly. Jo held her in place as her legs shook before she finally collapsed.

They lay together silently, joined in the shared intimacy. It was a first for Jo, and she wanted more of this closeness. The sex she'd had before was functional—lust and desire to be sated quickly and efficiently. This was different, and she wondered how Toni saw it.

It didn't matter. Ultimately, whatever this thing between them was, it didn't matter. It was temporary. Jo closed her eyes and pushed those thoughts away. She needed to enjoy the moment for what it was.

"When we heard the shots firing yesterday, what did you think?" Toni broke the delicate silence.

Jo had never had to talk to anyone about what she was thinking. She struggled to find words. "Is this one of our personal in the dark conversations? One that doesn't leave this tent?" How honest should she be with a reporter in her bed? Plenty of movies had been made about the disastrous outcome of whispers in the dark.

"We could start something new, post-sex conversations. Very personal." Toni ran her fingertips along Jo's spine. "I wondered about yesterday because I was so frightened. I didn't know what was happening and what we'd do. I wanted to know if you were scared and what you were thinking as things unfolded."

"I suppose I'd be lying if I said there wasn't a part of me that was frightened. Before I go out on patrol, I have a mix of fear and adrenaline. But I've learned to control it, because it's what I'm expecting to happen, and I know the feeling. It's like an old friend. I understand that I'll have to live with the consequences of my actions. I rely on my training too. Find out what the situation is, where the firing is coming from, remind myself where my men are, and then deal with what's in front of me. I moved through the things I needed to know to decide on what we would do." When she set it out like that, Jo had been in control throughout the engagement. No matter what the outcome of the rumors, Jo had done what was necessary.

"Did you have options? I mean, was there only one way things had to go?" Toni asked.

"Yes and no. It could have been the situation was too far away for us to help. Or it could have already been dealt with, and there was no need for us to go at all. We could've decided to commit some soldiers and move the rest away. There are endless scenarios. I ran through them in my head as HQ gave us each piece of information on what was happening."

"Did it make you nervous?"

"Nervous, no. Once it's all over, I try to work out what I'd do different next time—if anything. I was lying here earlier going through the day. I suppose my biggest concern was you," Jo said.

"Me? Was that because I was tying up some of your men?"

"No. It's because I was involving you in something dangerous and could see no way of making it less so. If I left you where you were in the ditch, it was quite possible that insurgents could have come up behind you, and there would have been an even bigger fight. Particularly if they found out you were press."

"Killed or taken hostage, right?" Toni shuddered a little.

"Whatever they might have planned to do, I wasn't giving them an option. I wanted to keep you with us. It was the safest plan. Despite you trying to put yourself in danger on the roof. I didn't need that extra argument," Jo said, not censoring the slight reprimand.

"I was conscious of you through it all though. You were like my safety beacon in the distance. I knew that I'd be safe with you there," Toni said.

Jo's stomach turned over, and her heart beat like a war drum. She could hardly think straight. "I don't think I've ever been a beacon before. Well, no one has ever told me so anyway. I think the men trust me to get them out of whatever we find ourselves in, whether it's something that happens to us, or something we put ourselves into." Jo wanted to be honest, but the words were all tangled up. "I wanted you to be safe. If anything happened to you, I'd be devastated." Had she said too much? And yet, there was more she wanted to say. But those words wouldn't—couldn't—make it to the light of day.

"Am I important to you?" Toni asked.

Jo decided to stay professional rather than personal. "You know you are. Without you, the story of the women in the villages wouldn't have such impact, and the sacrifices we're making, the soldiers' stories, all of it—wouldn't be out in the world," she said.

"What about to you personally?" Toni said.

She'd probably worked out Jo's strategy to pin her down. But she'd never had these feelings and wondered if it was too early to start trying to put thoughts into words. "I find I have feelings for you."

"You do?" Toni almost squeaked when she spoke. "What kind of feelings?'

Jo was once again grateful for the dark and the sense of safety it provided, false though it might be. "I'm happy when I'm with you, and it's made me think of other things I want to do with you. And to you. Not only sex though. I was looking at you earlier, wondering what it would feel like to wake up with you in my arms."

"I've wondered that myself, although that's not likely to happen here. I think trying to fit two of us in this bed for more than a couple of hours will be impossible. Now I know why they provide such narrow beds: to discourage lesbians from spending the night together." Toni cuddled Jo in her arms.

Her laughter vibrated through Jo's body and echoed around the room.

"Yesterday I wanted to hold you in my arms and keep you safe, which isn't what I was supposed to be thinking. It was hard to stay disciplined." Jo would never forget standing in the middle of a firefight arguing with Toni. Her stomach sank at the thought of Toni being on the roof, and her heart raced as fast as the machine-gun fire. "That kind of distraction could have cost lives. And I don't know what I'd have done if something had happened to you."

There was a long moment of silence as Toni seemed to take that in. "I care about you too," she said eventually, clearly unable to engage with the issue of Jo's divided attention.

Jo sighed. "You'll care about me until you disappear in a few weeks after the next big story that you're offered." Jo knew her way of thinking on this was good. Logical, practical, unemotional. Exactly the way she'd been trained to think.

"I may get offered a good story, but I'd hope that you and I would be able to work things out between us before that happens," Toni said. "We talked about this. I'm not going to be my mother." She pushed Jo away a few inches. "And while we're talking about problem areas, what about your hands-off approach?"

"My hands-off approach?" Jo loosened her arm around Toni, the return to the emotional making her wary.

"Yes. Your 'I can't have a relationship with you, I might lose my career' approach. Then you talk me into your bed, might I add."

"For a hands-on approach, I might suggest..." Jo grinned a little in the darkness, hoping it would change the direction of the conversation.

"But will we go back to the hands-off again tomorrow?" Toni asked.

She groaned. So much for redirection. "I don't know where we stand. We also have the issue of the rumor mill on base digging up issues that you want to print as an in-depth report. It could ruin my career," Jo said. "You're the one with power in our relationship. When it comes to what you say or do, when it comes to reporting about us, I have no control or say. That's not great when it comes to a healthy relationship, I don't think." She turned onto her back and drew Toni on to her. "At least the sex is good. You said you were feeling a little hung up with not getting any. We fixed that." Jo enjoyed making fun of Toni, even if the undertone to their conversation remained tense.

Toni's body relaxed a fraction against her. "Actually, yes, I did need sex with a gorgeous woman and here I am, sleeping on a narrow bed with one. But I'm also wondering if I could spend time with you out of uniform one day," Toni said.

"I'm hardly ever out of uniform. It's pretty much part of my being. I do little outside the Army. That's why I know so little about romance and relationships. I think we can agree I can handle sex though." Jo held one of Toni's breasts and stroked gently before kissing it.

"Oh, yeah, we seem to be on the same page in the sex manual.

Yes, there. That's good," Toni murmured softly. "But we can learn about relationship and romance together if we wanted to," she said.

"It sounds like you think I need convincing. I'm not a child you need to bribe to learn the piano." Jo wished Toni would drop it and just let the moment be what it was. She gave up paying attention to Toni's body in order to pay attention to her words. Damn stubborn woman wasn't about to give up, was she?

"I think you do though. How do I convince you that we could have something more than just sex?" Toni asked, settling against her again. "I mean, have you ever considered it with anyone?"

"I had offers from men and women when I was training, and quite a few since. But like I've said before, they were never long-term. You're making me think about things differently now. It's making me crazy."

"What's different now?"

Jo pondered how open she wanted to be. "The part of me that I shut down seems to have woken up despite me telling it to go away. I can't stop thinking about you." There was more silence as Jo thought about her life in the last few years, and Toni didn't rush her. "It can be difficult in the forces, that's why I've refused to consider these things in the past. Despite knowing that being gay is no longer a problem, I've always wanted to be a general, and that's not going to happen if I take risks with you and lose concentration on my work," Jo said. "I've spent the last ten years trying to be the best I can be, and I'm not sure I want to throw it all away. Or, at best, risk throwing it away for something that may not be worth it in the end. I'll be another notch on your bedpost, a story you think about one day. In the meantime, I've lost everything I worked so damn hard for."

"But I want more," Toni said. There was no mistaking the hurt in her voice.

"Do you really though?"

"Yes, much more. I won't lie and say I didn't want sex. You know I did. But I want to explore places together, to learn more about you and what you love, what makes you happy. Do you like cocktails on the patio as the sun's going down?" Toni asked, turning onto her side so they were face to face. "Do you like the way water sparkles under moonlight?"

"I don't know," Jo said. "I haven't really had time to think about those kinds of things."

"That's why I want to explore. I want to learn with you. I want to take you to my favorite places. I want to find out your favorite places and people," Toni said. "You'd be giving us a chance to see what we could be like out in the world. What if it is worth it?"

"But surely they're just pie in the sky dreams?" Jo asked, her stomach dropping. "I'm sorry. I just don't know if it's possible." She wanted those dreams to come true, but the chasm between them seemed too difficult to cross. She put her face to Toni's neck and breathed deeply to ground herself in the fragrance that was just her. Jo drew in a breath and let it out in a deep, silent sigh. Dreaming of a future that couldn't be was fun until you woke up the next morning to find the dream had evaporated under the desert heat.

CHAPTER TWELVE

SOMETIMES THE CLOCK MOVES slowly, particularly when life gets difficult. As Jo wrote yet another report, it was like she could feel every movement of the second hand on her watch. She needed to get this done and move on to other things. She considered their actions and what orders she'd given and the decisions she'd made. She'd never doubted herself quite as much as she did today. At the debrief, the colonel asked a number of questions that were on point but also appeared to be attacking her decision-making. It was as if he was looking for some error in her conduct. Toni's accusation from the night before continued to ring in her ears. What was going on?

Jo went through the whole debrief again. The colonel had questioned her placement of members of the patrol and particularly where Toni had been and who she was with. Jo decided he was making sure that if Toni reported the firefight, she would have nothing to say against his regiment. Once he'd finished the questions, he asked them again but phrased them differently. It became an interrogation, and Jo had done her best not to get defensive. She wasn't sure she'd managed it.

So now she was providing a written version of the events. Hopefully that would be the end of it. She took the report to the clerk in the colonel's office. He sat outside the colonel's office and was privy to all sorts of information. He was also known to be close-mouthed about what he knew, so she wasn't about to ask him about the rumors going around. Instead, Jo asked after the men who'd been injured.

"Corporal Alex Zenski was the soldier killed, and his family have now been informed," he said. "His body has already been moved to Fortress and will undoubtedly be on the way back to the UK soon. Sergeant Alan Green was seriously wounded and is in Fortress, but we think he'll be moved to the UK shortly, because he needs some specialist care. Private Warren and Corporal Miller are in sickbay and have only minor injuries. We hope they'll be released in the next few days."

"At least that's some good news," Jo said.

He tilted his head. "We need some. The colonel is doing a short memorial service later today to give the troops closure. Zenski was popular, and I know it was devastating to everyone. We went through basic together and ended up spending a lot of time together over the years. It's Rebecca and the kids I worry about. I wish I was at home to be there for her. But then, what could I do?"

Jo understood his sentiments, particularly the feeling of helplessness. "I'm sure Rebecca will have plenty of friends and family to support her. You could message her, so she knows you're there for her. But I suspect she'll take time to come to terms with things. If she asks for you, I'm sure the colonel will give you some leave," Jo said.

Jo handed him a tissue from the packet in her combat trouser pocket, surprised that he'd opened up to her and then began to cry. She wondered if it was because she was a woman, and he expected she would understand. Jo also understood that the service meant the memory of Zenski and his time in both the regiment and Helmand would give some meaning to his friends and colleagues as they remembered him.

She decided to go over to Foxtrot company lines to chat to their platoon commander. He would be able to talk about what happened in the firefight. It was one thing to debrief, and she'd even discussed it with Toni, but she needed an informal chat with someone with a commission. Someone who understood what had happened and what decisions they'd made. Someone who knew the truth.

She couldn't find any of the men or their leaders. She went to their company offices, where one of their clerks was sitting behind a desk made of a wooden plank resting on heaped wooden boxes.

"Good morning, corporal," she said. "Nice desk!"

He looked up at her and smiled. "Hello, ma'am. If it disappears, I'll know where to come. Well done yesterday, by the way, with helping our guys when they were in trouble." The clerk stood up and walked around his desk to shake her hand.

"It was what anyone would have done, and I hope if I ever get into that kind of trouble, someone will do the same for me," Jo said.

"What can I do for you?" he asked.

"I came to see the lieutenant and have a chat. I didn't get to meet him except to wave at the debrief," Jo said.

"I'm sorry, but he and the staff sergeant have been posted back to the UK. They were needed in the training wing as a couple of people had gone long-term sick, and they were two trainers down. They both left early this morning," he said.

"That's unusual." Them leaving so quickly seemed a bit too much of a convenient coincidence, and her stomach began to turn.

"It is but neither complained. Staff has a young family and the lieutenant's wife is seven months pregnant, so they were happy to be going home."

There was really no way to ask other than outright. "Have you heard the rumor that yesterday's casualties were friendly fire?"

The clerk worked with the leadership of the company and was likely to know anything that was being passed around the regiment.

He looked around and waved her closer. "I've heard it from a number of different places, but it's a rumor. Nothing more. No one has been able to point a finger or make a serious suggestion as to how it happened or why. Have you got anything?"

"No, I heard the rumor too and wanted to see if there was any substance to it. It would appear not." Jo almost breathed a sigh of relief. If the corporal had only heard rumors as well, there didn't appear to be anything that was well-founded. Maybe it was gossip after all. She'd pop to the sick bay next and put an end to it all.

When she got to the sickbay, she was directed to the soldiers' ward. The all-encompassing smell of a medical facility brought her up short. Like most soldiers, she thought sickbays were places to avoid at all costs. They made her think of injury and death and the fact that living in a war zone was a risky business. In a flash, she could become a patient. She drew her thoughts up close and moved to the ward.

"Sorry, ma'am. Colonel's orders. No one is to disturb these soldiers as they recover," the military policeman standing outside the door said as Jo went to walk past him. He didn't physically stop her, but he was obviously serious about his duty.

"When are visiting hours?"

"That's up to the colonel, ma'am, and he hasn't shared that with us."

Jo could see that he wasn't going to waver and let her in, so she left. She'd never known a patient to have a guard before. The heat added to her dry mouth as she left the air-conditioned sickbay and tried to work out what was happening.

She walked back and decided to stick with the version of events that came from her debrief. She met with her platoon and debriefed them with what she'd learned so far about the health of the wounded soldiers and the memorial service to take place later in the day. They were silent, and Toni looked tearful. She jotted down all the details, clarifying them with Jo to make certain she had them right for her article.

"Did you hear the rumor about yesterday's casualties being friendly fire?" Flash asked.

The other troops nodded. They'd obviously elected him as spokesman.

"Yes. The debrief yesterday made no mention of it, and I've been over to Foxtrot company this morning, and I found nothing that changes it. So unless you know something I don't, it's a rumor and nothing more." Jo put confidence and conviction that she didn't feel into her words. She didn't want the troops to worry about their colleagues taking potshots out of the sky at them. There were procedures in place to stop that happening. But Jo understood only too well that mistakes could happen. In this case, she was secretly wondering why the leaders of the patrol who were caught in the Taliban ambush yesterday had been posted back to the UK. Almost as though they didn't want them talking to anyone. Maybe, specifically, they didn't want Toni talking to them.

She mustn't start doubting her superiors. Living for a couple of months with Toni had her second-guessing things, and that wasn't how the military worked. "If any of you hear something that makes you doubt the official line, please let me know, and I'll follow it up. But I say again, there is nothing so far that makes me think this was friendly fire."

Toni was almost shaking, her hands were clenched, and her jaw was stiff. Her face was slowly going red. *She's about to blow.*

"So where are all these ideas about friendly fire coming from? If what they're saying is wrong, then what actually happened? And who keeps telling the story about friendly fire? Why haven't you got more information to tell us? We all need to know what's going on. Is there a cover-up?"

Jo's stomach did a somersault, and nausea threatened to rise. How dare Toni question her publicly and accuse her of inaction and dishonesty? Jo glared at her and then turned away. "I don't have more information because there isn't any. I've asked both at the HQ and at Foxtrot company offices, but there's nothing to suggest the rumor is true. If I hear anything different, I'll damn sure let you know. But unless we get something concrete, I ask that you all stop spreading rumors. Dismissed."

Jo left the briefing quickly and made her way to the officers' mess to get a large cup of coffee and to find somewhere quiet and out of the way to drink it. She needed to be alone to think. Toni was going to do what she needed to, even at the expense of their relationship. Damn it to hell. They didn't have a relationship.

They'd used each other for some company and a night of physical release. No matter how much she liked her, no matter what they'd established, they were who they were. And she wasn't about to let Toni destroy everything Jo had spent years building.

CHAPTER THIRTEEN

TONI WAS CERTAIN SOMETHING was being hidden, and she was going to get to the bottom of it. This was the sort of thing she was good at and why she'd become a reporter. She loved getting into someone's world and exploring the things that were wrong with it. There was something unscrupulous going on, and she would expose it and hold someone to account.

Although Jo insisted that there was no more information to give, Toni had a feeling she was holding back. When she got back to their tent, Jo wasn't there, nor had she been in the officers' mess when Toni went looking for her. Maybe she'd gone to the HQ offices. She'd have to wait until Jo returned.

Toni left to find Flash and the guys for a bit of company and fun. To her surprise, they didn't welcome her the way they had before. When she asked what was going on, they looked to Flash.

He ran his hand over his close-cropped hair. "You shouldn't have taken on the captain that way in front of everyone. She's one of us, you know. You were there that day. You know she did everything by the book, but you're treating her like she's the enemy." He looked at the others, who nodded their agreement. "We're all about respect, and we trust the captain one hundred percent. If she says there's no basis to it, then we believe her."

Toni bit her lip, not wanting to make a scene, but also feeling the fight rise in her. "Just because someone says they don't know anything doesn't mean it's true."

"Doesn't mean it isn't either. But maybe a reporter has to think bad about everyone, eh?" Wiffy said as he rolled a volleyball between his hands.

Toni backed away, shocked at how they'd rallied around Jo to the point they weren't even willing to consider the possibility of there being bigger things at stake.

"We're not saying you shouldn't ask questions," Flash said. "We're just saying you should ask the right people and not accuse the wrong ones."

Toni shook her head, then turned and fled back to the dining hall. She sipped a Coke and tried to stop her trembling. How unprofessional of her, to get emotional when someone didn't like what she was doing. She bet her mother never let her feelings get in the way. The thought made her blanch. Damn it. She wouldn't back down.

It was much later when she got back to the tent. Jo didn't greet her, and the tension was immediate. "Have you heard any more about the suggestion that the casualties were as a result of friendly fire?" Toni asked.

Jo looked up at her from her bed where she was doing paperwork. It was as if she could see right through her. She stared at Toni, saying nothing. Finally, she put her things down. Her face was white, and her lips thinned.

Okay, so maybe she hadn't gone about this the right way.

"I thought we were beginning to have something between us, some measure of care, security, and trust," Jo said.

"We have all those things," she said.

"No. We have our nighttime conversations that build trust, but then you ask me questions that imply I'm withholding information about something serious, something that has enormous implications," Jo said. "I've told you what I know. I've asked you not to print things until we're certain that families have been told. What else do you need me to say?" Her voice grew louder. "I get that you're a reporter, but what *you* don't get is that if we don't do this right, all the people you've talked to will have no jobs when you've finished. They'll also leave the military under a cloud and may be unable to find a decent job. You'll take away not only their livelihoods and careers, you'll also take away their futures. You'll get your name in lights though, and that's what's important, isn't it? Just like your mother. It's all about the story. The devastation to people's lives isn't your problem."

"I'm nothing like my mother, and I do care about people." Toni gritted her teeth. She wasn't going to let Jo's barbs find their target.

"Well, I'm not so sure. You questioned me in front of my platoon and embarrassed me. You accused me of lying, and then you come in here, our safe haven, without any apology or even polite conversation and start on me again," Jo said.

"I'm sure there's some sort of cover-up. Maybe you know about it, maybe you don't. I can't tell because you hide behind all these rules and regulations, about the way things are done, all the time furthering your career and being one of the boys," Toni said. "I get that your career is important to you, but sometimes you need to look beyond that and see what's happening."

"You've heard a vague rumor, and you tell me I can't see what's really happening? There's *nothing* happening, Toni. And incidentally, the military *is* all about rules and regulations. Do you really not know that yet?"

"Rumors start somewhere, and there's no sign of them stopping, which means that conversation is still happening somewhere. Someone knows something. I'll find them, and I'll find out the facts, and I'll report whatever it is I find," Toni said. "Your rules and regulations won't keep the truth at bay."

"You're not listening. You're not hearing what I'm asking. You really are your mother's daughter." Jo rubbed at her temples like Toni was giving her a headache.

Toni straightened, determined not to let Jo see how much that stung. "And I hope you're happy in your military career, blindly accepting everything you're told and doing it all alone for as long as it takes to get that promotion you're eager for, no matter the cost."

Jo stood. "I'm going to clear my head and maybe while I'm

gone, you'd like to rethink your position here on base. Perhaps it's time for you to leave. You have more than enough material to write things that won't blow up people's lives."

Jo marched out of the tent, and Toni was left open-mouthed. She'd never been under any illusion that Jo was happy about having her there, but then she'd said some nice things about Toni's work. Could she make Toni leave? If that was the case, she needed to talk to people fast. Her hurt and anger at Jo's declaration would have to wait. She had a job to do. The fact that that's exactly what her mother would say made her feel ill.

Maybe what she'd done to Jo wasn't right, but she wondered if the top brass knew something and were hiding it. Even from Jo. But would Jo tell her if she knew? Jo was so committed to the rules, and she wanted to be promoted, which gave her two good reasons to keep the status quo and not rock the boat.

Toni didn't want to consider that, so she decided to carry on with her investigation and set out to the company lines to interview the guys. The interviews didn't tell her much she didn't already know; she'd been there, after all. But when she put the pieces together, she created a timeline of what happened and who saw or heard what. She made an overlay with the information she'd gleaned from the photo and video evidence she had. It took longer than she expected and didn't give her any clear-cut information, but she did find she had a very good idea of the position of the various troops and the order that events happened. No one was conscious of any missiles being fired by the Taliban, but that didn't mean they were or weren't. Maybe what she knew would be useful later and help with whatever articles and reports she wrote. She knew that this story was going to be big, and it was important to get all her ducks in a row. Reporting was about the truth, and she wasn't about to let that get buried under layers of political maneuvering. Her hands trembled as she set the video camera down. What would the truth cost her though?

CHAPTER FOURTEEN

Jo stood in the colonel's office at attention, waiting for him to acknowledge her. He sat behind his big wooden desk paying no attention to her and reading from a file in front of him, as usual. He was treating her like a junior officer or soldier and not someone of her rank. A summons to the colonel's office had never been good for her whilst she was here, and it looked like nothing had changed.

Eventually he looked up. "Sit," he said, leaning back in his chair. "I've got some concerns about the friendly fire rumors. We need to keep a lid on them. There'll be an investigation in due course, and I want to ensure that the official line is known in order to give the investigation a clean run. Have you any problems or comments at this stage?"

"Yes, sir. What do you mean by keeping a lid on the situation if there's not been an investigation yet?" There was something not quite right with having an official line, and something about him was off too. He seemed...shifty somehow.

"Warn your lads that talking to the press is an offence, and the same goes for you. I want you to keep the press well away from the situation. Shut down Miss James, certainly before she gets to writing anything. And that's an order. I don't want anything out there that makes us look bad," he said.

"So you believe it was an enemy attack then, sir?" Jo asked.

He looked at her for a moment and then gave a sharp nod. "Yes. The facts as I've pieced them together are that the attack was from rockets launched by a group from behind the main Taliban force. They were firing at the tornado air support, and some rockets hit our positions. We didn't see the hidden rocket group, and they had us fooled with the heavy attack nearer in. In the confusion of everyone being pinned in place, we missed something major, and some soldiers were hit." He stood and leaned against his desk. "I don't want the press to learn we missed something as important as a hidden rocket launcher until it had harmed our troops. Makes us look weak and gives the insurgents ideas if they come across information like that," he said.

Something was wrong. Jo was a woman, someone he didn't want anywhere near his platoon, yet now he was acting like she was a colleague. His tone was conversational, and the information he'd provided hadn't been in any debrief she'd seen. Bile hit the back of her throat as her belief in the validity of the rumors rose. She swallowed it down.

"What do you think Miss James will do?" he asked.

"I think Miss James has already heard a lot of the rumors and is looking for something concrete." Jo had never been as conflicted about following orders and divulging information as she was now.

"You must encourage Miss James to accept what we're saying so that the stories about friendly fire stop, and she doesn't spread them further," he said. "If we send her away just when she's snooping around, it will look like we're hiding something, so that isn't an option. Provide enough information to get her off our backs, and that's it. You're clear about your orders?"

"Yes, sir. Very clear." She stood to attention, saluted, and left the office. Once outside, she walked until she was out near the landing zone and ducked down behind one of the hesco walls in a shady spot she used when she needed alone time. This wasn't going to end well. The order to shut down Toni's inquiry stank like a sewage pit. But she'd been given an order, and both that and talking to the press were court-martial offences. It didn't matter what she believed personally. And undoubtedly, the colonel would make sure she was prosecuted for something if anything at all went public. Even if she was found not guilty, the rumor would stick, and her promotion prospects would be over. She was the woman who'd been a thorn in his side commissioned in his ancient infantry regiment. She'd worked so fucking hard to make it this far, and now her future was in the hands of a reporter who wanted the truth at any cost. But it was Jo, and many others, who would pay the price.

***

Jo gathered the troop and asked Toni to come along, not bothering to ask why she looked so put out. "The colonel spoke to me earlier. He's heard the rumors about friendly fire and considers them background chatter and nonsense. It's totally unprofessional of us all to entertain it. There are no facts to support it. The official line seems to support that rockets were fired from a second group of Taliban held back to provide backup should more troops move in. They were shooting at the air support and hit our positions." Jo looked around at her men and felt sick. She wasn't sure the information was true and giving her men false intel felt wrong on every level. "The Taliban are moving out, and the large number holed up in Deh Lekay have probably been building up over time to give us a farewell gift of maximum casualties. But that was pre-empted when Foxtrot company found them. We've been congratulated on our handling of ourselves and the help we gave to them." Jo hadn't received any word on their performance, but she believed that the troops needed to hear the words the colonel wouldn't bother with.

"The colonel has also asked me to remind you all that talking to the press about operations is a court-martial offence, in case you should be tempted." Jo glanced at Toni. "Obviously, we've been talking to Toni freely about our lives and work, and that doesn't need to change. But with regard to specific operations and potentially useful information to the enemy, you need to refrain." There was no question the men looked uncomfortable, and Toni was stonily silent. "We'll be back on normal ops the day after tomorrow 0500, so get yourselves and your kit prepared. We're going back to Garmplis so that we can follow up on the women who had the chicks we took out. I want to see if they've been allowed to keep them or whether the men have killed them." Jo looked around the group. "Any questions? No? Dismissed."

The troops left, and she and Toni walked toward their accommodation together. Their easy and fun relationship was clearly a thing of the past, and her dreams of a future between them were so much dust in the wind.

"I don't believe the colonel," Toni said.

"Can we have this chat when we get somewhere more private?" It wasn't a question.

"Sure. But I still don't believe him," Toni said. "Can't you professionals tell the difference between Taliban rockets and bombs dropped out of a plane?"

"I'm not answering until we're back in our tent," Jo said.

They continued walking in silence. It sounded like Toni was holding her breath, trying not to speak. When they got to their tent and opened the flap, Toni released her barrage of words, almost tripping over each one.

"I *said* I still don't believe him," Toni said. "It must be possible for you to tell the difference between Taliban rockets and bombs dropped out of a plane. Even if you're a soldier on the ground, surely, you'd know the difference?"

Jo sat down, trying to make the conversation a little less high octane. "Of course. But when everything explodes around you and you're hit, you don't have any idea where it came from. But the truth is...I don't know." Jo was in dangerous territory, but she had to be honest. Toni was right; the colonel *was* lying. She was an Army professional, and she should know. She closed her eyes briefly, replaying the scene yet again. "There was a plane dropping bombs, and I didn't notice a rocket in all the commotion. I was firing to help the troops some distance away that were being overwhelmed, and I was looking after my own troops and you. The colonel told me the results of his investigation. He believes the friendly fire rumor is exactly that—a rumor. And as I said at the briefing, he wants us to stop being so unprofessional." She looked at Toni, silently pleading with her to let it go. "That's what I know, Toni. All of it." She couldn't bring herself to admit that she thought the bastard was lying too. She simply couldn't provide that kind of ammunition to someone who would throw it out into the world without having to deal with the repercussions.

Some of the fire went out of Toni as she put her arms around herself and sat down. "I don't think the rumors will stop because I think something happened. If something did go down, I need to know what happened," Toni said. "If you were ordered to do something that meant you'd have to compromise your personal beliefs, could you do it?"

Jo gave Toni her ideas as they came to her. She didn't pre-think her argument. "If I receive orders, it's my duty as a soldier to accept them and understand that I may not know all the facts surrounding those orders. It could be that the orders are made to protect people or countries. I'm low down the pecking order, so when an order comes along, I routinely only know a limited amount. That's the way the military works." She was being totally honest, which was easy given the nature of the conversation. This bit, anyway. "Think about the privates. They get an order from an even less knowledgeable viewpoint, often from their corporal, who gets the word from the sergeant. The sergeant may well get the word from someone like me, or if they're lucky, they may have direct access to someone higher up the chain of command. But often, there are even more layers. We all accept what we're told and follow the orders given. Otherwise, there would be anarchy. Do you understand?" The order from the colonel was an impossibility. Toni was fierce and dedicated, no less so than Jo herself. But that didn't mean she couldn't try. "Please, will you tell me if you decide you need to print something? I have to ensure that all the families already know their family members have been injured." She looked into Toni's eyes, ignoring for a moment how beautiful and expressive they were, and focusing on getting through to her. She considered how to continue, grateful that Toni seemed to be in a mood to listen. "When it comes to friendly fire, I think of how I'd feel if my child had been killed in action. It's always been contentious heading off to war in a fanfare of trumpets and glory to 'defend your wife and children, your family from the nasty invaders, and those people who want to inflict their religion or politics on you.' But then you come home to your family as a body in a coffin. It's devastating. Killed in action, and there's no glory to that. But there is a sense that the loss of life stood for something, be it protecting loved ones or country."

Toni nodded. "I get that."

"But with friendly fire, the sense of loss becomes more difficult to comprehend. They were killed by their *own* side. What went wrong? Who's to blame? People start to talk behind their hands, and there's almost embarrassment for the family already grieving their loss. Families struggle to cope when their loved ones were killed by *mistake*, when they weren't saving anybody."

Toni seemed to ponder that, and Jo let her think. There wasn't much more she could say that hadn't already been said. As conflicted as she was, she couldn't let Toni loose with information that could hurt people. She'd deal with her own doubts and worry about the truth on her own time.

Finally, Toni sighed. "If I decide to print something about friendly fire, I'll consider telling you first, but I can't promise. If I find out that it's true, that you've been lied to, along with the families and everyone else, then I have to say something. I'm sorry."

Frustration and sadness filled her, and it had nowhere to go. The only person she'd reached out to lately had been Toni, but the vibrant and strong woman she'd grown attached to had been replaced by a cold Amazon who was out to fight a battle against the odds. She couldn't stay here, so she left without another word.

She went to the officers' mess and sat at a table in the back. She held a mug tightly and stared into space, thinking about how things between her and Toni had developed into something good but were now so difficult. Inner turmoil and the deeper, uglier feeling of being so alone in the world made her neck ache with tension. She was only vaguely aware of time passing as she sat lost in her thoughts. Toni's question plagued her. What would you do if you were ordered to do something you didn't agree with? What would she do? She knew that Toni printing anything without facts was improbable. But she didn't understand... In the military, you followed orders. If you didn't, there were dire and direct consequences. Jo had always trusted in the people above her to play fair and do the right thing. Now though...

Toni pulled out a chair and sat next to her. "I know things are stupidly complicated. There's a lot I didn't think about. I'm not my mother, Jo. I don't want to hurt people for a story. But I do believe in the truth. I don't want to lose you. Lose us, whatever it is we are. Is there middle ground?" Toni wiped at the tears running down her cheeks.

Jo didn't dare move. There was a part of her that wondered if Toni was saying this to get information.

Toni took a deep breath. "I always feel safe with you, and you protect me. I trust you, and you're honorable and fair. I think about you, of being in the safety of your arms." Toni gulped. "So what am I supposed to do? Do I ignore a story, an issue that may be serious, in order to have something with you? Or do I follow the story and potentially lose someone who could, at the very least, be an amazing friend?"

Jo put down her mug and looked at Toni. "I feel as if I've been used. We got to know each other. I shared things I haven't shared with anyone. But you accused me of lying. I don't know what I can and can't say to you now."

Tears streamed down Toni's cheeks. "We seem to be getting further apart, and I'm not sure how we bridge the gap between us. I still don't understand how you don't question what you're told. It's how I live my life. I question everything."

They would probably never be able to get closer with the fundamentals of their lives and the way they lived them. They had too many opposing ideals. "I do question things, but I live a very different life to you. I live with rules that make life easy when, with no notice, everyone around me could be in danger. I need the confidence of knowing that we're all working to the same ideal. Asking 'who said that and why' doesn't work. It isn't necessary and to do so only messes up the order of things. You still don't understand the military way of life, even after being with us all this time." She wanted to put her arms around Toni and soothe away her tears. They did have something between them, their sex had been beautiful, but that wasn't going to make this work.

Toni rubbed her eyes. "I accept I don't understand every facet of your life in the Army, but I've been trying to. Please, Jo. There must be a way."

Jo rubbed her face with her hand. "How do I know I can trust you? And even if I do, I'm not sure I can live the life we might have together. I'd be posted anywhere the Army decides, and you'd go off around the world chasing some story or another. I'd still be going home at night alone, which is no different to what I do now. Having you as an absent partner would be too difficult. I mean, why not just stay single? I'd give up my promotion chances *and* have a life that is mostly unchanged except for being a little more lonely because I have a partner I never get to see. I can't be like your father. I just can't. The loneliness and a mundane daily existence just isn't me. At least the life I've been living is under my control. What you're asking for, Toni, it isn't fair." And there it was. Their connection was undeniable, but it came with difficulties that were impossible to overcome. She'd let Toni into her world, into her heart and mind, and she'd never be the same again. But when it came to having to give up everything when there was no promise of a forever, she simply couldn't bring herself to do it. She just had to learn to live with the ache of losing a woman who could have been her everything.

CHAPTER FIFTEEN

JO WASN'T KEEPING THE truth from her. She was telling Toni *her* truth. It may have been the official line, but Toni was sure Jo didn't know the full story. She decided to trace the source of the rumors and talk to the rest of the troops that had been at the firefight and see what came out of it. Maybe nothing, but she still couldn't leave it. Her journalistic nose wouldn't let her.

And if it came out that the truth had been hidden and she hadn't investigated fully, she'd be a professional laughing stock. She'd be back to writing about births, deaths, and marriages before she knew it. Toni had no choice but to follow her instinct and let the dice fall where they may.

Following orders without question wasn't only a military thing; Toni had seen it in the hospital investigation she'd done. Orders were given from on high and weren't questioned. That's what had given the hospital its problems. If more people had simply questioned the orders, if someone had lifted the lid and exposed the bad leadership, things would've been different. Maybe children wouldn't have died. If this case was friendly fire, then it needed someone to question the orders so that the soldiers could learn by what went wrong. They could then recognize how it had happened and how they could prevent it from happening again. She went over and over her reasons and touched them up against Jo's, but neither grouping ever fell. Both were valid.

But Toni wasn't military. She didn't have to follow orders that kept things in the dark.

She went to the company lines and found Flash. "Is it possible to get into the hospital and talk to the wounded soldiers? I've tried, but the guards outside their rooms wouldn't let me in. They said the wounded were resting and weren't to be disturbed." She let her expression tell him what she thought of that.

He looked around, frowning. "They've made an opening around the back of the tent, and they're chatting to their mates." He ducked his head and looked at the ground. "They're the ones with the information you need. I think the rumor is coming from them. They've only been allowed to talk to their families officially, but the stuff about friendly fire is coming from that direction," Flash said quietly.

"How do I get to the back of the sickbay to talk to them without anyone knowing?" Toni planned her possible movements. "If I went for a late evening run tonight, could one of your friends in Foxtrot company tell the guys I'll be coming?"

"Leave it with me," Flash said. "But, Toni, don't ask anyone other than me to help you. We were told not to talk to you about this stuff, and if we're caught, it's our asses on the line. I'll take the risk in case there's truth to it but don't involve anyone else." He raised his eyebrow until she nodded, and then he loped off across base.

She shoved her hands in her pockets and thought about what she was doing. Jo would be furious if she knew she'd dragged Flash into this, putting his career, and potentially his freedom, at risk. But he'd offered, and she wouldn't turn down the help. What did that say about her? Nothing good probably.

Toni waited until Jo left for a late briefing before she changed into her running clothes and picked up her bag of equipment. What she had with Jo felt special. Different. They were from different worlds and yet, Toni wanted to make Jo happy. She wanted time with her. She wanted more than the limited reality they existed in. To make sure nothing happened to mess things up, she would have to stop now. But she couldn't. It wasn't the way her DNA worked. She'd find out what the injured soldiers knew and then hope she could salvage something with Jo.

Toni slipped out of the tent and set off running. She put her kit at her water stash and set off on her usual route. She did one circuit, picked up her bag and diverted on her next lap to the back of the sickbay. Flash had given her instructions to find the correct wing and rooms, and it took her a while to get there. She could hear quiet voices inside. The bottom of the tent moved, and a head stuck out, smiling.

"Helloooo. Jack, there's a woman out here come to give us a treat. They won't let us talk to people, but we've got a good operation going here. We've managed pizza, friends, and now a lady. Things are looking up." He held up the flap and let her duck into the tent.

She sat on the floor beside an empty pizza box between their beds. "I'm Toni. I wanted to chat about what happened at the firefight. Did your friends tell you about me?" If they chose not to talk, she had no idea where to go next.

"They did. I'm Dusty, by the way. We know we're not supposed to talk to the press and could get in serious trouble, but we're being held here and don't know why. It's all a bit fishy." He motioned toward the door of the tent. Fortunately the sickbay was large, and they could speak quietly without the guards outside overhearing them.

"I'll record what you say and will let you know if I'm going to use it. Although if I find out anything that gives substance to what you find *fishy*, I may use what you tell me to make a case. I'll keep you out of it as best I can."

Dusty nodded, his deep blue eyes serious. "That's fair. Though what me and Jack have to say would mean that the brass would know where it came from anyway. We know the risk, and we've talked it over. Flash reckoned you're a good 'un. Do what you need to. We'll handle our end if it comes to it."

They could end up in prison or Army detention for a long spell if they said something out of line. But they were prepared to risk it. Was it fair to ask them to put themselves on the line this way? Plenty of people in the world talked to the press in order to right a wrong, and this was no different. They'd made their choice, so she would make hers. She was holding these soldiers' futures in her hands, and she would be mindful of the honor they had given her.

"Okay. Dusty, can I start with you?" Toni switched on her recorder. "Interview commenced 22 April at 2100 at the sickbay, FOB Sherwood. Interview by Toni James. Tell me who you are."

"I'm Corporal Anthony Miller. My mates call me Dusty. I'm in Foxtrot company, 2 Fizers."

"Were you involved in the firefight at Deh Lekay on 20 April?"

"Yep, I was there."

"Can you tell me what happened? From when you went out on patrol?"

"It was a routine patrol. We've been heading out from Sherwood into this valley along a number of different routes. The valley is wide there, so we vary our routes and the time of day we go out. It has been dead quiet since we've been in Helmand, and we were told that they thought the Taliban had moved out," Dusty said.

"Was there anything unusual about the day?" Toni asked.

"No. We headed along the route we'd been briefed to follow, and we could see the church in the distance. That's a disused compound of buildings marked on the maps, and it got its name because it's noticeable from a lot of points in the valley."

"Was that where you were headed that day?"

"No, we were headed across the valley from it. But we've been there a couple of times as part of our ops, and it's been empty," Dusty said. "This time, as we came along the wadi, we had to cross a track to move along the other side, and it was then we came under fire."

"Go on," Toni said. She would have liked to video this, but the light wasn't right, and she couldn't risk a studio light being seen by the guards.

"We all went down on our belt buckles, as usual. I called over to Jack, the sarge, and Alex to make sure they were okay. The lieutenant came over the radio to say he and the rest of the guys were a ways behind us, and they were also pinned down. The fire was coming from the building. It was heavy. This is my second tour out here, and the firing I'd seen before had been much more sporadic. There was little we could do against this kind of fire. We slid as best as we could into cover, such as there was. There were some bits of longer grass, and although it wasn't anything that would allow us to hide, it did mean we had something. It was better than being out in the open."

"Did you manage to fire back?" Toni asked.

"Once we got some decent cover, but it took a few minutes to get into position. The rest of the patrol managed to reply for us until we got going. It was impossible to move." He shook out his hands as though releasing the tension from them. "It was only a matter of time before we were killed or injured."

"So did the weapons fire cause all your injuries and kill Alex?" Toni asked gently.

He shook his head and looked at Jack, who looked equally serious. "No, we survived all that. We could hear chatter on the radio, and the lieutenant called for backup and air support almost straight away. We got backup help from the FEZ that you were with. It's always good when you know you're in a bad situation that someone's coming to help."

"So, what happened next?" Toni's adrenaline coursed through her veins; she was about to get her answers. She had to make sure she didn't push too hard in her excitement.

"We carried on firing, and I was using ammo fast and started wondering if I'd have enough. The firefight went on for quite some time. Don't ask how long, as I've no idea. When you're in the heat of battle, ten minutes can be two minutes or an hour," he said.

"I get that. I lost all sense of time that day," Toni said.

"We heard that air support was close, and we had to stop firing. I heard the plane in the distance, and I breathed a sigh of relief. I hoped they'd be able to hit the building, and we'd be able to move into cover. The plane got louder and louder, and they were firing at it from the ground, and I..." Dusty looked into the distance as if watching a movie. His face was a mask of quiet, and it transformed into rage as he watched their firefight's last moments. "I remembered thinking it sounded *too* close. Then I felt a burning sensation in my arm, and shit exploded all around us. Jack shouted that the sarge and Alex had been hit." Dusty looked at Jack, who gave him a supportive nod.

"Fire support came next, but I'm a little confused about that part. The firing from the building became sporadic and eventually stopped. I slid over to Jack and called for medevac. Jack had a head injury, and there was a lot of blood running down his face. He told me it wasn't serious. Alex wasn't moving, and his stomach area was a bloody mess. Sarge, who was across from him, wasn't moving, and I could see an injury to the side of his head. I could see bone." He took a long drink of water.

Jack passed a bottle to Toni, who gladly took a breather. Dusty's pain and confusion were almost tangible, and she could practically see the story he was telling.

"I called for the medics again before I went to the sarge and realized that his head injury was really bad. He was still breathing, but he was unconscious. I put a field dressing around his head to cover his wound. I had a kit for hypothermia and got out the reflective blanket and put it round him. I moved to Alex next. When I got close, I saw his body had been almost destroyed in the middle..."

Dusty couldn't speak, and Toni put out her hands to hold his. He cried, holding tight to Toni's hands. Jack came and put his arms around Dusty, crying as well. They all stayed like that for some time.

"I needed that. It's hard to let go, you know?" Jack wiped his eyes with his shirt sleeve.

"Me too." Dusty coughed and wiped his nose on the tissue that Toni handed him. He drew a deep breath. "Where was I? With Alex. I checked his pulse, but it was only just there. I always wondered what they meant when they said he had a thready pulse on the TV. Now I know. I screamed for the medevac over the radio. I knew he wasn't dead, but I didn't think he'd last long. Then I thought, you know medical guys are good these days, maybe they could save him."

Tears were running down Dusty's contorted face again, and his mouth was open as he breathed heavily, the only sound in the room apart from his voice. "I tried to put a field dressing on, but there was so much blood and so many wounds to cover. Someone came and moved me out of the way. Said they'd fix him."

"What happened next?" Toni asked softly when he drifted off again.

"I think I was in some kind of shock. Things get really muddled from there. There was a commotion, and then there were medics and helicopters, and I was in the air, and then here. Safe and alive. I'm one of the lucky ones. Flesh wound. I don't know if they can put the sarge's head back together, and Alex is now fighting his battles up there." Dusty pointed upward.

"Is that what you think happens?" It was strange to ask a question about spirituality right now, but Toni couldn't help but wonder how anyone kept faith in these surroundings.

"It's as good an idea as any. There may be someone up there looking out for us. I'm not convinced, but you need something solid when your whole world disintegrates around you. Being shut in here hasn't helped. We've had too much time to think, and there are only so many films you can watch. When we finish a movie, we come back down to earth with a bang. For a few hours, we didn't have to think about what happened."

"You should be able to get some help soon. You can talk it through with someone who understands and can help you," Toni said.

"They haven't offered yet, but to be honest, talking to you has helped. I'll be okay. I expect I'll be one of those who disappears into a bottle when it feels as if the pictures are coming back." He grinned as though to make light of it, but there was truth in his eyes.

"I need to ask—do you think you were hit by friendly fire?"

He and Jack looked at one another for a long moment. Finally, Dusty wrapped his arms around his legs and nodded. "Yeah. We weren't hit by stray bombs or enemy fire. Something went wrong, and the plane dropped on us instead of the church. We're sure of it."

"And have you told your superiors this in your report? Have the others who were also pinned down reported this fact?"

Dusty and Jack seemed to communicate silently again. "We can't speak for anyone else. But we put it in our reports." He frowned, his gaze searching hers. "That's why we're being held here, isn't it? They aren't happy about us saying it wasn't enemy fire."

Toni wasn't sure what to say, so she simply looked at him and said nothing. It was answer enough. His jaw tightened, and he shook his head.

"Thank you, Dusty, Corporal Miller. Interview concluded, 2125."

Toni interviewed Jack, who gave a similar account. They both believed that they were hit by friendly fire. This was the information Toni had been after. She thanked them and promised to keep their names out of it entirely if she could, but as they'd said, given the facts, it would be clear to anyone in the Army who she'd been speaking to.

They closed their makeshift opening behind her, and Toni picked up her bag and headed out. She jogged to her running route and stashed her bag before she did another lap. It was an ideal time to think through what she'd been told. It *was* friendly fire, and it *was* being covered up. What the hell was she going to do now? Exposing the soldiers who'd spoken to a reporter, specifically against orders, would put them at risk. Telling the world that a mistake like this one had been made would make the military look bad and maybe make people rethink joining in the first place. It would diminish trust among units who had to trust one another with their lives.

But the truth mattered. It meant things could be fixed. Letting things like this go under the radar meant people weren't held accountable for the death and injury of others. How was that acceptable?

And then there was Jo. They knew what sides they were on, but damn it, Toni didn't want them to be on separate sides at all. She wanted Jo to understand and agree with her. She wanted her to root Toni on, to tell her she was right to pursue the truth. But that wasn't going to happen. When this came out, there could be nothing between them ever again.

She headed back to the tent with a heavy heart. She had no idea it was going to be this hard to do a job she loved. What more would she have to give up?

CHAPTER SIXTEEN

Jo went to sort out the next morning's op and was told that HQ wanted another day with no one going into the villages. Taliban could still be in the area, and they could either set up another trap or harm the villagers.

"I'm not saying it's your fault, but it's because of what you're doing that the Taliban have decided to make a stand," the colonel said. "You've created a popularity contest between what you're offering and the old ways of the Taliban. They can't have you winning, so they're making us pay. That firefight occurred yesterday because you're pitting the villages against the Taliban. If it weren't for you and your outreach program, this wouldn't have happened."

One or two of the officers at the briefing looked at the colonel with surprise. Blaming someone for doing their job wasn't something done publicly in the Army and certainly not in such a manner.

"You went to help Foxtrot company because you felt guilty about what you're doing. Correct?"

Jo was aghast. *This isn't my fault.* "No, sir. The policy for helping the Afghan people and providing a viable alternative to the feudal way of the Taliban was a joint government decision. I don't feel guilty for doing my job, nor was helping Foxtrot anything to do with the mission to help the villagers. We assisted Foxtrot according to protocol." She wouldn't be the colonel's scapegoat, allowing the Fizers to get rid of her so he wouldn't have to command a female officer who weakened the regiment bloodline.

By going up against him and arguing her point, she would alienate him even more, but she couldn't just ignore the accusation that she'd acted out of emotion. She could only hope that the other officers in the meeting would ensure that she didn't get the complete blame.

"Dismissed." He waved her off without so much as a glance.

Jo left the briefing in turmoil. How was she going to deal with blame from a superior? She was still thinking about it as she reached her tent. She sat in the dark, trying to figure out what to do next.

Toni threw open the tent door, her eyes alight. "It's a cover-up; I have evidence." She was wearing her running kit and had a bag of her electronics with her but didn't look as if she'd run anywhere.

"Really?" Jo didn't want this on top of the rest of the mess. And yet... she'd never been one to back down from the truth. "What evidence do you have?"

"I interviewed the two soldiers in the sickbay. Did you know they're being guarded by the MPs and haven't been allowed visitors? They need time to recover apparently." Toni's eye roll expressed what she thought of that.

"How did you get to them?" Jo asked.

"They let me in through a gap they'd made to get pizza and to chat to their mates. *This* is why the friendly fire rumor never stopped. They know what happened."

"Can I listen to the interviews?"

Toni bit her lip and stared at Jo for a second. "I need to think about it. You're a part of the system denying there's a problem."

"I get that, and I understand. I don't want to be part of a system that's broken though," Jo said. "I need to work out how to fix this." Not just for the sake of the truth but quite possibly for the sake of her career.

"You also can't say anything about the interviews to anyone in charge because it will identify those two soldiers, and they'll get put in prison for speaking to the press about what happened. They spoke to me because Flash vouched for me as a friend." Toni crossed her arms. "Until you can tell me that you won't find a way to kill the story, I can't let you listen to the interviews."

Jo nodded, although she was fully aware she could demand the interviews based on the fact that they were, technically, military property at this point. But she'd hang onto that card and play it only if she absolutely had to. "Okay."

Toni sat on her bunk. "I hate being on opposite sides," she murmured, her gaze on her boots, and her hands clasped tightly in her lap. "I wish there was a way around it."

Jo didn't respond. What could she say? She lay back on her bed and closed her eyes. So many questions, so few answers.

The next morning, Jo strode to the colonel's office at 0730.

"I have a full day, Fitzgerald. I don't have time to talk to you now," the colonel said as he came down the corridor toward his office.

"I'd like a couple of minutes of your time. You'll want to hear what I have to say." Jo could be every bit as officious as the colonel.

"Going to give me some sob story about how the firefight wasn't your fault and how I've got it wrong, no doubt," the colonel said.

It wasn't a question of him being wrong. In fact, he might very well be right—the Taliban attacks were retaliatory as a result of her work. But her work was sanctioned, and she was doing her damn job. He couldn't gainsay that part but painting her as a villain would definitely tarnish her career. Arguing that right now wasn't the point though. She followed him into his office and shut the door.

Before he could sit, Jo moved directly in front of his desk. "I believe that the Fizer death and injuries may have been from friendly fire. I'd like my concerns to be on record and for the incident to be properly investigated."

The colonel looked at her quickly, his jaw clenched and his eyes narrowed. "You have your orders. What are they?"

She repeated what she'd been told before. "The deaths were due to a Taliban rocket launched from behind the main Taliban force, and no one is allowed to talk to the press."

"Those orders stand. What's the penalty for not obeying

orders?"

"It could be a court-martial," Jo said. "But if we aren't being told the truth—"

"A court-martial and the end of your career."

He approached Jo and stood close enough that she could see the spittle on his lips. His face reddened, and his eyes were fierce. He was close enough that Jo could smell the Old Spice aftershave he was wearing, mixed with sweat and frustration, and it was all she could do not to cover her nose.

"I don't want to hear the words 'friendly fire' coming out of your mouth again. You will obey your orders, or I will make sure you are dismissed from the battalion and the Army. Do you understand?"

Jo stared him down, her shoulders aching from the desire to smash something. "Yes, sir."

"Dismissed."

Jo turned and walked out of the office. Toni was right. Jo had seen it in the colonel's eyes. He wanted to bully her into silence, and he was doing the same by keeping the two injured soldiers from speaking to anyone. But what the hell was she going to do about it? She nodded at a couple of soldiers who said hello, but her mind was in full tactical mode. She needed to make a plan and go on the offensive instead of remaining in a passive position.

She went back to their tent and was pleased that Toni wasn't there. She didn't want to have a long conversation about why she didn't want her to accompany her. She needed to do this alone. No reporters determined to dig no matter the cost, and no superior officers determined to bury the truth.

She loaded up her day sack and headed out to get a ride to Camp Fortress. With all the daily traffic, she could pick up an ongoing flight to Kandahar. She landed only a short while later, having managed to get spaces on both flights. Throughout the journey, she went over the people she needed to talk to and the possible outcomes. None of them came out with her on top. So be it.

She went into the Air Controller's office. "Do you know where I'd be likely to find Flight Lieutenant Lilley today?"

The controller looked at his sheet. "He was due to fly today, but he's been scrubbed."

"Does that mean he'll be in his quarters?" Jo asked.

"Knowing him, I expect he'll be down in the lounge or the squadron offices. He and several of the pilots hang out there with the techs and engineers. You'll need to head to the back of the main workshop over there and keep going." He grinned. "We've got food in there, and it isn't your tent or the canteen, so it's popular."

"It's good to have a place like that. There ought to be more, but I suppose then it would be some kind of holiday camp and not a military operation."

"Yes, ma'am. There's no way we'd want us to be muddled up with a holiday camp."

Jo left, smiling. She remembered a TV program about the similarities of a British holiday village and the military. Accommodation blocks all looking the same, shared toilets and showers, and the dining facilities all shared too. But there was also the closeness of the people who were with each other twenty-four hours a day, seven days a week. How life was lived under the microscope of a multitude of eyes, each seeing what they expected or wanted to see and not what was happening. It had been funny at the time. Here in Helmand, it was a rich life experience but today she struggled to find humor in it.

She finished her musing as she crossed the maintenance bay that smelled of oil and grease. She passed a Tornado with the side off. A mechanic was deep in the workings and came up for air as Jo walked past. He smiled, his face smeared with oil across his forehead, took a sip from a water bottle, and disappeared back where he'd emerged. She was somehow reminded of a badger popping from its burrow to sniff the air, before deciding that the air wasn't quite right and turning back.

She reached the lounge at the back of the workshop and,

smelling cigarettes and cigar smoke, knew she was in the right place. She knocked on the door and opened it amid several cries of "Come in" and "Hope you have food."

She entered the darkened room. It had small openings close to the ceiling that let in light, and there was a desk at one end covered with magazines, coffee cups that had rarely seen washing-up liquid, and several overflowing ashtrays. Three men stood to attention in front of her.

A man in brown overalls saluted. He'd obviously washed his hands, but they still had a layer of grease in the cracks and fingernail beds. "Ma'am, are you a new pilot? We know our Annie down here, but she didn't say there was a new one. Are you looking for something? What do you need from us?" The man was obviously nervous, and his words came out in a barrage.

"As you were." She waited for him to relax. "Is Flight Lieutenant Lilley in here?" she asked.

He pointed to a man sitting in the corner who'd neither stood up nor acknowledged her presence. It was a breach in protocol but to be fair, he didn't seem aware of anything at all going on around him. "Sure, ma'am. We'll give you some space." He signaled to the other technicians to leave with him. "Perhaps I can give you some biscuits we have out here." He tilted his head for Jo to join him outside the snug. "Ma'am, have you come to help? He's been in a bit of a fug since the op, and he'll be fine eventually. But he's upset. The MO has been down, and they had a chat. When I asked Jeff about it, he said it was complicated." He waited, clearly hoping she'd shed some light on the issue.

"I'll talk to him and see what I can do that may help," Jo said. She had a feeling she knew what had left Jeff Lilley in a "fug." She didn't know him that well, but he'd spent time with her and Toni discussing the long distance walks he'd done around the world. The man sitting in the dirty easy chair looked nothing like the man they'd often talked to.

He was a dark-haired, bronzed, muscular man who wouldn't

have looked out of place on a special forces op. He had a lot of experience living out in the wild and was lively and sociable. But today, he slumped in a chair, and his always tidy hair was disheveled. His skin was pale with an almost yellow tinge to it. His eyes were red, and he was struggling to keep them open.

"Oh, dear. You look as if you're in a bad place," she said. She wasn't sure that was where she should start, but the words came out almost as if she were thinking aloud.

He looked at her then and rubbed his eyes. "I wanted to talk to you about what happened. Your colonel has given me orders not to speak to anyone. You were there though, right? I can talk to you?"

Her stomach turned at the despair in his eyes. "I was, although I didn't see what happened. The colonel has given me the same orders," Jo said. "Let's assume we can talk to each other, since we have the same orders." She leaned forward in her chair and looked at Jeff. "There's been all sorts of rumors going around the last forty-eight hours, so I wanted to get it from you. You're probably one of a small handful of people who knows what actually happened."

He almost seemed to grow smaller as his shoulders hunched forward. "Everything's fucked. Destroyed. I want things to go back to how they were last week. I was planning a trip along the Appalachian Trail and looking forward to some cool mountain air after months in this heat and sand," Jeff said. "But now..." He ran his hand through his hair and then dropped it limply back to his lap.

"What happened?" Jo asked.

His gaze grew distant. "It was a routine backup and support op. We used to get called to that valley a lot. Several times a week. We'd fly overhead and try to keep our troops safe, only using precision bombing as a last resort. We haven't been there much recently. The Taliban have headed back up the valley, so we don't need to be out."

"You got a call and set off?" Jo asked.

"Yes, we were up quickly. Annie and I pride ourselves on

getting up at speed when we're on standby. Annie's the pilot, the only woman in Afghanistan, and she's top notch. I'm sure it's not easy being the only woman, but I've enjoyed flying with her..."

She touched his arm. "Go on."

"I had the grid reference of where to drop my load. We were at the location in about ten minutes. I could see the derelict building, but my grid reference was still several meters away. I radioed HQ and questioned the grid reference, and it was confirmed. There was no red smoke visible to indicate our troops, or if there had been, I didn't see any. I dropped my load, and we returned here."

"Sounds straightforward to me. So where's the problem?" Jo asked the question though she already knew the answer. Someone had screwed up the drop-zone coordinates.

"The colonel told me I'd written down the wrong grid reference. No way, I told him. I couldn't have. I even queried it with HQ, because it didn't match what I was seeing. The building they said the insurgents were working from." His eyes welled with tears, and he brushed them away. "He told me it looked as if I'd killed and injured some of the Fizers. That I should speak to no one and he'd protect me." The look in his eyes was desperate as he turned to her. "Jo, I must have written it down wrong and queried the wrong grid reference or dropped the load on the wrong target. Something. I did *something* wrong. He said the visual of my drop clearly shows me hitting a target *in front* of the building." Jeff burst into tears, the pain of a deadly mistake shaking his body. "I want to die. I killed other soldiers. The corporal was doing his job, just like I was. His wife and kids are forever going to blame me for what I've done. I've left them without a husband and father. Oh, God..."

Jo's stomach heaved, and she struggled not to cry herself. *Friendly fire.* What an awful phrase for such a devastating thing. How would she cope if this or something similar happened to her? She forced herself to focus. Emotion would have to wait. "So, it's all down to the grid reference you were given by HQ ops. You wrote it down somewhere?"

"I wrote it on the plastic jot pad on my flying suit with a chinagraph pen. I showed the colonel so that he could see I was telling the truth. He said it was important evidence and took it away," Jeff said.

"So that was the only copy of the grid reference?" Her hope sank into her stomach with the weight of a bowling ball.

"The colonel asked me that last evening, and I said yes. At the time, I thought it was." Jeff sat up straighter. "Annie came to see me this morning, and I told her about the colonel's visit. She was angry. She said although I was navigating, she'd jotted it down on her flight suit too, just in case. She kept it safe. As soon as she heard the rumors of friendly fire, she wondered if we would have the investigators coming around to talk to us." He shrugged a little. "She's pretty messed up about it too."

"She's kept her note?" Jo's heart began to race.

He grimaced. "She told me I was nuts to hand over my only evidence to the colonel." His smile didn't reach his eyes. "I need some of Annie's balls."

"I know what the colonel can be like when he's after something. It wasn't like you had much choice." Jo recalled all her visits to the colonel which made her feel like a poor excuse for an officer. If she'd actually made a mistake like this one, what would she have done? "Jeff, you were given bad intel. You even double-checked that intel when you weren't sure. It's a terrible mistake, a tragedy, but he has no right to place all the blame on your shoulders."

"He was talking about my failure and my court-martial. To be honest, he frightened me, and there are only a few people I can say that about," Jeff said. "I wanted to come forward. I wanted to make an official report about what happened. But he said I wasn't to say anything to anyone. He told me the official story: that a rocket had been missed and that was what hit our guys." He shook his head, dashing at his wet cheeks again. "It isn't true, but I told myself I had to follow orders."

"But you were at a low point when he talked to you, so be fair to yourself. A senior officer throwing threats around when you're feeling vulnerable isn't good." How dare that bastard do that and devise a cover-up instead of helping someone under his command? Jo's decision was instantaneous. If she followed it, she would likely be removed from her post and could say goodbye to her career. But there was no way in hell she was going down without a fight. If the truth didn't matter, then what were they fighting for? "Toni would probably love to hear what happened. Would you tell her what you told me if she came over?"

"What about the colonel?" Jeff asked. "I mean, I'm already in the shit for being the cause of friendly fire injury, so it isn't like they can do much worse to me for disobeying orders and talking to a reporter. A court-martial and a prison sentence either way. But..." He shook his head, his shoulders falling. "I don't know what to do."

"I think the colonel will be too busy worrying about me not obeying orders to get to you." Jo held his hand. "This is your choice to make, and I'm not going to try to convince you. But if you let this ride, you'll live with it on your conscience, and the colonel will always have something to hold over you. Not only that, but it's a slippery slope. We allow assholes like him to scare us into submission, and it becomes a never-ending cycle. Who else does he bully and control?" Jo took a deep breath, knowing what she was saying applied as much to herself as it did to Jeff. "The truth matters. It has to."

He held on to Jo's arm. "Thank you for caring about me. I've felt so alone the last couple of days. I'm not saying you've made me feel better, but I know there's someone out there who understands," he said. "I can't ever fix my mistake, but at least I can take responsibility."

Although he'd taken the whole thing on his shoulders, she knew full well it wasn't entirely his fault. There were other people she needed to talk to. "I'll talk to Toni and get her to come over later today if she can."

Jeff jerked out of his seat and stood. He looked broken; there was no other word which would describe him. He saluted her although there was no official need to do so. Jo walked back into the workshop. She needed a copy of that grid reference from HQ, which meant she needed to talk to Annie. Should she head to HQ and talk to them next? At what point did she stop being a soldier and start being an investigator? But if the colonel had shut everyone down, then maybe it really was up to her to see it through.

No matter the cost.

The thought made her dizzy, and she fell against a shaded wall. Everything she'd worked for. Her whole future could go up in flames when she went against the colonel and opened this box of worms the Army top brass wanted to keep closed and buried. Was it worth it? She closed her eyes and moved back into the heat of the day, tilting her face toward the sun. She couldn't live with herself if she let this go. And she couldn't live with seeing the colonel every day and knowing what he'd done. If it cost her everything, at least she knew she'd done the right thing.

CHAPTER SEVENTEEN

JO WAS SITTING ON her bed when Toni came in. She looked upset, and her hands were shaking.

"Are you all right? Has something happened?" Toni's first concern was that they'd lost more soldiers.

"Yes, I'm fine." Jo gave a tired laugh. "No. Actually, I'm not."

Toni watched as a tear slowly rolled down her cheek like a single drop of rain on a windowpane. She sat beside her and took one of her hands into her own. It was ice-cold. "Can you share things with me?"

Jo sighed deeply. "I'm almost certain the incident *was* friendly fire and for some reason, the colonel is trying to hush things up."

Toni's heart raced. She'd already heard it firsthand, but hearing Jo admit to it made it real. "Why would he do that?"

"I don't know. Pride? Arrogance? You know we've been told to keep quiet. The navigator and pilot have been given the same orders. I saw Jeff today. He was the navigator."

"Jeff of the Camino de Santiago trail in France and Spain?" Toni asked, trying to follow. She wished she had her voice recorder on, but she couldn't break Jo's train of thought.

"Yes. He doesn't understand how he could have dropped bombs on our troops. He checked the grid reference with ops before he released his load because his references didn't line up," Jo said.

"Did he write it down anywhere?" Toni asked.

"Yes, but the colonel took it away as evidence. What the colonel doesn't know is that the pilot had a copy and has kept it safe." She swallowed hard, her hands still trembling. "I asked Jeff to talk to you."

"But won't his career be affected? A court-martial is a big deal and could ruin it." Toni didn't want to ask it, but it felt like the noble thing to do. What she really wanted to do was get on a plane and get to Jeff.

"Everyone who talks to you is going to be in big trouble. I'm sure the soldiers you've talked to have said the same thing. I think this is bigger than all of us though, and we all want to know the truth," Jo said.

Toni hesitated, making sure to hide her excitement about another element of the story breaking open properly for her. "This could be your career on the line too, couldn't it?" Her heart ached for Jo as she watched her struggle, the lines deep around her eyes, her skin pale.

"Yes. But the Army needs to be open about what we've done in a case like this. As you say, we should be learning from the mistakes we make so they don't get repeated... You'll create a hole in my hand if you keep rubbing that spot," Jo said with a small smile. "You've made me question so many things," Jo said softly. "I have a lot to think about, and I have plans to make." She finally looked into Toni's eyes. "I'm not sure how you and I will get through this, but I hope you'll be on the other side." Once again, she sighed and this time she let go of Toni's hands and leaned against the wall of the tent. "You have to talk to Jeff and see what you can find out," Jo said. "God forbid someone tells the colonel I've already been there, and he ships Jeff out or home."

Impulsively, Toni leaned down and gave Jo a kiss on the cheek. "What you're all doing is incredibly courageous. If you're brave enough to do this, I'll back you all the way."

Jo gave a tired nod.

Following Jo's directions, Toni went to Kandahar and to the snug at the back of the aircraft workshops. Toni had trouble recognizing the man before her as the same man she'd filmed and laughed and joked with.

Jeff stood when she went in, and Toni put her arms out. Jeff fell into her embrace like a man drowning and wept. Toni let him cry and said nothing.

Eventually, he lifted his head. "I'm okay. It's okay. When Jo said you'd be coming, I realized I needed you. As a friend, not a fellow soldier."

"Can I interview you?" Toni asked after she'd sat in an easy chair. "I know you're under orders not to speak, but I want to make a case, and I won't reveal your identity or anything that identifies you unless I have your specific permission. I'd like to do a short video about how you feel too."

"Go ahead. I trust you. Anyone who can get so excited talking to me about walking in Spain is worth trusting."

Toni smiled at the glimmer of the old Jeff coming through. He could claim his life back eventually, but she could see he'd have to work through the results of that op first. Jeff related the facts to Toni after she got the tech set up; they were the same as he'd told Jo.

"Tell me about grid references and why they're important," Toni said, wanting to make certain what he was saying was clear not only to her and to the military, but to her average reader.

"It's called the Military Grid Reference System, and we use it to ensure that we drop bombs on target. A correct grid reference, or GR, is vital. It gives you a point on the earth's surface that's correct to within about a meter. The smallest of errors, even by a single digit, can make a huge difference on the ground. It can be the difference between killing a target or children in a nearby school, for example." He swallowed hard and took a shaky breath. "Or in this case, your own men."

"And you were given this GR by headquarters," Toni said. How awful to make this kind of mistake because of someone *else's* mistake.

"I'm certain we fired to the GR we'd been given," Jeff said. "If it's feasible, the troops on the ground that are close to an enemy position will release a red smoke cannister so that any air attack can see where they are. It's the season of strong winds in the Afghan hills, and if there had been any smoke, it wasn't there when we arrived."

He went on to answer a few more of her questions and then came the final piece. He showed her Annie's note with the GR reference. She took a photo of it from several angles and had him tell her on camera what it was. When they were done, he tucked it in a locked box and put the key in his pocket.

Toni put her hand on his arm. "Thank you, Jeff. We'll get to the bottom of this." She hugged him hard when he stood. "I can't imagine what you're going through, but you don't have to do it alone." She held him at arm's length. "When this is done and you're free to talk, I hope you'll find someone to guide you through. And I'll be at the other end of the line if you need me."

Throughout the flight back, she made notes, checked the video recordings, and ran through the various permutations of the story in her head. Essential to all those thoughts was Jo. Sure, Toni would've gotten the story out based on the two soldiers' interviews, but it wouldn't have been as strong, and it would have been easy for the military to deny it. But now, with Jo on the side of truth, along with Jeff and Annie, the story had the kind of veracity a reporter could only dream of.

Once she got back to their accommodation, Toni sat with Jo and discussed the interview. "I want to do several articles about what's happened here and how no one knows what's going on. I won't name anyone or use anything soldiers have told me in confidence." She wasn't asking Jo's permission so much as letting her know what was about to happen.

Jo shrugged, her expression stony. "It's your story. It'll either change minds up the ladder, or we'll all get tarred with the same brush and lose our careers."

Toni couldn't help but worry about Jo and how this would all come down on her. The colonel seemed to have a brutal streak, particularly about the regiment and his *men*. He would undoubtedly do his best to ruin Jo.

"I think you should tell a general story as well about friendly fire, what it is and how often it happens," Jo said, her tone flat. "It won't matter, really, but it might mean Jeff and Annie aren't made scapegoats for something that isn't all that rare."

Toni listened halfheartedly. It was one thing to tell a story and bring up poor decisions, bad processes, or people who'd been badly treated or hurt, but this was different. This was bringing a process to the notice of the public so that more soldiers weren't killed in the future. But it was also going to ruin the lives of a number of people who were happy in the Army. Even worse, she'd be taking down a woman she had genuine feelings for. Feelings she wasn't sure she could figure out just yet.

Shit. Did she love her? Where had that come from? What if it wasn't really that? It might just be intense emotion based on forced proximity. She studied Jo, who'd lapsed into silence, lost in her own thoughts. She was beautiful, strong, capable, intelligent...and sexy, most definitely. She was also kind and honest, and because of all those qualities, she could lose it all. This was most definitely not the time for Toni to declare her devotion, and she could only hope that when the dust settled, Jo would still be interested in seeing if there was something between them.

"I'll put a note here to look into friendly fire statistics." Toni took a deep breath. She had to have the discussion with Jo. She couldn't plough on regardless. "This is going to ruin you and as much as I hate to say it, I could maybe find a way to back down. Find another way to tell the story somehow."

Jo shook her head hard. "No. I want to do this. You've made me look closely at my life, and I've found that the neat, ordered way I have of doing things in my mind, the way I look at rules and regulations, needs changing. I'm not saying that rules are meant to be broken, but because I'll always look at them carefully. But I think you've helped me to see that allowing myself and my men to be bullied isn't acceptable, and there are a number of instances in this whole story that have happened because people like me were too concerned about their promotion prospects and careers to question orders." Jo rested her hand on Toni's arm. "I don't want to be promoted if it means that I've covered up something like this. I realize now, that's not who I am. You've helped me see that. We need to do this."

"Are you sure? I worry that if I go ahead and we stay together, you'll get bitter and come to blame me for ruining your career and life."

"You've given me the decision, which I think was a courageous thing to do because I'm perhaps the only person that understands how much this means for you. I know you mean what you said about giving it all up. I'm certain I want you to keep going. Don't stop now."

Toni put her hand over Jo's and looked into her eyes. "So where do we go from here? What's our plan going forward? We still have a hole in our case. We don't know what's happened in HQ and how the grid reference was given incorrectly. Is there a way we can find that?"

Jo was silent for a moment, looking off into the distance. "I think I can fix that. I'll go to HQ and ask to see the logs or whatever they have. As an officer writing a report on the operation, I'll be allowed to look."

"And once we have that, I can burst into print and release my articles. I'll continue working on them, and we can decide what to release once you have more details."

After they settled down to sleep, Toni could hear Jo restlessly turning over and over. She climbed out of bed and went to Jo. "Can I sit with you for a moment?" she whispered.

"Please," Jo said.

"I'm sorry for all this. If I hadn't kept asking questions, if I hadn't kept pushing, you wouldn't be in this mess."

Jo grunted softly. "True. But we'd also be fostering a lie, and that's not right. So I'm worrying about what the colonel will do, and you're worrying about me. All in all, we make a fine pair." She chuckled wearily.

"I suppose it's good that we're both worrying for the right reasons. We care," Toni said. "Although I sometimes think life would be much simpler if I didn't care about things. I suppose I wouldn't write with such conviction if I didn't though."

"And I wouldn't think what I was doing was worth it either. A sleepless night or two won't matter if it means we get to the bottom of it all," Jo said. There was a moment of silence and then her hand slid up Toni's back. "I also find lying near you night after night the most difficult thing I've ever done. I want you next to me."

"Something else we have in common. What would happen now if I kissed you?" Toni asked. The change in subject was a welcome one. But was it wise? She didn't care at this point. With everything else on the line, why shouldn't they take this chance? When everything went down, they might not have each other.

"We'd both be one step closer to exploding. Maybe tonight we can exhaust ourselves with sex," Jo said.

"So if I lean over here and put my face here and kiss..." There was silence and then Jo actually giggled. "That was your nose. You did that on purpose." Toni was amazed at the playful Jo she was coming to know. The stoic, rule-based woman she'd met had layers of fun, sensuality, and courage she would never have known if they hadn't had this time together.

Jo cupped Toni's face in her hands and drew her onto the bed. The kiss was so gentle, their lips barely touching, that Toni almost sighed. This was something she'd never had before, and she'd been so close to never having it. She could only hope it wouldn't be the last time.

Toni leaned back into Jo and their lips met in a much stronger and longer kiss. Jo pushed her away. "Maybe you could get undressed while I check the tent is fastened securely," she said, moving swiftly to check their security before ditching her own clothing.

"Mm, I love to see your body like this," Toni said. She held Jo's hands. "You're beautiful on the inside as well as the out."

Jo held her tightly before laying her down on her bed. She moved her mouth from Toni's lips to her body, taking time with her exploration. Toni's breathing became heavy as she enjoyed the slow procession of exquisite feeling that culminated between her legs. Jo's mouth explored until she was between Toni's legs. Her clit hardened almost painfully under Jo's warm lips. Jo took her into her mouth and slid her tongue along the surrounding folds. Toni felt her release build to a crescendo, and her back arched as the orgasm crashed over her. She breathed out and met the look of adoration in Jo's eyes. They might not be able to define it yet, but this thing between them was special. "Come up here and let me be close to you for a moment."

Jo rested her head beside Toni. She could smell herself on Jo's mouth, and it made her need to return the favor. "I want you to feel as good as I do," Toni said. "I want to make you crave me the way I crave you."

"Connecting with you like that means that only a small touch from you and I'll explode," Jo said, her eyes dancing in the dim light.

"I have to have you anyway." Toni hardly touched her, and Jo came with a soft cry against Toni's neck, her hand buried in Toni's hair. She grabbed Toni and kissed her deeply, only letting her go when her body calmed.

"Maybe there will come a day when I can make the kind of noise I want to when you do that," Jo said and laughed.

They giggled like children having a sleepover in the dark, then lay together for some time, not speaking. Toni struggled to stay awake. She leaned over Jo and placed a kiss on each of her beautiful eyes. "Good night, you."

"Goodnight to you too," Jo said.

Reluctantly, Toni returned to her own bed and expected to fall asleep quickly. But thoughts of decisions and consequences began to cloud her mind, and as she lay there, watching Jo sleep, she wondered what was coming at them.

CHAPTER EIGHTEEN

JO OPENED HER EYES and knew exactly what she needed to do. Her dreams had brought her clarity, and there was no question about the next steps she needed to take.

Instead of looking for information at HQ, she needed to explain to someone who understood not only the military, but also Jo and her reasons for disobeying the colonel's orders. If he found out, she'd be arrested before she could get out of bed. She recognized that this could spell the end of her life in the Army but was resolute in her decision. Pre-Army, she'd been an engineer, so she could always go back to that as a civvy. Maybe someone could use a combat-trained engineer in their business. If that was the cost of honorable service, then she'd pay it.

She quietly got out of bed and looked across at Toni. Only a tuft of her brown hair showed above the covers. Jo dressed, picked up her gear, and left the tent on her tiptoes without Toni stirring. She didn't want Toni asking where she was going or trying to talk her out of it, or even worse, asking to go with her. Going to see the brigadier would put the final nail in her coffin as far as her career was concerned, but at least she would listen to what Jo had to say. Once she was kitted up, Jo headed to the heliport to sneak a place on an outgoing flight.

Luckily, there was a space on a helo just as she arrived. While flying the short distance to Fortress, she thought about what she would say and how she'd say it. The conversation in her dream had been so clear, so concise. Why didn't it come to her that way now? Her usual analytical and well-trained Army brain was falling short. Her interlude with Toni last night had been wonderful, but it wasn't helping her focus this morning.

Once she was at Fortress, she headed to HQ. The brigadier wasn't in the Operations room and when Jo looked at her watch, it was still only 0700. She decided to get breakfast and some tea. She'd finished her last piece of toast, hoping it would settle her stomach, when she saw the brigadier in the distance heading toward the Ops room.

Moving quickly, she caught up with her. "Morning, ma'am." Jo saluted. "I have an emergency and was hoping you could make time for me."

"Oh, hello, Jo. I wasn't expecting to see you until the end of the week. Let me head into Ops. I'll hand my duties to someone, so we can talk. Will you make me a coffee, please?"

"Thank you. The usual?"

"Yes, please."

Jo made the brigadier's drink and listened to the operational hum in the room, feeling a moment of calm. The worries of the night and the muddle of the flight were gone. This was her moment, and she would make her case. There was no question, no uncertainty at all that she was in the right. That had to count for something.

The brigadier led her into the same office she'd been in a few months ago when Jo had been lumbered with a reporter she wanted nothing to do with. She'd been worried that it would be difficult to manage the time bomb of a journalist and how likely it was to ruin her career if she wasn't careful. Now she was here ruining her career willingly because she believed in that same journalist. It might have been funny if it weren't so serious.

"What's the emergency then, Jo?" she asked, her expression quizzical. "You've always been self-sufficient, so it's unusual for you to have an emergency."

"It's a long story, ma'am. I was involved in the incident where the Fizers were held down by insurgent fire at Deh Lekay. My platoon happened to be close by and helped."

The brigadier's frown deepened. "Yes, I knew about that. It was a good job. I think they would've been in real trouble if you hadn't provided backup until fire and air support arrived. It's amazing how a small number of troops such as your platoon can make all the difference."

Jo nodded and held firm to her resolve. "Before I talk to you about the air support, I should say that Colonel Musgrove has given me orders that I've broken by talking to a number of people involved and by allowing Toni James, the reporter, access to them. When he finds out, I expect that I'll be removed from the regiment and, along with the pilot and navigator of the plane plus two of the injured Fizer soldiers, under threat of court-martial for leaking confidential information to the press."

"Court-martialed? You?" She looked genuinely bemused. "What have you been doing?"

"Perhaps I should start at the beginning." Jo went on to explain the situation in detail. "After we returned, rumors began of friendly fire."

The brigadier steepled her fingers beneath her chin. "That's interesting. Nothing has reached us here. Carry on with your account, please."

"The colonel called me in and ordered me to stop the rumors. He informed me that the official report stated that the dead and injured had been hurt by a wayward Taliban rocket fired at the air support from the mountainside behind the derelict building. He particularly mentioned Toni James and said I should ensure that she didn't print anything with regard to the friendly fire rumors."

"And what did you do?"

Jo explained the various people she'd talked to, including Jeff.

The brigadier stared at her for a long moment. "What did Toni James say? How were you going to keep her from writing about what you'd found out? And, presumably, what she found out herself?"

Jo nodded. "She did her own interviews and the soldiers from Foxtrot confirmed the rumors. It was friendly fire, which Jeff confirmed not long after. However, the colonel has taken Jeff's handwritten copy of the grid reference as evidence." Jo was far enough down the rabbit hole that she needn't bother tiptoeing. "I feel his behavior and unwillingness to investigate are suspicious."

"And now I'm suspicious too." The brigadier gave her a small smile. "Anything else?"

"I suspect we'll find that the recording and any film that was taken by the tech on board the plane will have been seized by the colonel. But with the interviews and information we have, I had to come to you. I'm handing myself in to you for disobeying the colonel's orders and allowing Toni James access to information that he considered was restricted. I hope you'll take into consideration the extenuating circumstances."

"Disobeying orders is a serious business, captain."

Jo tried to keep her breathing calm as she looked at the brigadier. Her career had been so promising, but that didn't matter now. She could hear Colonel Musgrove crowing to his friends about the uselessness of women in the Regiment. Letting the brigadier down was what was most upsetting though. She was someone special, and her respect meant a lot to Jo.

"However, I'd like to talk to the people involved before I say anything else. Given your suspicions and the information you've gathered, you were right to come to me. Let's get to the bottom of this. We've heard nothing about this here, so it's clearly been swept under the carpet at Sherwood. I understand why you're concerned about it. We'll go to Sherwood now and see what's going on."

Before Jo could take stock of what was happening, the force that was Brigadier McQueen in action was out of the door, picking up her kit and pistol on the way, and heading toward the heliport. They stopped on the way at the security office. "You may as well wait for me here," she said.

Jo nodded, wondering if the brigadier had changed her mind and was going to place her in custody. She was surprised when the brigadier came out followed by John Fletcher, a Military Police

Major, and they both strode off, clearly expecting Jo to follow. At the heliport, the brigadier asked the controller if he had space for them to go to Sherwood. When he shook his head, she suggested he bump three passengers, which he promptly did, and moments later, they were in the air. Jo's heart beat hard enough to match the thrum of the engine. She was trying to control a rising tide of nausea, and the sweat pouring off her added to her discomfort. This wasn't what she'd expected. Now she was going to have to face the colonel directly, showing that she'd gone over his head.

The helo landed, and they headed straight for the sickbay. The arrival of the brigadier created a flurry amongst the staff as they arrived.

"I need to see the injured soldiers," she said.

"I'm sorry, ma'am, but they've been examined and confirmed as fit. They're heading for Checkpoint Gresham," said the medic colonel who had rushed out of an office when the brigadier arrived, obviously startled by her appearance. His face was red with embarrassment, and he fiddled with the stethoscope around his neck.

"When did they leave?" the brigadier asked.

Jo was happy letting her take the lead. It was important that she find out what she wanted herself.

"I'm surprised you didn't see them when you came in. They were leaving directly; their guards were escorting them to get their kit and then they'd be off."

"Ring the heliport, colonel, and tell them to delay the flight to Gresham. My orders. Keep the soldiers and their escort there, and I'll be there shortly."

"Yes, ma'am."

"Come on, captain. Let's head back to the heliport. I hope we can get there in time," the brigadier said.

She retraced her steps, with Jo and Major Fletcher following behind her like a retinue racing along behind a queen. They reached the heliport, and the brigadier swept into air traffic control.

"Have you delayed the Gresham flight?" she asked.

She looked imperious, and Jo couldn't help but admire her attitude and presence.

"Yes, ma'am. The incoming flight hasn't arrived yet, so it will leave a little later than expected. The passengers are waiting behind the hesco wall."

Jo led the brigadier into the sheltered passageway, and they eventually arrived where the passengers waited. Among them were two military police and their charges.

"You haven't done anything wrong. We're making sure you get on the flight for your posting as your new orders demand," one of the MPs said.

"The whole base thinks we're under fucking arrest," one of the detained soldiers said. "We've never had to be escorted to our posting before."

"Attention, troops. Brigadier present," Jo said loudly, deciding that it was best to announce the brigadier's presence before things got any more difficult.

The soldiers jumped to attention.

"Captain, bring the MPs and their charges to the sickbay. I'd like to have a chat with them."

"Yes, ma'am." Jo motioned to them all. The MPs looked confused, whereas the two soldiers looked ill at ease. She tried to give them a reassuring smile but knew it fell flat. She was far from reassured herself.

Once they arrived at the sickbay, the brigadier requested the medic colonel find them a private space. Within moments, they were in a side ward.

"Sit, please. You're not in trouble, but I'd like to have a chat," the brigadier said.

"Corporal Stevens, is it?" The brigadier read his name printed on his shirt. "You're the military policeman in charge?"

"Yes, ma'am. We were briefed personally by Colonel Musgrove." His eyes darted from the brigadier to John Fletcher, who still hadn't said a word.

"What were your orders?"

"He told us to go to the sickbay and collect the two soldiers being held under guard. The two soldiers were not to talk to anyone, as they were under orders to keep quiet. He said that they were to leave here for an extended posting to Gresham, and we were to escort them as they collected their kit, and to ensure they caught the transport. That's all we know, ma'am," Stevens said. He looked at his colleague.

"Yes, ma'am. I can confirm he has it right, ma'am. That's what the colonel told us to do, so we did it."

"Major Fletcher, I think Corporals Stevens and Hill should stay here in sickbay until we complete our chat. What do you think?" the brigadier said.

"I agree. Could you both wait in the room next door, please. It could be a while. I'll see that you get breaks and food. I expect you to be here for a few hours. We're speaking confidentially here, hence our decisions. If anyone, including the colonel, comes to speak with you, please tell them to come talk to us first." Major Fletcher opened the door to another room. "Private Warren, perhaps you'll also wait with them. We'll call you in a minute."

"Corporal Miller, tell me about what happened at the incident at Deh Lekay when Sergeant Green was injured and Corporal Zenski was killed." The brigadier smiled gently at the corporal.

He blanched. "The colonel said I wasn't to discuss this with anyone, ma'am, otherwise I'll get court-martialed," Dusty Miller said, his eyes wide with fear.

"I'm senior to the colonel, so you're allowed to talk to me," the brigadier said. "Tell me what happened."

Dusty recounted the story including how the colonel had put guards outside their room in the sickbay ever since they got back.

"I'm sure it's been difficult," the brigadier said. "What happened today?"

"The colonel came to our room this morning. He said that he'd received our orders and wanted to tell us personally. We were told that we were being sent on an extended posting to Checkpoint Gresham, which we think is somewhere way north of here and in the heat of the fighting." He paused and glanced at Jo. "I feel as if I've done something wrong, and I'm being punished. We're only six weeks from going home on this posting. I don't want any trouble."

"Thank you, corporal. I'm not aware of you doing anything wrong. I want to find out exactly what happened on the 20th and what has happened since. I'll make sure you get the results of my inquiries. Please assume for now that this new posting won't be happening."

Dusty visibly relaxed and let out a big breath. "Thank you, ma'am."

"Please go and wait with the MPs for now, and I'll work out what to do next. I want to talk to your colleague first. Major Fletcher, if you'll sort them out."

A moment later, the seat was filled with a pale-faced Private Warren.

"Please tell me about the incident on the 20th at Deh Lakey and what's happened since," the brigadier said. Jack Warren told his story, which tallied with Dusty Miller's.

"I'll inform the corporal that neither of you will be posted up country. I'd like you to remain here for a short while. I have a few more enquiries to make," the brigadier said.

Major Fletcher showed the soldier into the room with the other soldiers. He returned looking grim. "Where to next, ma'am?"

The brigadier looked at Jo. "Let's get the pilot and navigator here, John. Once we hear what they have to say for ourselves then we can decide the way forward. Meanwhile, let's have a morning coffee."

Annie and Jeff arrived just as the brigadier finished her coffee. They told their account of the operation, and Annie showed the copy of the grid reference to them all.

"Thanks for coming so quickly and helping us. Please stay here so that we can get your statements," the brigadier said as she stood and headed to the door. "John. Jo. I think we should pay the colonel a visit next."

Jo's heart raced as they neared the colonel's office. This was it. The moment in a movie when the bullied had to face the bully. She was grateful that she wasn't doing it alone. But would he do what he'd done in the meeting and make it look like it was all her fault? She glanced at the brigadier. So far, she'd been the ally Jo needed. If that changed, things were going to get ugly fast.

CHAPTER NINETEEN

The small group of officers headed for the Regimental HQ and went straight to the colonel's office. His clerk looked up as they arrived.

Seeing the brigadier, he jumped to attention and stood ramrod stiff. He saluted. "The colonel is in his office, ma'am. I'll announce—"

"That won't be necessary, corporal. I'll head in." The brigadier was already two steps into the colonel's office, closely followed by Major Fletcher and Jo.

"Good morning, ma'am." The colonel stood and gave a weak salute. "And to what do I owe this pleasure?" He looked beyond the brigadier and saw Jo and the military police major. His face flushed from his neck upward, and his eyes narrowed ever so slightly.

"Colonel, I'm here investigating some things I've been told. I thought I'd give you the opportunity to give me your side of the story."

The colonel leaned on his desk, and Jo could see the white of his fingers as he grasped the edge. "What's the captain been saying now? She's been nothing but trouble since she arrived. The Fizers would be well to get rid of her, as I told you last time we spoke."

Jo clenched her jaw. She struggled not to leap forward and punch him, hard. A well-placed fist to the nose should do it. She reined herself in. She wouldn't go to a court-martial with a charge of assaulting a senior officer as well as breaking his orders.

"And as I told you then, Captain Fitzgerald is doing an excellent job here. Her work is exemplary, and she's ensured that Toni James has had access to and reported on the Fizers well. The coverage in both the UK and around the world has been excellent. Her conduct isn't the question here. I want to talk about the incident at Deh Lekay on the 20th."

He clenched his hands even tighter on the desk. "You've talked, haven't you? You've released confidential information. You disobeyed my orders."

"Yes, sir."

"I'll see you court-martialed for this," the colonel said, almost as though he'd forgotten there were other people in the room.

"I want to know why you're covering up a friendly fire incident and silencing everyone who was there," the brigadier said.

His attention snapped back to her. "My investigations showed it to be a rocket launched by insurgents from behind the insurgents' building."

"That's interesting. I questioned the soldiers who were injured, and they've said the same as the soldiers in the platoon providing backup. They didn't see any rocket being launched or landing. And both the pilot and navigator have confirmed what the soldiers on the ground said. That's a lot of people who were actually there giving credence to the so-called rumors, colonel. Which makes me wonder where your information came from."

He flinched, his jaw clenching and unclenching. "I must have been mistaken then, ma'am. I'm sure there's a sensible answer to this." He swallowed, obviously aware he hadn't answered her implied question. "It's probably something this woman," he said, tilting his head toward Jo, "has made up to get me in trouble. It's like I said in a briefing recently. It's her fault that the Taliban are riled up. She's going into villages and creating an uproar." When he saw the brigadier's raised eyebrow, he seemed to rethink his position. It was, after all, one of the brigadier's projects. "I warned her to stay in her lane and not talk to anyone about this, which she's clearly ignored. I want to insist that she's court-martialed." He looked at Major Fletcher. "Major, please take her into custody."

Major Fletcher shook his head.

There was silence as the brigadier folded her hands in her lap and stared at the colonel. It became heavy with things being left unsaid, and finally, with sweat dripping down his face, the colonel slapped the desk.

"I heard it was friendly fire and made a decision for the good of the Army."

"But why make up this story about the rocket?" the brigadier asked, rolling right past the fact that he was falling apart in front of her.

"I didn't want an incident where the soldiers blamed the pilots and searched them out to cause trouble."

"Do you know of an incident where that's happened before? The brigadier tilted her head slightly. "A time when soldiers have acted violently or otherwise to the pilots and navigators who spend their lives providing them cover and support?"

"No, I can't say that I have," the colonel said.

"So let me get this right. You knew it was friendly fire, and you made up a story about rockets that no one appears to have believed, to save the troops from violence between your soldiers and the airmen protecting them?" the brigadier asked.

The colonel didn't so much as blink at the comment. His face remained straight. "Yes, that's it in a nutshell."

"You saw the navigator's note of the grid reference on his flight overalls and seized them for evidence. Where are they now?" the brigadier asked.

For the first time, the colonel looked flustered. "I'm not certain. They may be in a filing cabinet in the outer office," he said.

"Why keep it there? Do you have other evidence that it was friendly fire or documentation that would necessitate a file?"

"No," the colonel said.

"The navigator checked the grid reference with HQ while in flight and the pilot wrote it down. So luckily, HQ will have evidence of the grid reference," the brigadier said, punching a hole into his cover-up with impressive nonchalance. "You believe the air crew got it wrong, resulting in the friendly fire incident?"

"Yes," the colonel said.

"Sadly, the video evidence from the plane has gone missing. However, I have the recording of the conversation from HQ."

Jo was certain she didn't. There hadn't been time to get it. She was bluffing, based on Jo's information and certainty. Fucking hell, she hoped she wasn't wrong about anything.

"The recording is clear; the navigator was given the wrong grid reference." The brigadier sounded certain that what she was saying was true. "And why would that wrong grid reference concern you enough to go in search of it and then hide it away? We both know your reasoning is illogical when it comes to the threat of violence. Why have you swept this under the rug, colonel? No more lies, please. I'm extremely busy."

He deflated like a beach ball with a puncture. He rocked on his feet before he walked back around his desk and almost fell into his chair. "My nephew works in the Ops room, and he gave the navigator the wrong grid reference. He called me and asked me what he should do. I decided to help him out."

"That's a lot of effort to 'help your nephew out.' You went against all protocol and, instead of making it clear that a tragic mistake was made, you created an improbable story, blamed the captain, and kept the injured soldiers in solitary. Does that sound right?" the brigadier asked.

"Our family has been in the service for generations. Friendly fire deaths are something that linger long in people's memories. My nephew is likely to be charged with manslaughter and such a mistake will be forever linked with our name," the colonel said. "The Fizers and the Musgrove name have always played an honorable part in British history. I didn't want that tarnished. If that damned reporter hadn't come and the captain had done her fucking job and followed orders—"

The brigadier walked around the desk. "Stand up."

The colonel slowly stood, rage and frustration seeming to

compete with despair in his expression.

"I'm taking you into custody for the offences of blackmail, kidnapping, and the dissemination of information intended to deceive your superiors and the British Army." She raised her hand to cut him off when it was clear he was going to start ranting. "There is no doubt in my mind that the Fizers and the Musgrove name will be forever linked. Major Fletcher will escort you to your quarters, where you'll remain under guard until we organize a flight to Fortress."

Major Fletcher escorted the colonel out of the office, and the brigadier turned to Jo. "This has been a strange morning in more ways than one. I had no idea I'd be arresting one of my colonels for insubordination, among other things. What do you think we should take away from all this?" She motioned for Jo to take a seat. "While you think about it, I need food. Breakfast seems a long while ago."

Jo watched the brigadier stride out of the office and couldn't imagine eating anything with the way her stomach was flipflopping. The brigadier's belief in her was pretty incredible. She still wasn't in handcuffs but recognized that could change. Even though the colonel had lied, Jo had still disobeyed orders. She didn't have long to think before the brigadier returned and placed a cup of tea in Jo's hands.

"Tell me, Jo, why did you come forward?" the brigadier asked when she sat down.

"There are various reasons, really. I've had a strange few days, and this morning solidified my logic," Jo said. "Senior officers have significant power over their men and should use it wisely. It's perhaps rather trite to say, but in this case had he been successful in cleverly bullying his subordinates, the colonel could have gotten away with it and ruined a lot of lives. It needed someone to stand up and be counted. I realized that I wouldn't want to be in an organization that didn't hold to the truth and integrity that it's supposed to be all about. I couldn't stand by and watch others being bullied into silence." Jo met the brigadier's gaze. "I've come to realize that as an officer, I shouldn't follow orders blindly. I should consider *why* they were given. If they appear to be poorly thought through or make me wonder as to the reason, then I should open a discussion about it."

"But what about getting a reputation about undermining discipline? Disobeying orders?" the brigadier asked.

"Yes, ma'am, that's what would happen in all probability," Jo said. "But I've always been taught that a good order will be followed without question. As an officer, if I was getting questions, it would be because my orders weren't clear or were causing problems." She took a swig of her tea to allow her to get her ideas in order. "There are some things I'd have to draw the line at. We're allowed to disobey orders if they're unconstitutional or illegal. I'd also say we need to talk to our superiors if we feel there's an element of risk to people's welfare."

"Is that why you decided to disobey the colonel's order?"

"Ah. Yes." Jo took another swig of her tea. All this talk of disobeying orders was making her mouth dry. "The colonel threatened me with a court-martial. But I saw the way the men were being treated. I saw what state Jeff was in, and I couldn't stand by and allow it."

"The colonel certainly understood how to bully his way through rules and regulations," the brigadier said.

"I probably would have let it go if the colonel hadn't put guards on the soldiers in the sickbay. That's what made me consider something was wrong," Jo said. She wasn't about to drag Toni into this, though she'd been the one to set it all in motion.

"I also think we should all be grateful to Toni James for following her instincts and getting into sickbay to see the soldiers," the brigadier said.

There was something about her gaze, something knowing, that made Jo shift uncomfortably. "I agree. What happens next, ma'am? Will we still be court-martialed?" Better to simply ask the question outright than wait for it to happen.

"No." The brigadier smiled. "I'm going to hand the information over to Major Fletcher to follow up. To do that, he'll probably need you all to make yourselves available. Can you see to that, please?"

Jo nodded. The relief was dizzying.

"We need to make sure it doesn't happen again, and we need to put measures in place to stop this sort of trouble." The brigadier wiped her hands on her paper napkin and placed it on the empty plate in front of her. "You did the right thing, captain. We'll see to it that this mess is dealt with properly."

Jo didn't know what to say. She wasn't being arrested but what did that mean for her career overall? The brigadier seemed happy enough. Was her future solid after all?

The brigadier set her cup down, her expression thoughtful. "I need to see Toni James first though. I need to make sure she recognizes what can be written now and what can be written later. I need her to understand the friendly fire case will be fully investigated, and I expect her evidence will be called for. I'm sure she'll be allowed to print the whole story once the investigation is finished." The brigadier stood. "I'll commandeer the colonel's office. Can you find Ms. James and bring her here as soon as possible?"

Jo hurried to her accommodation, hoping she'd catch Toni writing her article, but the tent was empty. She looked at Toni's belongings to see if she could guess what she was wearing and thus what she was doing. Her uniform was still on her bed, as well as her electronics and her wash kit. That meant she was either playing sports or eating. Jo made her way to the volleyball court and sure enough, there was a tousled, brown head in the middle of the crowd at the far end of the court. They were cheering one of the teams on although Jo had no idea who they were.

Toni caught sight of her and waved. She'd obviously been playing hard; her top was sweat-stained, and she was glowing in the early afternoon sun.

"Where have you been all day? I woke up this morning, and you were gone. I didn't know what to think. My first thought was that you'd been arrested by the colonel. I went to the company lines to see what I could find out and met Flash on his way to breakfast. He assured me we'd all know if that happened. Then I decided you'd gone to HQ to do some investigating. I eventually had breakfast with Flash and the guys and got invited to an all-day volleyball tournament." Toni looked at her more closely. "What is it?"

Jo wanted to put her arms around her and breathe in her confidence and optimism. "Well, I haven't been arrested, although that was in question first thing this morning. Anyway, I need you to come with me right away. I'll explain as we go."

"Let me tell the guys," Toni said. She jogged over and responded good-naturedly to the groans and jibes, and then returned to Jo.

"I'll talk quietly as we walk, but you need to shower and change quickly. The brigadier wants to see you in the colonel's office as soon as you're done," Jo said quietly, glancing around to make certain they wouldn't be overheard. "I went to Fortress this morning, and I told the brigadier that I'd helped you and why. I told her everything."

"You didn't?" The color drained from Toni's face, and she stopped walking. "That means you'll be court-martialed for sure. Going over your commander's head is bad news too, isn't it?"

Jo carried on walking and waited for her to catch up. "I decided that I'd rather tell her what I'd done and why, and that I'd rather be arrested, court-martialed, and thrown out of the regiment for releasing information to the press than stand by and do nothing," she said. "It gave me an element of control over whatever was going to happen."

'You're still here, so I guess the brigadier believed what you were telling her," Toni said.

Jo secured the entrance of the tent and took Toni in her arms. "I missed you today as well." She gently kissed Toni. "I realized that life is too lonely not to share it with someone, and while you're infuriating on many levels, I want more time with you." She released her and stepped back. "We're short on time just now though; the brigadier wants us as soon as possible. I'll tell you the rest while we walk to the HQ offices."

After Jo filled her in on, Toni sat on the bed beside her, brow furrowed.

"I know what that must have cost you this morning. I know you don't believe I could understand completely, and maybe that's true, but if I had to stop my reporting and do something else, it would hurt. Even if it was for something I believed was right. So I get why you were hoping it wasn't true, and why you did the right thing even though it could cost you everything."

Jo pulled Toni closer. They only had a moment, and Jo wanted much, much longer. "We've got to go. The brigadier is waiting for us. She wants to discuss what you write, when, and how much."

Toni screwed up her face. "So now the brigadier is the keeper of the story. Will we have to be quiet again? Is that why she hasn't arrested you? She's going to shut us both up?"

"I didn't get that impression." She thought about their conversation. "Strangely, I got more of a feeling that I was having a job interview." She shook her head at the silly notion.

"Well, I'll wait to be surprised then. Let's go," Toni said.

Jo was mostly an extra appendage in the meeting. Brigadier McQueen answered Toni's questions about protocol, orders, and even about the issue of friendly fire. Jo couldn't help but smile at Toni's ability to get people to talk. She watched her and emotions she was unfamiliar with battled for her attention. Could they make this work? What would she give up for a chance to stay in Toni's orbit? When she thought her future in the military was over, she'd been prepared to approach Toni with the idea that they see what they could be together. Now though, would Toni want to take that chance with someone who could be stationed anywhere at any time? The question was the only one left unanswered, and it was the only one that could break her heart.

CHAPTER TWENTY

SWEAT SLID IN RIVERS down Toni's back, and she was no more used to it now than she'd been when she arrived. As they walked, she thought back to her first practice patrol and how she worried her legs might not last through all the ducking and weaving. But then, she'd grown in so many ways. She was much stronger now and didn't think she'd drop to the ground every ten seconds. But the major difference was that she'd been ignorant of how truly precarious life was in a war situation. Reporters had been killed and injured covering them, and she'd never forget the sound of the first rifle shot she'd heard. A single crack. She had tasted her own fear, knowing that she or one of the troops could have lost their lives to that one bullet.

They were making their way to her favorite village, one of the first she'd visited, and one she'd been to with Jo a few times since. Their party included an extra person. Laura was a lieutenant attached to the Tennent's regiment who were taking over from the Fizers, and she'd be performing Jo's role when the Fizers moved out soon. She'd have her own troop to protect her, but Jo wanted her to meet the women in the villages she'd developed close ties with. Laura had been on a crash course to learn Pashto and was excited to have the chance to meet Afghan women who needed help.

The village greeted them happily as usual, and although Jo took the lead and did much of the talking, Toni enjoyed her time with the villagers who had become like friends. She discussed some of their sewing and showed them stitches she remembered from her days learning needlework. She'd managed to get a couple of yards of material sent to her for the women but wasn't sure who she should give it to because there wasn't enough for everyone. She got Jo to talk to the women at a shura. They voted that Larmina, who was newly married and loved sewing, should have some and the rest should go to Moska who made clothes for the children.

Toni played games with the children, and she'd brought a bagful of sweets and small chocolate bars that were a hit, as they always had been. Some of the men even sent their kids to get them a bar. She was going to miss these people. It wasn't as if she'd be able to write letters; nothing would come of them. There was no way she would ever see them again and with a sinking heart, she said her goodbyes. This was something she'd have to get used to, and she allowed the ache to be something special, a reminder of the vastness of the world and the people who touched her life.

The women held their hands and wished them a happy future while the children hung on to their legs. It was sad in some ways but in others, it was good.

These were the knotty problems they'd only begun to explore. The women were keen on getting the medical side of things sorted. There were only two or three gynecologists in the whole of western Afghanistan, and they'd been forced underground when the Russians left. Some women knew where to find them, but the gynecologists lived in constant fear for their lives and had almost no medical products to use. Toni was so pleased they'd managed to get a British Army nurse out to meet one of them, and she'd made a list of supplies that the Army could get for the women's medical network.

As she watched Jo interact with the women of the village, as well as with her own troops, Toni was once again reminded of what a special person she was. She'd managed to keep her compassion, empathy, and desire for change even through all the conflict she'd seen. But what did it mean when it came to *them*? Her chest hurt at the thought of walking away from Jo as surely as they were walking away from this village. Would she be just another person who'd touched her life?

"You need to be as aware as you always have been," Flash said, encouraging her to keep her eyes searching the surroundings as they left the village behind. "We all get jumpy at the end of a tour. We worry that lady luck is going to give us a bad hand, and we'll be injured or killed right at the end."

Toni nodded, conscious of all she needed to do as she covered the ground and made sure she wasn't blasé, especially as they neared Sherwood.

Once they were back, Jo did her usual briefing though this one including instructions for the battalion leaving. "Most of you will be pulling out tomorrow. You need to get your kit together and be ready to leave by 0900. Lieutenant Travers will be in charge of the platoon as I'll be staying a couple of extra days. Ms. James will also be staying. Thank you all for your efforts to help me get much needed assistance to Afghan women. You'll be able to look back with pride at what we've managed to do here. It's been a pleasure working with you all, and you'll have the lieutenant all to yourself in the future because when we get back to the UK, I'll be moved on."

Jo gave the lieutenant a handful of money. "Pizza and drinks are on me tonight. Don't stay up too late."

Toni followed Jo to their accommodation, and they shucked out of their outer kit and kitbags. "Shower, long drink of water, and then a chat?" Toni asked.

"Mm, sounds good," Jo said.

A few hours later, they each lay on their beds with a cup of tea that Jo had picked up along with some digestive biscuits that seemed to be a great favorite with the Fizers.

"Have you tried these with cheese? Any cheese will do, but they go best with a strong one like Stilton and Roquefort. Although I suspect cheese connoisseurs would call me a philistine for that." Jo held up the dry, unremarkable cookie like it was a trophy. "Dunk it in your tea and pull it out quickly. Don't leave it too long, or you'll lose the biscuit entirely. When you get to the bottom of the cup, there'll be this thick layer of dead digestive."

Toni smiled at Jo's simple delight. "In some ways I'm going to miss this place. I get to do something I love, and I enjoy lying here chatting with you. I'm comfortable. I know we were both struggling at the start, but I can't think of anyone I'd rather spend time with."

"You make me sound like an old slipper," Jo said.

"I promise you don't look like one." Toni squawked when Jo threw her deodorant across the small room at her.

"I checked with the troop movements office, and the main regiment move will be tomorrow. I need to get my final reports done for HQ and staying a few extra days will give me the opportunity. We'll only have our rear party here plus the Tennent's battalion as they arrive. Once I get the word that the main troop movements are over tomorrow, we'll make arrangements to leave. We'll stay a couple of nights in Fortress and complete our meetings with the brass about your reports, what you've done so far, and what they can expect. I guess we'll be slotted in for movement to the UK on Thursday."

"Sounds good to me. That's the official side done and dusted. But I'd like to know about us. What are you thinking we might do?" Toni's held her breath, not sure she was ready for the answer. Her big worry was that Jo didn't share her strong feelings. Toni could see them making their relationship work. She wanted to go on dates and spend nights together back in the UK. She'd never felt this way before, and she wanted it more than she'd ever wanted anything. Jo gave her stability and safety, and Toni knew she cared for her. Their sex together had been a little hurried out of necessity, and she wanted them to take their time exploring each other physically. But Jo might not want any of those things.

"I thought we'd spend the afternoon walking in Hyde Park and Kensington Gardens, and then go out for supper in a little place I know in Knightsbridge." Jo looked at her, her eyes dancing with mischief. "And then spend the rest of the evening in a nearby hotel having a...nightcap. That'd be the first day of my leave and depending on what we decide, perhaps the next few days will follow a similar pattern. What do you think?"

The stress and worry floated away from her shoulders. She was full of excitement, enthusiasm, and yes, lust. "Yes, please. A million times yes. I'm serious about wanting to see where this goes."

"I don't know how we'll make it work. There's no question it'll be long distance a lot of the time, and maybe it will feel impossible sometimes. But for now, I have plenty of leave, and I want to spend it with you. I want to explore your body for hours and hours before, during, and after we're doing other things so I can get to know you even better."

"You do?" Toni choked, and her words came out as a squeak.

Jo's smile was sweet. "I know what I want, and I'm going for it. I've been worried about what being gay would do to my career. I've had to fight my way up the ladder, and I've been worried about everything from being strong enough to being able to hold my own against the big guys." Jo shrugged. "This situation has taught me that I'm more than strong enough. I know what I'm doing, and I know what matters." She looked Toni over and gave her a dirty grin. "You matter."

Toni gave a little shiver of desire. "Get up and get packed. I want to be on that plane to London as soon as possible so I can make use of every dirty thought going through your mind."

The future wasn't certain. No future could be, since they were both in careers born of chaos. But for now, there was promise, and Toni would hold onto it with both hands.

CHAPTER TWENTY-ONE

WHEN THEY GOT BACK to the UK, Toni suggested that Jo stay at her mother's house with her. Her mother was away as usual, in Brunei or the Philippines somewhere, following a difficult story about child pornography and body snatching.

Toni showed her around the large home and finished in the master bathroom. "The bathtub is big enough for two, and I'm hoping you'll make the most of that with me very, very soon. We'll have to go out to eat until we've been shopping."

Jo stood and looked around. The luxury and space overwhelmed her for a moment. It was a far cry from the plastic-wrapped shower cubicles she was used to. Coming back from deployment always hit her hard.

"You okay?" Toni asked.

"I'm fine. Just acclimatizing to the ordinary." She smiled. "It'll be nice to go shopping for our own food... It's the small things, you know?"

Toni nodded. "I get it."

"I only have my deployment clothes, so you'll have to put up with me in an old T-shirt and jeans today. We can go to my place tomorrow to replenish my wardrobe."

"Speaking of clothing..." Toni tugged the hem of Jo's shirt, then pulled it slowly over her head. "Let's get dirty."

Within seconds, they were naked and standing under the hot water, and Jo ran her hands over Toni's body, pressing her lips to Toni's wet skin. Jo stood behind Toni as she pushed inside her and reveled in the freedom of her crying out Jo's name as she thrust deeper until Toni sagged against the wall, breathing hard.

It wasn't until the water ran cold that they got out, toweling each other and taking their time getting dressed. She let Toni take her hand to lead her down to the kitchen.

"I have American coffee. Obviously I didn't get much being embedded with the British. My second luxury after the hot water is a pot of American coffee, made the way my daddy makes it. He sent me Topeca Time Blend from Tulsa at Christmas." Toni peered at the coffee pot as though to make it run faster.

"I think I could go with one of your American coffees if I'm not stealing your supply?" Jo laughed, picked up the bag of coffee, and hid it under her shirt.

Toni grabbed at her, trying to tickle Jo under her arm. She was ticklish, but Toni hadn't known that until now. Jo was helpless with laughter and crumbled under her onslaught, surrendering the coffee bag.

Jo put her arm around Toni. She didn't consciously think about it; the touch seemed right. Toni put her arms around Jo's neck, and the rightness of the moment made Jo's heart beat faster. Being able to kiss when they felt like it and not have to hide was a freedom so sweet.

She slid her tongue along Toni's lips, and the emotion that rose wasn't just one of desire.

"So where were we? Coffee," Toni said. "I think we both need the day to de-stress and to walk outside knowing we're not going to be shot at. I don't know if I remember how to walk in a straight line."

"As much as I want more of this," Jo touched her finger to Toni's lips gently, "I get what you're saying. I was looking for my weapon earlier even though I handed it in before I left Afghanistan. A day being ordinary, boring people will do me good. Though I'm taking a rain check on this." She pulled Toni closer. "And just to clarify, you're anything but ordinary or boring."

Toni grinned. "Glad to hear you say so. I could get a complex. Now let me pour you a cup of my Tulsa coffee. It's going to explode on your taste buds; your tea wilts in comparison."

They spent the rest of the day walking through London parks and talking, holding hands and enjoying soft kisses.

This was what Jo wanted. The closeness and easy chat that came with love. *Love?* She couldn't ignore it. This was what she'd always believed love was, although she never expected to feel it. They made it to the Italian restaurant in Knightsbridge and enjoyed eating at a slow pace and with few worries, so different from chowing down as much as possible in as short a time as possible. The emotional revelation was on her mind, though she wasn't sure what to do with it just yet. She could be brave in the face of a firefight. She could be brave enough to walk into a superior's office and blow the lid off a cover-up. But was she brave enough to love? "Do you have scotch at your place?" Jo asked, thinking it might give her some courage.

"Yeah. Mother has the good stuff. Is that a sneaky way of checking we're going to get dirty before bed?"

"Maybe. I'm so focused on us being together tonight, I'm making the whole day about it," Jo said. Toni nestled one of her feet against the inside of Jo's leg, increasing Jo's desperation to get Toni's body next to hers soon. Jo stood quickly; she needed control of her body. She couldn't concentrate, and her mind was whirling. What were they talking about? The heat was stifling, her breathing was erratic, and she was wet—so wet. Toni looked at her with a knowing smile. Toni knew exactly what she was doing. Jo grinned and shook her head at the wicked gleam in Toni's eyes.

"Let's go. I want that scotch and more of what we started earlier," Toni said.

When they got home, Jo sat on the couch. Toni poured them each a tumbler of Benriach and placed them on a neat coffee table at the side of her. "Where shall I sit?' she asked, her finger to her lips as she looked around at the selection of chairs and footstools.

"Right here." Jo patted the sofa next to her. "As close to me as you can get, please." She actually wanted her on her lap but next to her would work.

"I think this is better. Don't you?" Toni said and plonked herself on Jo's lap.

"Can you read my mind? I was hoping you might sit here." Jo pushed her back slightly and twisted around to kiss her. When they came up for air, Jo reached for Toni's drink. "We'll have to sit still so that we can get the value from this expensive scotch," she said.

She took her own glass and took a mouthful. "Wow... It's so smooth and mellow. Maybe we should live here. I could get a taste for this." Jo dipped her finger in the drink and painted it along Toni's lips.

Jo kissed her. The sweet flavor of the scotch was a perfect match to her soft lips. Jo could feel the heat of Toni's body as she ran her hand over her leg. She stopped when she reached her waist.

"Why on earth would you stop?" Toni asked, her eyes half-lidded.

Jo took another sip of scotch and kissed her again, sharing the sip between them. She moved her hand up until she could feel the soft curve of Toni's breast through her bra. "Could we go to bed and explore each other slowly? I want to be able to see you. As good as this is, I want more. I want to feel us skin to skin."

Toni got up, held out her hand, and led Jo up to her room. Jo inhaled the scent of Toni's perfume and wiggled her toes in the lush carpet. In the corner by the window was an old desk which looked out of place amongst the modern furniture. "That seems incongruous to the rest of your decor."

"I wanted something that gives me a sense of history while I write. I searched for a few months 'til I found what I was looking for." She looked a little embarrassed, like she was admitting to something childish.

"I like it. When you move, you'll have to find a house that fits your desk." Jo laughed. "One minute I want us to move in for the scotch and the next I want us to move out to give your desk a home."

"The drink has gone to your head. It almost sounds like you're saying we should live together." Toni pulled her toward the bed. "Do you want me to undress while you watch? Or would you rather take my clothes off yourself?"

Jo swallowed, not trusting herself to speak. She'd been dreaming of this for so long. She nodded and sat on the bed, letting Toni take that as her answer.

Toni slowly removed her clothes until she was down to her lacy pink underwear. Jo leaned back on her elbows, unable to take her eyes away. Toni's nipples pushed through the lacy bra, perfectly formed and begging her to touch them. Toni peeled off her bra, and the sight of her naked breasts took Jo's breath away. Once Toni had removed her panties, Jo finally made eye contact.

"Like what you see?" Toni asked, her eyes shining.

"Let me show you how much." Jo held out her hand.

Toni pulled her to her feet. "I want to lie on the bed and watch you now. And *don't* rush. I want to enjoy this too."

Jo would've done a military strip in twenty seconds, so she was glad for the instruction. She breathed slowly and started her own tease. By the time she was down to her boxers and sports bra, her hands were shaking uncontrollably. She wasn't as curvaceous as Toni; she had small breasts and was much more solidly built, but it was clear from the raw desire in Toni's eyes that she liked what she saw. Very much.

Jo pulled off her boxer shorts and flexed her leg muscles, making Toni laugh.

Toni held up her hands. "Lie with me."

She did as asked and gently placed her hand on Toni's stomach before slowly moving up toward her breasts. Back in the desert, she'd enjoyed looking at Toni's cleavage and the way her sweat-soaked tank tops had clung to her breasts in the heat. Now she could touch them and really take her time to appreciate them. She placed soft kisses along Toni's curves, drawing her soft sighs .

"Can't have you having all the fun." Toni pushed Jo onto her back and began her exploration.

As Toni took Jo's nipple into her mouth, Jo knew she wouldn't last long. Toni's hot wet lips on her body had her coming undone. She was wet and wanted pressure where she needed it most. She shifted to get Toni to move to the right place, but Toni put one hand on Jo's stomach to keep her in place. She moved her hand down inch by inch until she reached Jo's center. The pressure there and Toni's mouth on her stopped all sensible thought. The orgasm crashed over her, and she held Toni to her, feeling as though she couldn't get close enough.

She settled into the warmth of Toni's embrace and must have dozed off. She awoke and she was exactly where she'd been, nestled in Toni's arms. "I'm sorry I fell asleep," she said, wondering if Toni would be all right with that.

"You were only out for a bit. You obviously needed a moment's respite." Toni grinned and ran her fingertips up Jo's spine.

"Can we swap places? I have my own exploring to do." Jo leaned in and kissed Toni, putting all her feeling into it. She needed Toni to understand that she, and this, were important to her. Her sense of power as Toni arched into her touch gave her extra courage. She was in love, and she wanted Toni to feel it with every breath. Toni pushed into her hand, and Jo responded. Jo felt the heat and the softness and looked for the spot inside that took her over the edge every time. Toni cried out, and Jo was certain she was only a breath away herself. She continued what she was doing until Toni put out her hand to stop her.

Jo pulled her into her arms. Overwhelmed with what they'd shared, with the way she was feeling, she whispered into Toni's hair, "You're so beautiful. Thank you for giving me this wonderful gift. You're always safe in my arms. I love you."

She froze as the words left her lips. *Damn.* This was going to make things difficult; she hadn't meant to say that. But the moment of lovemaking had weakened her. She waited, holding her breath, but Toni didn't respond. Maybe she hadn't heard her. She relaxed, both disappointed and relieved.

Toni's breathing evened out as she drifted to sleep in Jo's arms. It was right where she wanted her to be. But would she stay there?

She awoke to the light sliding beneath the curtains and nestled into the heat coming from Toni's body lying on her. It was a delicious way to wake up.

"I think you could say we both had a good night's sleep," Toni said, her voice hoarse.

"That echoed through your chest."

"I'm not surprised, you and my chest bonded during the night."

Toni moved up and leaned over Jo. "Good morning, my love."

"I do like being your love," Jo said. It gave her a warm feeling in her soul.

"I like calling you my love, especially since I *do* love you," Toni said. She leaned in for a deep and passionate kiss. "You didn't know I heard you last night, did you?"

Jo shook her head.

Toni cupped Jo's cheek in her palm. "When you said it to me, I was startled, and I didn't want you thinking I said it back on a whim. But it was the first thing I thought of this morning. *She loves me.* I want you to wake up with that feeling tomorrow. I love you so much. You're everything I want, even when you're driving me crazy."

Jo leaned on her elbow and looked at Toni. "I was attracted to you from the start, but you annoyed me, and I was worried about what you'd do to my career. But as I got to know you, I saw a woman who was intelligent, strong, capable, and damn near everything I'd fantasized about for years." She swallowed hard. "When I thought I'd lose my career, it hurt a little bit less because I thought maybe we could have something out here, in the real world. If I had to choose between you and my career..." She kissed Toni's palm. "I want you at my side. I love you, and you've shown me that life is so much bigger, so much more beautiful than I'd allowed myself to see."

Toni's eyes were full of tears, and she laughed as she kissed

Jo repeatedly, placing little kisses on her cheeks, eyelids, and lips. "And you taught me to think deeper. To consider more than just the story without thinking about the cost to the people around me." She sobered for a moment, looking at the comforter. "And you taught me that not only do I not have to impress my mother, I also don't need to be anything other than who I am. And that I can do that my way." She sighed and laid her head on Jo's chest. "I love you."

Jo stroked her back for a while, taking in the momentous occasion. Her stomach rumbled, and they laughed. Toni placed a food order for delivery, and then they took their time once more in the shower. Jo would never get enough of Toni's curves under her hands.

As they were serving dinner later, Jo brought up the last worry on her mind. "Will love be enough?" When Toni raised her eyebrows while slurping up a noodle, Jo smiled. "God knows where I'll be stationed next. Or the time after that. And you'll be chasing stories wherever the wind takes you." She set her fork down and frowned. "How do we make that work?"

Toni took a sip of her drink, her expression thoughtful. "People have long-distance relationships all the time. People work crazy hours and hardly see each other. We don't have to have some traditional white picket fence romance. We live our best lives and chase our dreams. And when we're together, we'll appreciate one another that much more because we know our time is limited."

Jo's smile grew as she took in Toni's pragmatic viewpoint. She was right. They could create the relationship that worked for them. Love would make them stronger than steel, and Jo couldn't wait to see how amazing their future was going to be.

EPILOGUE

"Will you stay with me until the last possible minute before you need to go and take your seat? I need you here," Toni said.

"Of course, my love." Jo gently unclasped Toni's hands and kissed her knuckles. "I'm so proud of you. Your articles about the friendly fire incident have been brilliant. That extra supplement in the Global News Sunday paper was extraordinary and with all the articles and work you produced about your time with the Fizers, you deserve every award you get." Jo put her arms around Toni's waist and kissed her gently. "I'll try not to take any lipstick off."

"There's no way you won't. My lipstick gets well used when you're in a kissing mood." Toni stole another kiss anyway and sighed. "Remember that first kiss in the dark?"

"I'll never forget it. One kiss, and you whisked me away, forever to be lost amidst the warmth and sweet love you shared with me," Jo said. "I'll show you tonight when we get to our honeymoon, at last."

"Work pressures have a lot to answer for. Who could have known when we set the date that Brigadier McQueen would make full general? Even more so that she'd want you as her staff officer? You being promoted to major is just icing on the cake and the start of your journey to the senior ranks. I love hearing your name, Major Fitzgerald." She tugged a little on Jo's tie.

Jo smiled. It was nice hearing it too. "And now you're an award-winning go-to person for everyone. I love that Global News have given you a free choice of stories and that we have a sound base in London now. The gift your parents gave us and the money we got for selling my place have been great for buying our own home.

At last, we've got somewhere that suits your antique desk and my scotch cabinet." Moving in with Toni had been a dream come true, even when they clashed about the way to do things. Whereas Jo had a system based on order, Toni's was chaos trapped in a tornado.

It worked perfectly.

"The colonel's court-martial was reported in the paper this morning." Jo's energy dipped a little as she recalled the ordeal. "I know you haven't seen the article yet. The judge advocate sentenced him to be dismissed from the Army, stripped of rank, and to serve ten years in prison. The end of an era." Jo held Toni's hand. "And since the nephew got seven years for manslaughter, everyone has full closure."

"It's also good that the Army has tightened up their friendly fire processes and demonstrated that they've learned from this incident," Toni said, moving into Jo for a kiss. "And letting me report on it as well. It was perfect."

There was a knock on the door, and it opened a crack. "Toni Fitzgerald. Time to get to the anteroom."

"Thank you." Toni headed toward the door then turned back to Jo. "I still have to get used to my new name. Thank you for sharing it with me."

"I'm with you, always. Break a leg, beautiful."

Jo entered the presentation auditorium and looked around to get her bearings. She was in full dress uniform with her major's insignia and all her medals. Her boots shone like glass. She saw Toni's parents on the far end of the stage, and her father waved. Toni's parents side by side was an unusual occurrence, but they'd spent the last three months in Tulsa together. Jo and Toni had chatted about it, and Toni wondered if her mother was getting to the age where she wanted to spend time on the ranch enjoying life instead of chasing down a story.

Jo wasn't certain. They'd spent a couple of weeks at the ranch earlier in the year, and she was still trying to get her head around

Toni's mother. She'd only grudgingly acknowledged Toni's recent awards. And even with this one, the top of the pile, she was no more joyful. Charles, Toni's father, made up for it though; he'd collected every word she'd written online and in print and was the proudest father imaginable.

Charles walked over to her and put his arms around her. "Whoops. Is it all right to hug you when you're dressed up like this?" he asked, his wrinkled eyes twinkling. He reminded Jo of a large teddy bear.

"You can hug me anytime. Your hugs are priceless."

"So how was she?' he said. "Is she okay?"

Toni's mother joined them. "Hello, Jo. You look nice."

"Thank you. I wanted to look my best today." She turned her attention back to Charles. "Toni's nervous but otherwise good. She's ready to go. This has always been one of her dreams, so being here is amazing. She's worked out what to say—it's all good." Jo sounded as nervous as Toni was. She wanted this night to be perfect for her.

"It's a big moment for her. They'll record the whole thing, so she'll have a copy to look at later. I expect she'll struggle to remember a lot of it," Charles said. He looked at Toni's mother, who remained stoic as she gave a slight smile.

"Best take our seats. Things are happening." Jo considered for a moment, and then gave an internal shrug. Toni deserved to be happy. "You know," she said to Toni's mother, "she started down this path hoping to make you proud. She had a hard time living up to you and your expectations. Maybe at some point you could show her that you're proud of her, instead of allowing her to guess that you being here tonight means that."

Toni's mother looked taken aback and didn't respond. Charles grinned and looked toward the stage. The lights dimmed, and they took their seats. Jo had said her piece, and if it made Toni's life any better, that would be great. She'd stand up to anyone in the world if it meant making Toni smile.

With her heart in her throat, Jo watched as Toni received the Pulitzer Prize for her work on reporting British military operations from Afghanistan. Through their travails, through the doubts and struggles, they'd made their dreams come true. The best thing of all was that they'd done it together, and the future held nothing but promise.

Other Great Butterworth Books

Dead Ringer by Robyn Nyx
Three bodies. One killer. No motive?
Available on Amazon (ASIN B0CPQ8HFK7)

Medea by JJ Taylor
Who will Medea become in her battle for freedom?
Available from Amazon (ASIN B0CK2FB7GW)

Virgin Flight by E.V. Bancroft
In the battle between duty and desire, can love win?
Available from Amazon (ASIN B0CKJWQZ45)

Fragments of the Heart by Ally McGuire
Love can be the greatest expedition of all.
Available on Amazon (ASIN B0CHBPHR6M)

Here You Are by Jo Fletcher
.Can they unlock their hearts to find the true happiness they both deserve?
Available on Amazon (ASIN B0CBN935ZB)

Stunted Heart by Helena Harte
A stunt rider who lives in the fast lane. An ER doctor who can't take chances. A passion that could turn their worlds upside down.
Available on Amazon (ASIN B0C78GSWBV)

Dark Haven by Brey Willows
Even vampires get tired of playing with their food...
Available on Amazon (ASIN B0C5P1HJXC)

Green for Love by E.V. Bancroft
All's fair in love and eco-war.
Available from Amazon (ASIN B0C28F7PX5)

Call of Love by Lee Haven
Separated by fear. Reunited by fate. Will they get a second chance at life and love?
Available from Amazon (ASIN B0BYC83HZD)

Where the Heart Leads by Ally McGuire
A writer. A celebrity. And a secret that could break their hearts.
Available on Amazon (ASIN B0BWFX5W9L)

Stolen Ambition by Robyn Nyx
Daughters of two worlds collide in a dangerous game of ambition and love.
Available on Amazon (ASIN B0BS1PRSCN)

Cabin Fever by Addison M Conley
She goes for the money, but will she stay for something deeper?
Available on Amazon (ASIN B0BQWY45GH)

Zamira Saliev: A Dept. 6 Operation by Valden Bush
They're both running from their pasts. Together, they might make a new future.
Available from Amazon (ASIN B0BHJKHK6S)

The Helion Band by AJ Mason
Rose's only crime was to show kindness to her royal mistress...
Available from Amazon (ASIN B09YM6TYFQ)

That Boy of Yours Wants Looking At by Simon Smalley
A riotously colourful and heart-rending journey of what it takes to live authentically.
Available from Amazon (ASIN B09V3CSQQW)

Sapphic Eclectic Volume Four edited by Nyx & Willows
A little something for everyone...
Available free from Butterworth Books website

Of Light and Love by E.V. Bancroft
The deepest shadows paint the brightest love.
Available from Amazon (ASIN B0B64KJ3NP)

An Art to Love by Helena Harte
Second chances are an art form.
Available on Amazon (ASIN B0B1CD8Y42)

Music City Dreamers by Robyn Nyx
Music brings lovers together. In Music City, it can tear them apart.

Available on Amazon (ASIN B0994XVDGR)

Let Love Be Enough by Robyn Nyx
When a killer sets her sights on her target, is there any stopping her?
Available on Amazon (ASIN B09YMMZ8XC)

Dead Pretty by Robyn Nyx
An FBI agent, a TV star, and a serial killer. Love hurts.
Available on Amazon (ASIN B09QRSKBVP)

Nero by Valden Bush
Banished and abandoned. Will destiny reunite her with the love of her life?
Available from Amazon (ASIN B0BHJKHK6S)

Warm Pearls and Paper Cranes by E.V. Bancroft
A family torn apart by secrets. The only way forward is love.
Available from Amazon (ASIN B09DTBCQ92)

Judge Me, Judge Me Not by James Merrick
One man's battle against the world and himself to find it's never too late to find, and use, your voice.
Available from Amazon (ASIN B09CLK91N5)

Scripted Love by Helena Harte
What good is a romance writer who doesn't believe in happy ever after?
Available on Amazon (ASIN B0993QFLNN)

Call of Love by Helena Harte
Sometimes the call you least expect is the one you need the most.
Available on Amazon (ASIN B08D9SR15H)

What's Your Story?

Global Wordsmiths, CIC, provides an all-encompassing service for all writers, ranging from basic proofreading and cover design to development editing, typesetting, and eBook services. A major part of our work is charity and community focused, delivering writing projects to under-served and under-represented groups across Nottinghamshire, giving voice to the voiceless and visibility to the unseen.

To learn more about what we offer, visit: www.globalwords.co.uk

A selection of books by Global Words Press:
Desire, Love, Identity: with the National Justice Museum
Aventuras en México: Farmilo Primary School
Times Past: with The Workhouse, National Trust
Young at Heart with AGE UK
In Different Shoes: Stories of Trans Lives

Self-published authors working with Global Wordsmiths:
Steve Bailey
Ravenna Castle
Jackie D
CJ DeBarra
Dee Griffiths
Iona Kane
Maggie McIntyre
Emma Nichols
Dani Lovelady Ryan
Erin Zak